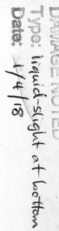

My Uncle Oswald

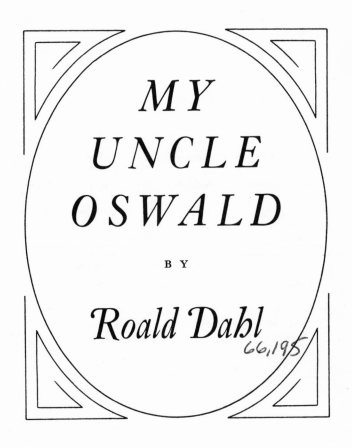

MY
UNCLE
OSWALD

BY

Roald Dahl

ALFRED A. KNOPF   *New York*   1980

Library of Congress Cataloging in Publication Data

Dahl, Roald.   My Uncle Oswald.

I. Title.
PZ3.D1373MY   1980[PR6054.A35]   823'.9'14   79-19811
ISBN 0-394-51011-9

Manufactured in the United States of America
FIRST EDITION

My Uncle Oswald

I

I AM BEGINNING, once again, to have an urge to salute my
Uncle Oswald. I mean, of course, Oswald Hendryks
Cornelius deceased, the connoisseur, the bon vivant, the
collector of spiders, scorpions and walking-sticks, the
lover of opera, the expert on Chinese porcelain, the
seducer of women, and without much doubt the greatest
fornicator of all time. Every other celebrated contender
for that title is diminished to a point of ridicule when his
record is compared with that of my Uncle Oswald.
Especially poor old Casanova. He comes out of the con-
test looking like a man who was suffering from a severe
malfunction of his sexual organ.

Fifteen years have passed since I released for publication in 1964 the first small excerpt from Oswald's diaries.
I took trouble at the time to select something unlikely to
give offence, and that particular episode concerned, if you
remember, a harmless and rather frivolous description of
coitus between my uncle and a certain female leper in the
Sinai desert.

So far so good. But I waited a full ten years more (1974)
before risking the release of a second piece. And once
again I was careful to choose something that was, at any
rate by Oswald's standards, as nearly as possible suitable

for reading by the vicar to Sunday school in the village church. That one dealt with the discovery of a perfume so potent that any man who sniffed it upon a woman was unable to prevent himself from ravishing her on the spot.

No serious litigation resulted from the publication of this little bit of trivia. But there were plenty of repercussions of another kind. I found my mailbox suddenly clogged with letters from hundreds of female readers, all clamouring for a drop of Oswald's magic perfume. Innumerable men also wrote to me with the same request, including a singularly unpleasant African dictator, a British left-wing cabinet minister, and a cardinal from the Holy See. A Saudi-Arabian prince offered me an enormous sum in Swiss currency, and a man in a dark suit from the American Central Intelligence Agency called on me one afternoon with a briefcase full of hundred-dollar bills. Oswald's perfume, he told me, could be used to compromise just about every senior Russian statesman and diplomat in the world, and his people wanted to buy the formula.

Unfortunately, I had not one drop of the magic liquid to sell, so there the matter ended.

Today, five years after publication of that perfume story, I have decided to permit the public yet another glimpse into my uncle's life. The section I have chosen comes from Volume XX, written in 1938, when Oswald was forty-three years old and in the prime of life. Many famous names are mentioned in this one, and there is obviously a grave risk that families and friends are going to take offence at some of the things Oswald has to say. I can only pray that those concerned will grant me indulgence and will understand that my motives are pure. For this is a document of considerable scientific and historical

importance. It would be a tragedy if it never saw the light
of day.

Here then is the extract from Volume XX of the Diaries
of Oswald Hendryks Cornelius, word for word as he
wrote it:

London, July 1938

HAVE JUST RETURNED from a satisfactory visit to the
Lagonda works at Staines. W. O. Bentley gave me lunch
(salmon from the Usk and a bottle of Montrachet) and
we discussed the extras for my new V12. He has promised
me a set of horns that will play Mozart's *"Son già mille e
tre"* in perfect pitch. Some of you may think this to be a
rather childish conceit, but it will serve as a nice incentive
to be reminded, every time I press the button, that good
old Don Giovanni had by then deflowered 1003 buxom
Spanish damsels. I told Bentley that the seats are to be up-
holstered in fine-grain alligator, and the panelling to be
veneered in yew. Why yew? Simply because I prefer the
colour and grain of English yew to that of any other wood.

But, what a remarkable fellow this W. O. Bentley is.
And what a triumph it was for Lagonda when he went
over to them. It is somehow sad that this man, having
designed and given his name to one of the finest cars in
the world, should be forced out of his own company and
into the arms of a rival. It means, however, that the new
Lagondas are now peerless, and I for one would have no
other machine. But this one isn't going to be cheap. It is
costing me more thousands than I ever thought it possible
to pay for an automobile.

Yet who cares about money? Not me, because I've always had plenty of it. I made my first hundred thousand

pounds when I was seventeen, and later I was to make a lot more. Having said that, it occurs to me that I have never once throughout these journals made any mention of the manner in which I became a wealthy man.

Perhaps the time has come when I should do this. I think it has. For although these diaries are designed to be a history of the art of seduction and the pleasures of copulation, they would be incomplete without some reference also to the art of money-making and the pleasures attendant thereon.

Very well, then. I have talked myself into it. I shall proceed at once to tell you something about how I set about making money. But just in case some of you may be tempted to skip this particular section and go on to juicier things, let me assure you that there will be juice in plenty dripping from these pages. I wouldn't have it otherwise.

Great wealth, when uninherited, is usually acquired in one of four ways—by chicanery, by talent, by inspired judgement, or by luck. Mine was a combination of all four. Listen carefully and you shall see what I mean.

In the year 1912, when I was barely seventeen, I won a scholarship in natural sciences to Trinity College, Cambridge. I was a precocious youth and had taken the exam a year earlier than usual. This meant that I had a twelve-month wait doing nothing, because Cambridge would not receive me until I was eighteen. My father therefore decided that I should fill in the time by going to France to learn the language. I myself hoped that I should learn a fair bit more than just the language in that splendid country. Already, you see, I had begun to acquire a taste for rakery and wenching among the London débutantes. Already, also, I was beginning to get a bit bored with these young English girls. They were, I decided, a pretty pithless lot, and I was impatient to sow a few bushels of wild oats in foreign fields. Especially in France. I had been reliably informed that Parisian females knew a thing or two about the act of lovemaking that their London cousins had never dreamed of. Copulation, so rumour had it, was in its infancy in England.

On the evening before I was due to depart for France, I gave a small party at our family house in Cheyne Walk. My father and mother had purposely gone out to dinner at seven o'clock so that I might have the place to myself. I had invited a dozen or so friends of both sexes, all of them about my own age, and by nine o'clock we were sitting around making pleasant talk, drinking wine, and consuming some excellent boiled mutton and dumplings. The front doorbell rang. I went to answer it, and on the doorstep there stood a middle-aged man with a huge moustache, a magenta complexion, and a pigskin suitcase. He introduced himself as Major Grout and asked for my father. I said he was out to dinner. "Good gracious me," said Major Grout. "He has invited me to stay. I'm an old friend."

"Father must have forgotten," I said. "I'm awfully sorry. You had better come in."

Now I couldn't very well leave the Major alone in the study reading *Punch* while we were having a party in the next room, so I asked him if he'd care to come in and join us. He would indeed. He'd love to join us. So in he came, moustache and all, a beaming jovial old boy who settled down among us quite comfortably despite the fact that he was three times the age of anyone else present. He tucked into the mutton and polished off a whole bottle of claret in the first fifteen minutes.

"Excellent vittles," he said. "Is there any more wine?"

I opened another bottle for him, and we all watched with

a certain admiration as he proceeded to empty that one as
well. His cheeks were swiftly turning from magenta to
a very deep purple and his nose seemed to be catching on
fire. Halfway through the third bottle, he began to loosen
up. He worked, he told us, in the Anglo-Egyptian Sudan
and was home on leave. His job had to do with the Sudan
Irrigation Service, and a very hot and arduous business it
was. But fascinating. Lots of fun, y'know. And the wogs
weren't too much trouble so long as one kept the old
shambok handy all the time.

We sat round him, listening and not a little intrigued by
this purple-faced creature from distant lands.

"A great country, the Sudan," he said. "It is enormous.
It is remote. It is full of mysteries and secrets. Would you
like me to tell you about one of the great secrets of the
Sudan?"

"Very much, sir," we said. "Yes, please."

"One of its great secrets," he said, tipping another glass
of wine down his throat, "a secret that is known only to a
few old-timers out there like myself and to the natives,
is a little creature called the Sudanese Blister Beetle or to
give him his right name, *Cantharis vesicatoria sudanii*."

"You mean a scarab?" I said.

"Certainly not," he said. "The Sudanese Blister Beetle
is a winged insect, as much a fly as a beetle, and is about
three-quarters of an inch long. It's very pretty to look at,
with a brilliant iridescent shell of golden green."

"Why is it so secret?" we asked.

"These little beetles," the Major said, "are found only in
one part of the Sudan. It's an area of about twenty square
miles, north of Khartoum, and that's where the hashab
tree grows. The leaves of the hashab tree are what the
beetles feed on. Men spend their whole lives searching for

these beetles. Beetle hunters, they are called. They are very sharp-eyed natives who know all there is to know about the haunts and habits of the tiny brutes. And when they catch them, they kill them and dry them in the sun and crunch them up into a fine powder. This powder is greatly prized among the natives, who usually keep it in small elaborately carved Beetle Boxes. A tribal chief will have his Beetle Box made of silver."

"But this powder," we said, "what do they do with it?"

"It's not what *they* do with *it*," the Major said. "It's what *it* does to *you*. One tiny pinch of that powder is the most powerful aphrodisiac in the world."

"The Spanish Fly!" someone shouted. "It's the Spanish Fly!"

"Well, not quite," the Major said, "but you're on the right track. The common Spanish Fly is found in Spain and southern Italy. The one I'm talking about is the *Sudanese Fly*, and although it's of the same family, it's a different kettle of fish altogether. It is approximately ten times as powerful as the ordinary Spanish Fly. The reaction produced by the little *Sudanese* fellow is so incredibly vicious it is dangerous to use even in small doses."

"But they do use it?"

"Oh God, yes. Every wog in Khartoum and northwards uses the old Beetle. White men, the ones who know about it, are inclined to leave it alone because it's so damn dangerous."

"Have *you* used it?" someone asked.

The Major looked up at the questioner and gave a little smile under his enormous moustache. "We'll come to that in a moment or two, shall we?" he said.

"What does it actually do to you?" one of the girls asked.

"My God," the Major said, "what doesn't it do to you? It builds a fire under your genitals. It is both a violent aphrodisiac and a powerful irritant. It not only makes you uncontrollably randy but it also guarantees you an enormous and long-lasting erection at the same time. Could you give me another glass of wine, dear boy?"

I leaped up to fetch more wine. My guests had suddenly become very still. The girls were all staring at the Major, rapt and motionless, their eyes shining like stars. The boys were staring at the girls, watching to see how they would react to these sudden indiscretions. I refilled the Major's glass.

"Your father always kept a decent cellar," he said. "And good cigars, too." He looked up at me, waiting.

"Would you like a cigar, sir?"

"That's very civil of you," he said.

I went to the dining-room and fetched my father's box of Montecristos. The Major put one in his breast pocket and another in his mouth. "I will tell you a true story if you like," he said, "about myself and the Blister Beetle."

"Tell us," we said. "Go on, sir."

"You'll like this story," he said, removing the cigar from his mouth and snipping off the end of it with a thumbnail. "Who has a match?"

I lit his cigar for him. Clouds of smoke enveloped his head, and through the smoke we could see his face dimly, but dark and soft like some huge over-ripe purple fruit.

"One evening," he began, "I was sitting on the veranda of my bungalow way upcountry about thirty miles north of Khartoum. It was hot as hell and I'd had a hard day. I was drinking a strong whiskey and soda. It was my first that evening, and I was lying back in the deck chair with my feet resting on the little balustrade that ran round the veranda. I could feel the whiskey hitting the lining of my stomach, and I can promise you there is no greater sensation at the end of a long day in a fierce climate than when you feel that first whiskey hitting your stomach and going through into the bloodstream. A few minutes later, I went indoors and got myself a second drink, then I returned to the veranda. I lay back again in the deck chair. My shirt was soaked with sweat but I was too tired to take a shower. Then all of a sudden I went rigid. I was just about to put the glass of whiskey to my lips and my hand froze, it literally froze in mid-air, and there it stayed with my fingers clenched around the glass. I couldn't move. I couldn't even speak. I tried to call out to my boy for help but I couldn't. Rigor mortis. Paralysis. My entire body had turned to stone."

"Were you frightened?" someone asked.

"Of course I was frightened," the Major said. "I was bloody terrified, especially out there in the Sudan desert miles from anywhere. But the paralysis didn't last very long. Maybe a minute, maybe two. I don't really know. But when I came to as it were, the first thing I noticed was a burning sensation in the region of my groin. 'Hullo,' I said, 'what the hell's going on now?' But it was pretty obvious what was going on. The activity inside my trousers was becoming very violent indeed and within another few seconds my member was as stiff and erect as the mainmast of a topsail schooner."

"What do you mean, your *member*?" asked a girl whose name was Gwendoline.

"I expect you will catch on as we go along, my dear," the Major said.

"Carry on, Major," we said. "What happened next?"

"Then it started to throb," he said.

"What started to throb?" Gwendoline asked him.

"My member," the Major said. "I could feel every beat of my heart all the way along it. Pulsing and throbbing most terribly it was, and as tight as a balloon. You know those long sausage-shaped balloons children have at parties? I kept thinking about one of those, and with every beat of my heart it felt as if someone was pumping in more air and it was going to burst."

The Major drank some wine. Then he studied the ash on his cigar. We sat still, waiting.

"So of course I began trying to puzzle out what might have happened," he went on. "I looked at my glass of whiskey. It was where I always put it, on top of the little white-painted balustrade surrounding the veranda. Then my eye travelled upward to the roof of the bungalow and to the edge of the roof and suddenly, presto! I'd got it! I knew for certain what must have happened."

"What?" we said, all speaking at once.

"A large Blister Beetle, taking an evening stroll on the roof, had ventured too close to the edge and had fallen off."

"Right into your glass of whiskey!" we cried.

"Precisely," the Major said. "And I, thirsting like mad in the heat, had gulped him down without looking."

The girl called Gwendoline was staring at the Major with huge eyes. "Quite honestly I don't see what all the fuss was about," she said. "One teeny weeny little beetle isn't going to hurt anyone."

"My dear child," the Major said, "when the Blister Beetle is dried and crushed, the resulting powder is called cantharidin. That's its pharmaceutical name. The Sudanese variety is called cantharidin sudanii. And this cantharidin sudanii is absolutely deadly. The maximum safe dose for a human, if there is such a thing as a safe dose, is one minim. A minim is one four-hundred-eightieth of a fluid ounce. Assuming I had just swallowed one whole fully grown Blister Beetle, that meant I'd received God knows how many hundreds of times the maximum dose."

"Jesus," we said. "Jesus Christ."

"The throbbing was so tremendous now, it was shaking my whole body," the Major said.

"A headache, you mean?" Gwendoline said.

"No," the Major said.

"What happened next?" we asked him.

"My member," the Major said, "was now like a white-hot rod of iron burning into my body. I leaped up from my chair and rushed to my car and drove like a madman for the nearest hospital, which was in Khartoum. I got there in forty minutes flat. I was scared fartless."

"Now wait just a minute," the Gwendoline creature said. "I'm still not quite following you. Exactly why were you so frightened?"

Boy, what a dreadful girl. I should never have invited her. The Major, to his great credit, ignored her completely this time.

"I dashed into the hospital," he went on, "and found the casualty room where an English doctor was stitching up somebody's knife wound. 'Look at this!' I cried, taking it out and waving it at him."

"Waving *what* at him, for heaven's sake?" the awful Gwendoline asked.

"Shut up, Gwendoline," I said.

"Thank you," the Major said. "The doctor stopped stitching and regarded the object I was holding out to him with some alarm. I quickly told him my story. He looked glum. There was no antidote for Blister Beetle, he informed me. I was in grave trouble. But he would do his best. So they stomach-pumped me and put me to bed and packed ice all around my poor throbbing member."

"Who did?" someone asked. "Who's they?"

"A nurse," the Major answered. "A young Scottish nurse with dark hair. She brought the ice in small rubber bags and packed it round and kept the bags in place with a bandage."

"Didn't you get frostbite?"

"You can't get frostbite on something that's practically red hot," the Major said.

"What happened next?"

"They kept changing the ice every three hours day and night."

"Who, the Scottish nurse?"

"They took it in turns. Several nurses."

"Good God."

"It took two weeks to subside."

"Two weeks!" I said. "Were you all right afterwards, sir? Are you all right now?"

The Major smiled and took another sip of wine. "I am deeply touched," he said, "by your concern. You are obviously a young man who knows what comes first in this world, and what comes second. I think you will go far."

"Thank you, sir," I said. "But what happened in the end?"

"I was out of action for six months," the Major said, smiling wanly. "But that is no hardship in the Sudan. Yes, if you want to know, I'm all right now. I made a miraculous recovery."

That was the story Major Grout had told us at my little party on the eve of my departure for France. And it set me thinking. It set me thinking very deeply indeed. In fact, that night, as I lay in bed with my bags all packed on the floor, a tremendously daring plan began rapidly to evolve in my head. I say "daring" because by God it damn well was daring when you consider I was only seventeen years old at the time. Looking back on it now, I take my hat off to myself for even contemplating that sort of action. But by the following morning, my mind was made up.

2

I BADE FAREWELL to my parents on the platform at Victoria Station and boarded the boat train for Paris. I arrived that afternoon and checked in at the house where my father had arranged for me to board. It was on the avenue Marceau, and the family, who were called Boisvain, took paying guests. Monsieur Boisvain was a civil servant of sorts and as unremarkable as the rest of his breed. His wife, a pale woman with short fingers and a flaccid rump, was in much the same mould as her husband, and I guessed that neither of them would give me any trouble. They had two daughters—Jeanette, aged fifteen, and Nicole, who was nineteen. Mademoiselle Nicole was some kind of a freak, for while the rest of the family were typically small and neat and French, this girl was of Amazonian proportions. She looked to me like a sort of female gladiator. She could not possibly have stood less than six feet three in her bare feet, but she was nonetheless a well-made young gladiator with long, nicely turned legs and a pair of dark eyes that seemed to hold a number of secrets. It was the first time since puberty that I had encountered a woman who was not only tremendously tall but also attractive, and I was much impressed by what I saw. Since then, over the years, I have naturally sampled many a lofty wench and I must say that I rate them higher, on the whole, than their more diminutive sisters. When a woman is very tall, there is greater power and greater traction in her limbs for one thing, and of course there is also a good deal more substance to tangle with.

In other words, I do enjoy a tall woman. And why shouldn't I? There's nothing freakish about that. But what *is* pretty freakish, in my opinion, is the extraordinary fact that women in general, and by that I mean all women everywhere, go absolutely dotty about tiny men. Let me explain at once that by "tiny men" I don't mean ordinary tiny men like horse-jockeys and chimney-sweeps. I mean genuine dwarfs, those minuscule bow-legged characters you see running around in circus arenas wearing pantaloons. Believe it or not, any one of these little fellows can, if he puts his mind to it, drive even the most frigid woman to distraction. Protest all you like, you lady readers. Tell me I'm crazy, misguided, ill-informed. But before you do that, I suggest you go away and talk to a female who has actually been worked over by one of these little men. She will confirm my findings. She will say yes yes yes, it's true, I'm afraid it's true. She will tell you they are repulsive but irresistible. An exceedingly ugly middle-aged circus dwarf who stood no more than three feet six inches tall once told me that he could always have his pick of any woman in any room at any time. Very odd I find that.

But to go back to Mademoiselle Nicole, the Amazonian daughter. She interested me at once, and as we shook hands, I applied a touch of extra pressure to her knuckles and watched her face. Her lips parted and I saw the tip of her tongue push out suddenly between her teeth. Very well, young lady, I told myself. You shall be number one in Paris.

In case this sounds a bit brash coming from a seventeen-year-old stripling like me, I think you should know that even at that tender age, fortune had endowed me with far more than my share of good looks. Going back now over the family photographs of the time, I can see that I was a youth of quite piercing beauty. This is no more than a simple fact and it would be silly to pretend it wasn't true. Certainly, it had made things easy for me in London, and I could honestly say that up to then I had not received a single snub. But I had not, of course, been playing the game for very long, and no more than fifty or sixty young birds had come into my sights.

In order to carry out the plan which the good Major Grout had put into my head, I straightaway announced to Madame Boisvain that I would be leaving first thing in the morning to stay with friends in the country. We were still standing in the hall and we had just completed the handshakes. "But Monsieur Oswald, you have only this minute arrived!" the good lady cried.

"I believe my father has paid you six months in advance," I said. "If I am not here, you will save money on food."

Arithmetic like that will mollify the heart of any landlady in France, and Madame Boisvain made no further protest. At seven p.m. we sat down to the evening meal. It was boiled tripe with onions. This I consider to be the second most repulsive dish in the entire world. The *most* repulsive dish is something that is eaten with gusto by jackaroos on sheep stations in Australia. These jackaroos—

and I might as well tell you about it so that you can avoid it if ever you should go that way—these jackaroos or sheep cowboys invariably castrate their male lambs in the following barbaric manner: two of them hold the creature upside down by its fore and hind legs. A third fellow slits the scrotum and squeezes the testicles outside the sac. He then bends forward and takes the testicles in his mouth. He closes his teeth on them and jerks them free from the unfortunate animal and spits this nauseating mouthful into a basin. It's no good you telling me these things don't happen because they do. I saw it all last year with my own eyes on a station near Cowra in New South Wales. And these idiots went on to inform me with pride that three competent jackaroos could castrate sixty lambs in sixty minutes and go on doing it all day long. A little jaw ache was all one got, they said, but it was well worth it because the rewards were great.

"What rewards?"

"Ah ha," they said, "you just wait!" And in the evening I had to stand and watch while they fried the spoils in a pan with mutton fat over a wood fire. This gastronomic miracle is, I can assure you, the most revolting, the toughest, the most nauseating dish it is possible to imagine. Boiled tripe comes second.

I keep digressing. I must get on. We are still in the Boisvain household having boiled tripe for supper. Monsieur B went into ecstasies over the stuff, making loud sucking noises and smacking his lips and shouting *"Délicieux! Ravissant! Formidable! Merveilleux!"* with every mouthful. And then, when he had finished—would horrors never cease?—he calmly removed his entire set of false teeth and rinsed them in his fingerbowl.

At midnight, when Monsieur and Madame B were well

asleep, I slipped along the corridor and entered the bedroom of Mademoiselle Nicole. She was tucked up in an
enormous bed and there was a candle burning on the table
beside her. She received me, oddly enough, with a formal
French handshake, but I can assure you there was nothing
formal about what followed after that. I do not intend to
dwell upon this little episode. It has nothing at all to do
with the main part of my story. Let me just say that every
rumour I had ever heard about the girls of Paris was sub-
stantiated during those few hours I spent with Mademoiselle Nicole. She made the glacial London débutantes
seem like so many slabs of petrified wood. She went for me
like a mongoose for a cobra. She suddenly had ten pairs
of hands and half a dozen mouths. She was a contortionist
to boot, and more than once, amidst the whirring of limbs,
I caught a glimpse of her ankles locked around the back of
her neck. The girl was putting me through the wringer.
She was stretching me beyond the point of endurance. I
was not really ready at my age for such a severe examination as this, and after an hour or so of unremitting activity,
I began to hallucinate and I remember imagining that my
entire body was one long well-lubricated piston sliding
smoothly back and forth within a cylinder whose walls
were made of the smoothest steel. God only knows how
long it went on, but at the end of it all I was suddenly
brought back to my senses by the sound of a deep calm
voice saying, "Very well, monsieur, that will do for the
first lesson. I think, though, that it will be a long time
before you get out of the kindergarten."

I staggered back to my room, bruised and chastened, and
fell asleep.

The next morning, in order to carry out my plan, I said
farewell to the Boisvains and took a train for Marseilles. I

had on me the six months' expense money my father had provided before I left London, two hundred pounds in French francs. That was a lot of money in the year 1912.

At Marseilles, I booked a passage for Alexandria on a French steamship of nine thousand tons called *L'Impératrice Josephine*, a pleasant little passenger boat that ran regularly between Marseilles, Naples, Palermo, and Alexandria.

The trip was without incident except that I encountered on the first day out yet another tall female. This time she was a Turk, a tall dark-skinned Turkish lady who was so smothered in jewellery of all sorts that she tinkled as she walked. My first thought was that she would have worked wonders on top of a cherry tree to keep the birds away. My second thought, which followed very soon after the first, was that she had an exceptional shape to her body. The undulations in the region of her chest were so magnificent that I felt, as I gazed at them across the boat deck, like a traveller in Tibet who was seeing for the first time the highest peaks in the Himalayas. The woman returned my gaze, her chin high and arrogant, her eyes travelling slowly down my body from head to toe, then up again. A minute later, she calmly strolled across and invited me to her cabin for a glass of absinthe. I'd never heard of the stuff in my life, but I went willingly, and I stayed willingly and I did not emerge again from that cabin until we docked at Naples three days later. I may well, as Mademoiselle Nicole had said, have been in the kindergarten and Mademoiselle Nicole herself was perhaps in the sixth form, but if that was so then the tall Turkish lady was a university professor.

Things were made more difficult for me during this encounter by the fact that all the way between Marseilles and Naples, the ship seemed to be battling against a terrible storm. It pitched and rolled in the most alarming manner and more than once I thought we were going to capsize. When at last we were safely anchored in the Bay of Naples, and I was leaving the cabin, I said, "Well by gosh, I'm glad we made it. That was some storm we went through."

"My dear boy," she said, hanging another cluster of jewellery round her neck, "the sea has been calm as glass all the way."

"Oh no, madame," I said. "It was a tremendous storm."

"That was no storm," she said. "It was me."

I was learning fast. I had learned above all—and I have confirmed this many times since—that to tangle with a Turk is like running fifty miles before breakfast. You have to be fit.

I spent the rest of the voyage getting my wind back and by the time we docked at Alexandria four days later, I was feeling quite bouncy again. From Alexandria I took a train to Cairo. There I changed trains and went on to Khartoum.

By God, it was hot in the Sudan. I was not dressed for the tropics but I refused to waste money on clothes that I would be wearing only for a day or two. In Khartoum, I got a room at a large hotel where the foyer was filled with Englishmen wearing khaki shorts and topis. They all had moustaches and magenta cheeks like Major Grout, and every one of them had a drink in his hand. There was a Sudanese hall porter of sorts lounging by the entrance. He was a splendid handsome fellow in a white robe with a red tarboosh on his head, and I went up to him.

"I wonder if you could help me?" I said, taking some French banknotes from my pocket and riffling them casually.

He looked at the money and grinned.

"Blister Beetles," I said. "You know about Blister Beetles?"

Here it was, then. This was *le moment critique*. I had come all the way from Paris to Khartoum to ask one question, and now I watched the man's face anxiously. It was certainly possible that Major Grout's story had been nothing more than an entertaining hoax.

The Sudanese hall porter's grin became wider still. "Everyone knows about Blister Beetles, sahib," he said. "What you want?"

"I want you to tell me where I can go out and catch one thousand of them."

He stopped grinning and stared at me as though I'd gone balmy. "You mean *live* beetles?" he exclaimed. "You want to go out and catch yourself one thousand *live* Blister Beetles?"

"I do, yes."

"What you want live beetles for, sahib? They no good to you at all, those old live beetles."

Oh my God, I thought. The Major has been pulling our legs.

The hall porter moved closer to me and placed an almost jet-black hand on my arm. "You want jig-a-jig, right? You want stuff to make you go jig-a-jig?"

"That's about it," I said. "More or less."

"Then you don't want to bother with them *live* beetles, sahib. All you want is *powdered* beetles."

"I had an idea I might take the beetles home and breed them," I said. "That way I'd have a permanent supply."

"In England?" he said.

"England or France. Somewhere like that."

"No good," he said, shaking his head. "This little Blister Beetle he live only here in the Sudan. He needs very hot sun. Beetles will all die in your country. Why you not take the powder?"

I could see I was going to have to make a slight adjustment in my plans. "How much does the powder cost?" I asked him.

"How much you want?"

"A lot."

"You have to be very, very careful with that powder, sahib. All you take is the littlest pinch; otherwise you get into *very serious trouble*."

"I know that."

"Over here, we Sudanese men measure up one dose by pouring the powder over the head of a pin and what stays on the pinhead is one dose exactly. And that is not very much. So you better be careful, young sahib."

"I know all about that," I said. "Just tell me how I go about getting hold of a large quantity."

"What you mean by large quantity?"

"Well, say ten pounds in weight."

"Ten pounds!" he cried. "That would take care of all the people in the whole of Africa put together!"

"Five pounds then."

"What in the world you going to do with *five pounds* of Blister Beetle powder, sahib? Just a few *ounces* is a lifetime supply even for a big strong man like me."

"Never mind what I'm going to do with it," I said. "How much would it cost?"

He laid his head on one side and considered this question carefully. "We buy it in tiny packets," he said. "Quarter ounce each. Very expensive stuff."

"I want five pounds," I said. "In bulk."

"Are you staying here in the hotel?" he asked me.

"Yes."

"Then I see you tomorrow with the answer. I must go around asking some questions."

I left it at that for the time being.

The next morning the tall black hall porter was in his usual place by the hotel entrance. "What news of the powder?" I asked him.

"I fix," he said. "I find a place where I can get you five pounds in weight of pure powder."

"How much will it cost?" I asked him.

"You have English money?"

"I can get it."

"It will cost you one thousand English pounds, sahib. Very cheap."

"Then forget it," I said, turning away.

"Five hundred," he said.

"Fifty," I said. "I'll give you fifty pounds."

"One hundred."

"No. Fifty. That's all I can afford."

He shrugged and spread his palms upward. "You find the money," he said. "I find the powder. Six o'clock tonight."

"How will I know you won't be giving me sawdust or something?"

"Sahib!" he cried. "I never cheat anyone."

"I'm not so sure."

"In that case," he said, "we will test the powder on *you* by giving you a little dose before you pay me. How's that?"

"Good idea," I said. "See you at six."

One of the London banks had an overseas branch in Khartoum. I went there and changed some of my French francs for pounds. At six p.m., I sought out the hall porter. He was now in the foyer of the hotel.

"You got it?" I asked him.

He pointed to a large brown-paper parcel standing on the floor behind a pillar. "You want to test it first, sahib? You are very welcome because this is the absolute top class quality Beetle powder in the Sudan. One pinhead of this and you go jig-a-jig all night long and half the next day."

I didn't think he would have offered me a trial run if the stuff hadn't been right, so I gave him the money and took the parcel.

An hour later, I was on the night train to Cairo. Within ten days, I was back in Paris and knocking on the door of Madame Boisvain's house in the avenue Marceau. I had my precious parcel with me. There had been no trouble with the French customs as I disembarked at Marseilles. In those days, they searched for knives and guns but nothing else.

3

I ANNOUNCED to Madame B that I was going to stay for quite a while but that I had one request to make. I was a science student, I told her. She said she knew that. It was my wish, I went on, not only to learn French during my stay in France, but also to pursue my scientific studies. I would therefore be conducting certain experiments in my room which involved the use of apparatus and chemicals that could be dangerous or poisonous to the inexperienced. Because of this, I wished to have a key to my room, and nobody should enter it.

"You are going to blow us all up!" she cried, clutching her cheeks.

"Have no fear, madame," I said. "I am merely taking the normal precautions. My professors have taught me always to do this."

"And who will clean your room and make your bed?"

"I will," I said. "This will save you much trouble."

She muttered and grumbled a fair bit, but gave way to me in the end.

Supper with the Boisvains that evening was pigs' trotters in white sauce, another repellent dish. Monsieur B tucked into it with all the usual sucking noises and exclamations of ecstasy, and the glutinous white sauce was smeared over his entire face by the time he had finished. I excused myself from the table just as he was preparing to transfer his false teeth from mouth to fingerbowl. I went upstairs to my room and locked the door.

For the first time, I opened my big brown-paper parcel. The powder had been packed, thank goodness, in two large biscuit tins. I opened one up. The stuff was pale grey and almost as fine as flour. Here before me, I told myself, lay what was probably the biggest crock of gold a man could ever find. I say "probably" because as yet I had no proof of anything. I had only the Major's word that the stuff worked and the hall porter's word that it was the genuine article.

I lay on my bed and read a book until midnight. I then undressed and got into my pyjamas. I took a pin and held it upright over the open tin of powder. I sprinkled a pinch of powder over the upright pinhead. A tiny cluster of grey powder grains remained clinging to the top of the pin. Very carefully, I raised this to my mouth and licked off the powder. It tasted of nothing. I noted the time by my watch, then I sat on the edge of the bed to await results.

They weren't long coming. Precisely nine minutes later, my whole body went rigid. I began to gasp and gurgle. I froze where I was sitting, just as Major Grout had frozen on his veranda with the glass of whiskey in his hand. But because I'd had a much weaker dose than he had, this period of paralysis lasted only for a few seconds. Then I felt, as the good Major had so aptly put it, a burning sensation in the region of my groin. Within another minute, my member—and again the Major has said it better than I can—my member had become stiff and erect as the mainmast of a topsail schooner.

Now for the final test. I stood up and crossed to the door. I opened it quietly and slipped along the passage. I entered the bedroom of Mademoiselle Nicole, and surely enough, there she was tucked up in bed with the candle already lit, waiting for me. "*Bon soir, monsieur,*" she whispered, giving me another of those formal handshakes. "You have come along for your lesson number two, yes?"

I didn't say anything. Already, as I got into bed beside her, I was beginning to slide off into another of those weird fantasies that seem to engulf me whenever I come to close quarters with a female. This time I was back in the middle ages and Richard Coeur de Lion was King of England. I was the champion jouster of the country, the noble knight who was once more about to display his prowess and strength before the King and all his courtiers in the field of the Cloth of Gold. My opponent was a gigantic and fearsome female from France who had butchered seventy-eight valiant Englishmen in tournaments of jousting. But my steed was brave and my lance was of tremendous length and thickness, sharp-pointed, vibrant, and made of the strongest steel. And the King shouted out, "Bravo, Sir Oswald, the man with the mighty lance! No one but he has the strength to wield so huge a weapon! Run her through, my lad! Run her through!" So I went galloping into battle with my giant lance pointed straight and true at the Frenchy's most vital region, and I thrust at her with mighty thrusts, all swift and sure, and in a trice I had pierced her armour and had her screaming for mercy. But I was in no mood to be merciful. Spurred on by the cheers of the King and his courtiers, I drove my steely lance ten thousand times into that writhing body and then ten thousand times more, and I heard the courtiers shouting, "Thrust away, Sir Oswald! Thrust away and keep on thrusting!" And then the King's voice was saying, "Begad, methinks the brave fellow is going to shatter that great lance of his if he doesn't stop soon!" But my lance did not shatter, and in a glorious finale, I impaled the giant Frenchy female upon the spiked end of my trusty weapon and went galloping around the arena, waving the body high above my head to shouts of "Bravo!" and "Gadzooks!" and "*Victor ludorum!*"

All this, as you can imagine, took some time. How long, I had not the faintest idea, but when I finally surfaced again, I jumped out of the bed and stood there triumphant, looking down upon my prostrate victim. The girl was panting like a stag at bay and I began to wonder whether I might not have done her an injury. Not that I cared much about that.

"Well, mademoiselle," I said. "Am I still in the kindergarten?"

"Oh no!" she cried, twitching her long limbs. "Oh no, monsieur! No, no, no! You are ferocious and you are marvellous and I feel like my boiler has exploded!"

That made me feel pretty good. I left without another word and sneaked back along the corridor to my own room. What a triumph! The powder was fantastic! The Major had been right! And the hall porter in Khartoum had not let me down! I was on my way now to the crock of gold and nothing could stop me. With these happy thoughts, I fell asleep.

The next morning, I immediately began to set matters in train. You will remember that I had a science scholarship. I was, therefore, well versed in physics and chemistry and several other things besides, but chemistry had always been my strongest subject.

I therefore knew already all about the process of making a simple pill. In the year 1912, which is where we are now, it was customary for pharmacists to make many of their own pills on the premises, and for this they always used something called a pill-machine. So I went shopping in Paris that morning, and in the end I found, in a back street on the Left Bank, a supplier of second-hand pharmaceutical apparatus. From him I bought an excellent little pill-machine that turned out good professional pills in groups of twenty-four at a time. I bought also a pair of highly sensitive chemist's scales.

Next, I found a pharmacy that sold me a large quantity of calcium carbonate and a smaller amount of tragacanth. I also bought a bottle of cochineal. I carried all this back to my room and then I cleared the dressing-table and laid out my supplies and my apparatus in good order.

Pill making is a simple matter if you know how. The calcium carbonate, which is neutral and harmless, comprises the bulk of the pill. You then add the precise quantity by weight of the active ingredient, in my case cantharidin powder. And finally, as an excipient, you put in a little tragacanth. An excipient is simply the cement that makes everything stick together and harden into an attractive pill.

I weighed out sufficient of each substance to make twenty-four fairly large and impressive pills. I added a few drops of cochineal, which is a tasteless scarlet colouring matter. I mixed everything together well and truly in a bowl and fed the mixture into my pill-machine. In a trice, I had before me twenty-four large red pills of perfect shape and hardness. And each one, if I had done my weighing and mixing properly, contained exactly the amount of cantharidin powder that would lie on top of a pinhead. Each one, in other words, was a potent and explosive aphrodisiac.

I was still not ready to make my move.

I went out again into the streets of Paris and found a commercial box maker. From him, I bought one thousand small round cardboard boxes, one inch in diameter. I also bought cotton-wool.

Next, I went to a printer and ordered one thousand tiny round labels. On each label the following legend was to be printed in English:

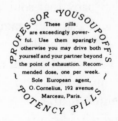

PROFESSOR YOUSOUPOFF'S POTENCY PILLS

These pills are exceedingly powerful. Use them sparingly otherwise you may drive both yourself and your partner beyond the point of exhaustion. Recommended dose, one per week. Sole European agent, O. Cornelius, 192 avenue Marceau, Paris.

The labels were designed to fit exactly upon the lids of my little cardboard boxes.

Two days later, I collected the labels. I bought a pot of glue. I returned to my room and stuck labels onto twenty-four box lids. Inside each box, I made a nest of white cotton-wool. Upon this I placed a single scarlet pill and closed the lid.

I was ready to go.

As you will have guessed long ago, I was about to enter the commercial world. I was going to sell my Potency Pills to a clientele that would soon be screaming for more and still more. I would sell them individually, one only in each box, and I would charge an exorbitant price.

And the clientele? Where would they come from? How would a seventeen-year-old boy in a foreign city set about finding customers for this wonder pill of his? Well, I had no qualms about that. I had only to find one single person of the right type and let him try one single pill, and the ecstatic recipient would immediately come galloping back for a second helping. He would also whisper the news to his friends, and the glad tidings would spread like a forest fire.

I already knew who my first victim was going to be.

I have not yet told you that my father, William Cornelius, was in the diplomatic service. He had no money of his own, but he was a skillful diplomat and he managed to live very comfortably on his pay. His last post had been ambassador to Denmark, and he was presently marking time with some job in the Foreign Office in London before getting a new and more senior appointment. The current British ambassador to France was someone by the name of Sir Charles Makepiece. He was an old friend of my father's, and before I left England my father had written a letter to Sir Charles asking him to keep an eye on me.

I knew what I had to do now, and I set about doing it straightaway. I put on my best suit of clothes and made my way to the British Embassy. I did not, of course, go in by the chancery entrance. I knocked on the door of the ambassador's private residence, which was in the same imposing building as the chancery, but at the rear. The time was four in the afternoon. A flunkey in white knee breeches and a scarlet coat with gold buttons opened the door and glared at me. I had no visiting card, but I managed to convey the news that my father and mother were close friends of Sir Charles and Lady Makepiece and would he kindly inform her ladyship that Oswald Cornelius Esquire had come to pay his respects.

I was put into a sort of vestibule where I sat down and waited. Five minutes later, Lady Makepiece swept into the room in a flurry of silk and chiffon. "Well, well!" she cried, taking both my hands in hers. "So *you* are William's son! He always had good taste, the old rascal! We got his letter and we've been waiting for you to call."

She was an imposing wench. Not young, of course, but not exactly fossilized either. I put her around forty. She had one of those dazzling ageless faces that seemed to be carved out of marble, and lower down there was a torso that tapered to a waist I could have circled with my two hands. She sized me up with one swift penetrating glance, and she seemed to be satisfied with what she saw because the next thing she said was, "Come in, William's son, and we shall have a dish of tea together and a chat."

She led me by the hand through a number of vast and superbly appointed rooms until we arrived at a smallish, rather cosy place furnished with a sofa and armchairs. There was a Boucher pastel on one wall and a Fragonard watercolour on another. "This," she said, "is my own private little study. From here I organize the social life of the embassy." I smiled and blinked and sat down on the sofa. One of those fancy-dress flunkeys brought tea and sandwiches on a silver tray. The tiny triangular sandwiches were filled with Gentleman's Relish. Lady Makepiece sat beside me and poured the tea. "Now tell me all about yourself," she said. There followed a whole lot of questions and answers about my family and about me. It was all pretty banal, but I knew I must stick it out for the sake of my great plan. So we went on talking for maybe forty minutes, with her ladyship frequently patting my thigh with a jewelled hand to emphasize a point. In the end, the hand remained resting on my thigh and I felt a slight finger pressure. Ho-ho, I thought. What's the old bird up to now? Then suddenly she sprang to her feet and began pacing nervously up and down the room. I sat watching her. Back and forth she paced, hands clasped together across her front, head twitching, bosom heaving. She was like a tightly coiled spring. I didn't know what to make of it. "I'd better be going," I said, standing up.

"No, no! Don't go!"

I sat down again.

"Have you met my husband?" she blurted out. "Obviously you haven't. You've just arrived. He's a lovely man. A brilliant person. But he's getting on in years, poor lamb, and he can't take as much exercise as he used to."

"Bad luck," I said. "No more polo and tennis."

"Not even Ping-Pong," she said.

"Everyone gets old," I said.

"I'm afraid so. But the point is this." She stopped and waited.

I waited, too.

We both waited. There was a very long silence.

I didn't know what to do with the silence. It made me fidget. "The point is what, madame?" I said.

"Can't you see I'm trying to ask you something?" she said at last.

I couldn't think of an answer to that one, so I helped myself to another of those little sandwiches and chewed it slowly.

"I want to ask you a favour, *mon petit garçon*," she said. "I imagine you are quite good at games?"

"I am rather," I said, resigning myself to a game of tennis with her, or Ping-Pong.

"And you wouldn't mind?"

"Not at all. It would be a pleasure." It was necessary to humour her. All I wanted was to meet the ambassador. The ambassador was my target. He was the chosen one who would receive the first pill and thus start the whole ball rolling. But I could only reach him through her.

"It's not much I'm asking," she said.

"I am at your service, madame."

"You really mean it?"

"Of course."

"You did say you were good at games?"

"I played rugger for my school," I said. "And cricket. I'm a pretty decent fast bowler."

She stopped pacing and gave me a long look.

At that point a tiny little warning bell began tinkling somewhere inside my head. I ignored it. Whatever happened, I must not antagonize this woman.

"I'm afraid I don't play rugger," she said. "Or cricket."

"My tennis is all right, too," I said. "But I haven't brought my racquet." I took another sandwich. I loved the taste of anchovies. "My father says anchovies destroy the palate," I said, chewing away. "He won't have Gentleman's Relish in the house. But I adore it."

She took a great big deep breath and her breasts blew up like two gigantic balloons. "I'll tell you what I want," she whispered softly. "I want you to ravish me and ravish me and ravish me! I want you to ravish me to death! I want you to do it now! Now! Quickly!"

By golly, I thought. Here we go again.

"Don't be shocked, dear boy."

"I'm not shocked."

"Oh yes you are. I can see it on your face. I should never have asked you. You are so young. You are far too young. How old are you? No, don't tell me. I don't want to know. You are very delicious, but schoolboys are forbidden fruit. What a pity. It's quite obvious you have not yet entered the fiery world of women. I don't suppose you've ever even touched one."

That nettled me. "You are mistaken, Lady Makepiece," I said. "I have frolicked with females on both sides of the Channel. Also on ships at sea."

"Why, you naughty boy! I don't believe it!"

I was still on the sofa. She was standing above me. Her big red mouth was open and she was beginning to pant. "You do understand I would never have mentioned it if Charles hadn't been . . . sort of past it, don't you?"

"Of course I understand," I said, wriggling a bit. "I understand very well. I am full of sympathy. I don't blame you in the least."

"You really mean that?"

"Of course."

"Oh, you gorgeous boy!" she cried and she came at me like a tigress.

There is nothing particularly illuminating to report about the barney that followed, except perhaps to mention that her ladyship astounded me with her sofa work. Up until then, I had always regarded the sofa as a rotten romping ground, though heaven knows I had been forced to use it often enough with the London débutantes while the parents were snoring away upstairs. The sofa to me was a beastly uncomfortable thing, surrounded on three sides by padded walls and with a horizontal area that was so narrow one was continually rolling off it onto the floor. But Lady Makepiece was a sofa wizard. For her, the sofa was a kind of gymnastic horse upon which one vaulted and bounced and flipped and rolled and achieved the most remarkable contortions.

"Were you ever a gym teacher?" I asked her.

"Shut up and concentrate," she said, rolling me around like a lump of puff-pastry.

It was lucky for me I was young and pliable, otherwise I'm quite sure I would have suffered a fracture. And that got me thinking about poor old Sir Charles and what he must have gone through in his time. Small wonder he had chosen to go into mothballs. But just wait, I thought, until he swallows the old Blister Beetle! Then it'll be *her* that starts blowing the whistle for time out, not him.

Lady Makepiece was a quick-change artist. A couple of minutes after our little caper had ended, there she was, seated at her small Louis Quinze desk, looking as well-groomed and as unruffled as when I had first met her. The steam had gone out of her now, and she had the sleepy contented expression of a boa constrictor that has just swallowed a live rat. "Look here," she said, studying a piece of paper. "Tomorrow we're giving a rather grand dinner party because it's Mafeking Day."

"But Mafeking was relieved twelve years ago," I said.

"We still celebrate it," she said. "What I'm saying is that Admiral Joubert has dropped out. He's reviewing his fleet in the Mediterranean. How would you like to take his place?"

I only just stopped myself from shouting hooray. It was exactly what I wanted. "I would be honoured," I said.

"Most of the government ministers will be there," she said. "And all the senior ambassadors. Do you have a white tie?"

"I do," I said. In those days, one never travelled any-where without taking full evening dress, even at my age.

"Good," she said, writing my name on the guest list. "Eight o'clock tomorrow evening, then. Good afternoon, my little man. It was nice meeting you." Already she had gone back to studying the guest list, so I found my own way out.

4

THE NEXT EVENING, sharp at eight o'clock, I presented my-self at the embassy. I was fully rigged up in white tie and tails. A tail-coat, in those days, had a deep pocket on the inside of each tail, and in these pockets I had secreted a total of twelve small boxes, each with a single pill inside. The embassy was a blaze of lights, and carriages were rolling up at the gates from all directions. Uniformed flunkeys were everywhere. I marched in and joined the receiving line.

"Dear boy," said Lady Makepiece. "I'm so glad you could come. Charles, this is Oswald Cornelius, William's son."

Sir Charles Makepiece was a tiny little fellow with a full head of elegant white hair. His skin was the colour of biscuits, and there was an unhealthy powdery look about it, as though it had been lightly dusted over with brown sugar. The entire face, from forehead to chin, was criss-crossed with deep hair-line cracks, and this, together with the powdery, biscuity skin, made him look like a terra-cotta bust that was beginning to crumble. "So you are William's boy, are you?" he said, shaking my hand. "How are you making out in Paris? Anything I can do for you, just let me know."

I moved on into the glittering crowd. I seemed to be the only male present who was not smothered in decorations and ribbons. We stood around drinking champagne. Then we went in to dinner. It was quite a sight, that dining-room. About one hundred guests were seated on either side of a table as long as two cricket pitches. Small place cards told us where to sit. I was between two incredibly ugly old females. One was the wife of the Bulgarian ambassador and the other was an aunt of the King of Spain. I concentrated on the food, which was superb. I still remember the large truffle, as big as a golf ball, baked in white wine in a little earthenware pot with the lid on. And the way in which the poached turbot was so superlatively undercooked, with the centre almost raw but still very hot. (The English and the Americans invariably overcook their fish.) And then the wines! They were something to remember, those wines!

But what, pray, did seventeen-year-old Oswald Cornelius know about wines? A fair question. And yet the answer is that he knew rather a lot. Because what I have not yet told you is that my own father loved wine above all other things in life, including women. He was, I think, a genuine expert. His passion was for burgundy. He adored claret, too, but he always considered even the greatest of the clarets to be just a touch on the feminine side. "Claret," he used to say, "may have a prettier face and a better figure, but it's the burgundies that have the muscles and the sinews." By the time I was fourteen, he had begun to communicate some of this wine passion to me, and only a year ago, he had taken me on a ten-day walking tour through Burgundy during the *vendange* in September. We had started out at Chagny and from there we had strolled in our own time northward to Dijon, so that in the week that followed we traversed the entire length of the Côte de Beaune and the Côte de Nuits. It was a thrilling experience. We walked not on the main road but on the narrow rutted tracks that led us past practically every great vineyard on that famous golden slope, first Montrachet, then Meursault, then Pommard, and a night in a wonderful small hotel in Beaune where we ate *écrevisses* swimming in white wine and thick slices of foie gras on buttered toast. I can remember the two of us the next day eating lunch while sitting on the low white wall along the boundary of Romanée-Conti—cold chicken, French bread, a *fromage dur*, and a bottle of Romanée-Conti itself. We spread our food on the top of the wall and stood the bottle alongside, together with two good wineglasses. My father drew the cork and poured the wine while I did my best to carve the chicken, and there we sat in the warm autumn sun, watching the grape pickers combing the rows of vines, filling their baskets, bringing them to the heads of the rows, dumping the grapes into larger baskets, which in turn were emptied into carts drawn by pale creamy-brown horses. I can remember my father sitting on the wall and waving a half-eaten drumstick in the direction of this splendid scene and saying, "You are sitting, my boy, on the edge of the most famous piece of land in the whole world! Just look at it! Four and a half acres of flinty red clay! That's all it is! But those grapes you can see them picking at this very moment will produce a wine that is a glory among wines. It is also almost unobtainable because so little of it is made. This bottle we are drinking now came from here eleven years ago. Smell it! Inhale the bouquet! Taste it! Drink it! But never try to describe it! It is impossible to put such a flavour into words! To drink a Romanée-Conti is like having an orgasm in the mouth and the nose both at the same time."

I loved it when my father got himself worked up like this. Listening to him during those early years, I began to realize how important it was to be an enthusiast in life. He taught me that if you are interested in something, no matter what it is, go at it full speed ahead. Embrace it with both arms, hug it, love it, and above all become passionate about it. Lukewarm is no good. Hot is no good, either. White hot and passionate is the only thing to be.

We visited Clos de Vougeot and Bonnes Mares and Clos de la Roche and Chambertin and many other marvellous places. We went down into the cellars of the châteaux and tasted last year's wine from the barrels. We watched the grapes being pressed in gigantic wooden screw presses that required six men to turn the screw. We saw the juice being run off from the presses into the great wooden vats, and at Chambolle-Musigny, where they had started picking a week earlier than most of the others, we saw the grape juice coming alive in the colossal twelve-foot-high wooden vats, boiling and bubbling as it began its own magic process of converting sugar into alcohol. And while we actually stood there watching, the wine became so fiercely active and the boiling and bubbling reached such a pitch of frenzy that several men had to climb up and sit upon the cover of each vat to hold it down.

I have wandered again. I must get back to my story. But I did want to demonstrate to you very quickly that despite my tender years, I was quite capable of appreciating the quality of the wines I drank that evening at the British Embassy in Paris. They were indeed something to remember.

We started with a Chablis Grand Cru Grenouilles. Then a Latour. Then a Richebourg. And with the dessert, a d'Yquem of great age. I cannot remember the vintage of any one of them, but they were all pre-phylloxera.

When dinner was over, the women, led by Lady Makepiece, left the room. Sir Charles shepherded the men into a vast adjoining sitting-room to drink port and brandy and coffee.

In the sitting-room, as the men began to split up into groups, I quickly manoeuvred myself alongside the host himself. "Ah, there you are, my boy," he said. "Come and sit here with me."

Perfect.

There were eleven of us, including me, in this particular group, and Sir Charles courteously introduced me to each one of them in turn. "This is young Oswald Cornelius," he said. "His father was our man in Copenhagen. Meet the German ambassador, Oswald." I met the German ambassador. Then I met the Italian ambassador and the Hungarian ambassador and the Russian ambassador and the Peruvian ambassador and the Mexican ambassador. Then I met the

French minister for foreign affairs and a French army general and lastly a funny little dark man from Japan who was introduced simply as Mr. Mitsouko. Every one of them spoke English, and it seemed that out of courtesy to their host they were making it the language of the evening.

"Have a glass of port, young man," Sir Charles Makepiece said to me, "and pass it round." I poured myself some port and carefully passed the decanter to my left. "This is a good bottle. Fonseca's eighty-seven. Your father tells me you've got a scholarship to Trinity. Is that right?"

"Yes, sir," I said. My moment was coming any second now. I must not miss it. I must plunge in.

"What's your subject?" Sir Charles asked me.

"Science, sir," I answered. Then I plunged. "As a matter of fact," I said, lifting my voice just enough for them all to hear me, "there's some absolutely amazing work being done in one of the laboratories up there at this moment. Highly secret. You simply wouldn't believe what they've just discovered."

Ten heads came up and ten pairs of eyes rose from port glasses and coffee cups and regarded me with mild interest.

"I didn't know you'd already gone up," Sir Charles said. "I thought you had a year to wait and that's why you're over here."

"Quite right," I said. "But my future tutor invited me to spend most of last term working in the Natural Sciences Lab. That's my favourite subject, natural sciences."

"And what, may I ask, have they just discovered that is so secret and so remarkable?" There was a touch of banter in Sir Charles's voice now, and who could blame him?

"Well, sir," I murmured, and then purposely, I stopped.

Silence for a few seconds. The nine foreigners and the British ambassador sat still, waiting politely for me to go on. They were regarding me with a mixture of tolerance and amusement. This young lad, they seemed to be saying, has a bit of a nerve to be holding forth like this in front of us. But let's hear him out. It's better than talking politics.

"Don't tell me they are letting a fellow of your age handle secrets," Sir Charles said, smiling a little with his crumbling terra-cotta face.

"These aren't *war* secrets, sir," I said. "They couldn't help an enemy. These are secrets that are going to help all of mankind."

"Then tell us about them," Sir Charles said, lighting a huge cigar. "You have a distinguished audience here and they are all waiting to hear from you."

"I think it's the greatest scientific breakthrough since Pasteur," I said. "It's going to change the world."

The foreign minister of France made a sharp whistling sound by sucking air up through his hairy nostrils. "You have another Pasteur in England at this moment?" he said. "If so, I would very much like to hear about him." He was a sleek oily Frenchman, this foreign minister, and sharp as a knife. I would have to watch him.

"If the world is about to be changed," Sir Charles said, "I'm a little surprised that this information hasn't yet found its way to my desk."

Steady on, Oswald, I told myself. You've hardly begun and already you've been laying it on too thick.

"Forgive me, sir, but the point is he hasn't published yet."

"Who hasn't? Who's *he*?"

"Professor Yousoupoff, sir."

The Russian ambassador put down his glass of port and said, "Yousoupoff? Iss he a Russian?"

"Yes, sir, he's a Russian."

"Then vy haven't *I* heard of him?"

I wasn't about to get into a tangle with this black-eyed, black-bearded Cossack, so I kept silent.

"Come on, then, young man," Sir Charles said. "Tell us about the greatest scientific breakthrough of our time. You mustn't keep us in suspense, you know."

I took a few deep breaths and a gulp of port. This was the great moment. Pray heaven I wouldn't mess it up.

"For years," I said, "Professor Yousoupoff has been working on the theory that the seeds of a ripe pomegranate contain an ingredient that has powerful rejuvenative properties."

"We have millions and millions of pomegranates in my country!" the Italian ambassador exclaimed, looking proud.

"Be quiet, Emilio," Sir Charles said. "Let the boy go on."

"For twenty-seven years," I said, "Professor Yousoupoff has been studying the seed of the pomegranate. It became an obsession with him. He used to sleep in the laboratory. He never went out socially. He never married. The whole place was littered with pomegranates and their seeds."

"Excuse me, please," said the little Japanese man. "But why the pomegranate? Why not the grape or the black currant?"

"I cannot answer that question, sir," I said. "I suppose it was simply what you might call a hunch."

"Hell of a long time to spend on a hunch," Sir Charles said. "But go on, my boy. We mustn't interrupt you."

"Last January," I said, "the Professor's patience was at last rewarded. What he did was this. He dissected the seed of a pomegranate and examined the contents bit by bit under a powerful microscope. And it was only then that he observed in the very centre of the seed a minuscule speck of red vegetable tissue that he'd never seen before. He proceeded to isolate this tiny speck of tissue. But it was obviously too small to be of any use on its own. So the Professor set out to dissect one hundred seeds and to obtain from them one hundred of these tiny red particles. This is where he allowed me to assist him. I mean by dissecting out these particles under a microscope. This alone occupied us for a whole week."

I took another sip of port. My audience waited for me to go on.

"So we now had one hundred red particles, but even when we put them all together on a glass slide, the result could still not be seen by the naked eye."

"And you say they were red, these little things?" said the Hungarian ambassador.

"Under the microscope they were a brilliant scarlet," I said.

"And what did this famous professor do with them?"

"He fed them to a rat," I said.

"A rat!"

"Yes," I said. "A big white rat."

"Vy vould anybody vish to feed deese little red bomegranate tings to a rat?" the German ambassador asked.

"Give him a chance, Wolfgang," Sir Charles said to the German. "Let him finish. I want to know what happened." He nodded for me to go on.

"You see, sir," I said, "Professor Yousoupoff had in the laboratory a lot of white rats. He took the one hundred tiny red particles and fed every one of them to a single large healthy male rat. He did this by inserting them, under a microscope, into a piece of meat. He then put the rat in a cage together with ten female rats. I remember very clearly how the Professor and I stood beside the cage watching the male rat. It was late afternoon and we were so excited we had forgotten all about lunch."

"Excuse me one moment, please," the clever French foreign minister said. "But why were you so excited? What made you think that *anything* was going to happen with this rat?"

Here we go, I thought. I knew I'd have to watch this wily Frenchman. "I was excited, sir, simply because the Professor was excited," I said. "He seemed to *know* something was going to happen. I can't tell you how. Don't forget, gentlemen, I was only a very young junior assistant. The Professor did not tell me all his secrets."

"I see," the foreign minister said. "Then let us proceed."

"Yes, sir," I said. "Well, we were watching the rat. At first, nothing happened. Then suddenly, after exactly nine minutes, the rat became very still. He crouched down, quivering all over. He was looking at the females. He crept toward the nearest one and grabbed her by the skin of her neck with his teeth and mounted her. It did not take long. He was very fierce with her and very swift. But here's the extraordinary thing. The moment the rat had finished copulating with the first female, he grabbed a second one and set about her in just the same way. Then he took a third female rat, and a fourth, and a fifth. He was absolutely tireless. He went from one female to another, fornicating with each in turn until he had covered all ten of them. Even then, gentlemen, he hadn't had enough!"

"Good gracious me!" Sir Charles murmured. "What a curious experiment."

"I should add," I went on, "that rats are not normally promiscuous creatures. They are in fact rather moderate in their sexual habits."

"Are you sure of that?" the French foreign minister said. "I thought rats were extraordinarily lascivious."

"No, sir," I answered firmly. "Rats are actually very intelligent and gentle creatures. They are easy to domesticate."

"Go on, then," Sir Charles said. "What did all this tell you?"

"Professor Yousoupoff got very excited. 'Oswaldsky!' he shouted—that's what he called me. 'Oswaldsky, my boy, I think I have discovered the absolutely greatest most powerful sexual stimulant in the whole history of mankind!'

" 'I think you have, too,' I said. We were still standing by the cage of rats and the male rat was still leaping on the wretched females, one after the other. Within an hour, he had collapsed from exhaustion. 'We give him too big a dose,' the Professor said."

"This rat," the Mexican ambassador said, "what came of him in the end?"

"He died," I said.

"From too much women, yes?"

"Yes," I said.

The little Mexican clapped his hands together hard and cried out, "That is exactly how I wish to go when I die! From too much women!"

"From too much goats and donkeys iss more like it in Mexico," the German ambassador snorted.

"That's enough of that, Wolfgang," Sir Charles said. "Let's not start any wars. We are listening to a most interesting story. Carry on, my boy."

"So the next time," I said, "we isolated only twenty of these tiny red microscopic nuclei. We inserted them in a pellet of bread and then went out looking for a very old man. With the help of the local newspaper, we found our old man in Newmarket—that's a town not far from Cambridge. His name was Mr. Sawkins, and he was one hundred and two years old. He was suffering from advanced senility. His mind was wandering and he had to be fed by spoon. He had not been out of bed for seven years. The Professor and I knocked on the door of his house and his daughter, aged eighty, opened it. 'I am Professor Yousoupoff,' the Professor announced. 'I have discovered a great medicine to help old people. Will you allow us to give some to your poor old father?'

" ' You can give 'im anything you damn well please,' the daughter said. 'The old fool doesn't know what's goin' on from one day to the next. 'E's a flamin' nuisance.'

"We went upstairs and the Professor somehow managed to poke the bread pellet down the old man's throat. I noted the time by my watch. 'Let us retire to the street outside and observe,' the Professor said.

"We went out and stood in the street. I was counting each minute aloud as it went by. And then—you won't believe this, gentlemen, but I swear it's exactly what happened—precisely on the dot of nine minutes, there was a thunderous bellow from inside the Sawkins house. The front door burst open and the old man himself rushed out into the street. He was in bare feet, wearing dirty blue-and-grey-striped pyjamas, and his long white hair was all over his shoulders. 'I want me a woman!' he bellowed. 'I want me a woman and by God I'm goin' to get me a woman!' The Professor clutched my arm. 'Don't move!' he ordered. 'Just observe!'

"The eighty-year-old daughter came rushing out after the father. 'Come back, you old fool!' she yelled. 'What the 'ell d'you think you're up to?'

"We were, by the way, in a little street with a row of

identical connected houses on either side. Mr. Sawkins ignored his daughter and ran, he actually ran, to the next-door house. He started banging on the door with his fists. 'Open up, Mrs. Twitchell!' he bellowed. 'Come on, my beauty, open up and let's 'ave a bit of fun!'

"I caught a glimpse of the terrified face of Mrs. Twitchell at the window. Then it went away. Mr. Sawkins, still bellowing, put his shoulder to the flimsy door and smashed the lock. He dived inside. We stayed out on the street, waiting for the next development. The Professor was very excited. He was jumping up and down in his funny black boots and shouting, 'We have a breakthrough! We've done it! We shall rejuvenate the world!'

"Suddenly, piercing screams and yells came issuing from Mrs. Twitchell's house. Neighbours were beginning to gather on the street. 'Go in and get 'im!' shouted the old daughter. ''E's gone stark starin' mad!' Two men ran into the Twitchell house. There were sounds of a scuffle. Soon, out came the two men, frog-marching old Mr. Sawkins between them. 'I 'ad er!' he was yelling. 'I 'ad the old bitch good and proper! I near rattled 'er to death!' At that point, the Professor and I moved quietly away from the scene."

I paused in my story. Seven ambassadors, the foreign minister of France, the French army general, and the little Japanese man were all now leaning forward in their seats, their eyes upon me.

"Is this *exactly* what happened?" Sir Charles asked me.

"Every word of it, sir, is the gospel truth," I lied. "When Professor Yousoupoff publishes his findings, the whole world will be reading what I have just told you."

"So what happened next?" the Peruvian ambassador asked.

"From then on, it was comparatively simple," I said. "The Professor conducted a series of experiments designed to discover what the proper absolutely safe dose should be for a normal adult male. For this, he used undergraduate volunteers. And you can be quite sure, gentlemen, that he had no trouble getting young men to come forward. As soon as the news spread around the university, there was a waiting list of over eight hundred. But to cut the story short, the Professor finally demonstrated that the safe dose was no more than five of those tiny microscopic nuclei from the pomegranate seed. So, using calcium carbonate as a base, he manufactured a pill containing exactly this quantity of the magic substance. And he proved beyond any doubt that just one of these pills would, in precisely nine minutes, turn any man, even a very old man, into a marvellously powerful sex-machine that was capable of pleasuring his partner for six hours nonstop, *without exception.*"

"*Gott in Himmel!*" shouted the German ambassador. "Ver can I get hold of ziss stuff?"

"Me too!" cried the Russian ambassador. "I haff priority claim because it voss invented by my countryman! I muss inform zee Tsar at vonce!"

Suddenly, they were all speaking at the same time. Where could they get it? They wanted it now! How much did it cost? They were willing to pay handsomely! And the little Japanese fellow sitting on my left leaned over and hissed, "You get me big supply of pills, yes. I give you very much money."

"Now just a moment, gentlemen," Sir Charles said, raising a wrinkled hand for silence. "Our young friend here has told us a fascinating story, but as he correctly pointed out, he was only a junior assistant to Professor whatever-his-name-is. I am quite sure, therefore, that he is

not in a position to supply us with this remarkable new
pill. Perhaps though, my dear Oswald"—and here Sir
Charles leaned toward me and placed a withered hand
gently on my forearm—"perhaps, my dear Oswald, you
could put me in touch with the great Professor. One of
my duties here at the embassy is to keep the Foreign Office
informed of all new scientific discoveries."

"I quite understand," I said.

"If I could obtain a bottle of these pills, preferably a
large bottle, I would send it straight to London."

"And I vould send it to Petrograd," said the Russian
ambassador.

"And me to Budapest."

"And me to Mexico City."

"And me to Lima."

"And me to Rome."

"Rubbish!" cried the German ambassador. "You vant
dem for yourselves, you dirty olt men!"

"Now then, Wolfgang," Sir Charles said, squirming a
bit.

"Vy not, my dear Sharles? I too vant dem for myself.
For zee Kaiser as well, of course, but me first."

I decided I rather liked the German ambassador. He was
honest anyway.

"I think it best, gentlemen," Sir Charles said, "if I myself
make all the arrangements. I shall write personally to the
Professor."

"The Japanese people," Mr. Mitsouko said, "are very
interested in all massage techniques and hot baths and in all
similar technological advances, especially the Emperor
himself."

I allowed them to finish. I was in control now and that
gave me a good feeling. I helped myself to another glass of

port but refused the huge cigar Sir Charles offered me. "Would you prefer a smaller one, dear boy?" he asked me eagerly. "Or a Turkish cigarette? I have some Balkan Sobranies."

"No, thank you, sir," I said. "But the port is delicious."

"Help yourself, dear boy! Fill your glass!"

"I have some interesting news," I said, and suddenly everyone became silent. The German ambassador cupped a hand behind his ear. The Russian leaned forward in his seat. So did all the rest of them.

"What I am about to tell you is extremely confidential," I said. "May I rely upon all of you to keep it to yourselves?"

There was a chorus of "Yes, yes! Of course! Absolutely! Carry on, young fellow!"

"Thank you," I said. "Now the point is this. As soon as I knew that I was going to Paris I decided I simply must take with me a supply of these pills, especially for my father's great friend Sir Charles Makepiece."

"My dear boy!" Sir Charles cried out. "What a generous thought!"

"I could not, of course, ask the Professor to give any of them to me," I said. "He would never have agreed to that. After all, they are still on the secret list."

"So what did you do?" asked Sir Charles. He was dribbling with excitement. "Did you purloin them?"

"Certainly not, sir," I said. "Stealing is a criminal act."

"Never mind about us, dear boy. We won't tell a soul."

"So vot did you do?" the German ambassador asked. "You say you haff dem and you didn't steal dem?"

"I made them myself," I said.

"Brilliant!" they cried. "*Magnifique!*"

"Having assisted the Professor at every stage," I said,

"I naturally knew exactly how to manufacture these pills. So I . . . well . . . I simply made them in his laboratory each day when he was out to lunch." Slowly, I reached behind me and took one small round box from my tail-coat pocket. I placed it on the low table. I opened the lid. And there, lying in its little nest of cotton-wool, was a single scarlet pill.

Everyone leaned forward to look. Then I saw the plump white hand of the German ambassador sliding across the surface of the table toward the box like a weasel stalking a mouse. Sir Charles saw it, too. He smacked the palm of his own hand on top of the German's, pinning it down. "Now, Wolfgang," he said, "don't be impatient."

"I vant zee pill!" Ambassador Wolfgang shouted.

Sir Charles put his other hand over the pill-box and kept it there. "Do you have more?" he asked me.

I fished in my tail-coat pockets and brought out nine more boxes. "There is one for each of you," I said.

Eager hands reached across, grabbing the little boxes. "I pay," said Mr. Mitsouko. "How much you want?"

"No," I said. "These are presents. Try them out, gentlemen. See what you think."

Sir Charles was studying the label on the box. "Ah-ha," he said. "I see you have your address printed here."

"That's just in case," I said.

"In case of what?"

"In case anyone wishes to get a second pill," I said.

I noticed that the German ambassador had taken out a little book and was making notes. "Sir," I said to him, "I expect you are thinking of telling your scientists to investigate the seed of the pomegranate. Am I not right?"

"Zatt iss exactly vot I am tinking," he said.

"No good," I said. "Waste of time."

"May I ask vy?"

"Because it's not the pomegranate," I said. "It's something else."

"So you lie to us!"

"It is the only untruth I have told you in the entire story," I said. "Forgive me, but I had to do it. I had to protect Professor Yousoupoff's secret. It was a point of honour. All the rest is true. Believe me, it's true. It is especially true that each of you has in his possession the most powerful rejuvenator the world has ever known."

At that point, the ladies returned, and each man in our group quickly and rather surreptitiously pocketed his pill-box. They stood up. They greeted their wives. I noticed that Sir Charles had suddenly become absurdly jaunty. He hopped across the room and splashed a silly sort of kiss smack on Lady Makepiece's scarlet lips. She gave him one of those cool what-on-earth-was-that-for looks. Unabashed, he took her arm and led her across the room into a throng of people. I last saw Mr. Mitsouko prowling around the floor inspecting the womanflesh at very close quarters, like a horse-dealer examining a bunch of mares on the market-place. I slipped quietly away.

Half an hour later, I was back at my boarding-house in the avenue Marceau. The family had retired and all the lamps were out, but as I passed the bedroom of Mademoiselle Nicole in the upstairs corridor, I could see in the crack between the door and the floor a flicker of candlelight. The little trollop was waiting for me again. I decided not to go in. There was nothing new for me in there. Even at this early stage in my career, I had already decided that the only women who interested me were new women. Second time round was no good. It was like reading a detective novel twice over. You knew exactly what was going to happen next. The fact that I had recently broken this rule by visiting Mademoiselle Nicole a second time was beside the point. That was done simply to test my Blister Beetle powder. And by the way, this principle of no-woman-more-than-once is one that I have stuck to rigorously all my life, and I commend it to all men of action who enjoy variety.

5

THAT NIGHT I slept well. I was still fast asleep at eleven o'clock the next morning when the sound of Madame Boisvain's fists hammering at my door jerked me awake. "Get up, Monsieur Cornelius!" she was shouting. "You must come down at once! People have been ringing my bell and demanding to see you since before breakfast!"

I was dressed and downstairs in two minutes flat. I went to the front door and there, standing on the cobblestones of the sidewalk, were no fewer than seven men, none of whom I had ever seen before. They made a picturesque little group in their many-coloured fancy uniforms with all manner of gilt and silver buttons on their jackets.

They turned out to be embassy messengers, and they came from the British, the German, the Russian, the Hungarian, the Italian, the Mexican, and the Peruvian embassies. Each man carried a letter addressed to me. I accepted the letters and opened them on the spot. All of them said roughly the same thing: *They wanted more pills.* They begged for more pills. They instructed me to give the pills to the bearer of the letter, etc. etc.

I told the messengers to wait on the street and I went back up to my room. Then, I wrote the following message on each of the letters: *Honoured Sir, these pills are extremely expensive to manufacture. I regret that in future the cost of each pill will be one thousand francs.* In those days there were twenty francs to the pound, which meant that I was asking exactly fifty pounds sterling per pill. And fifty pounds sterling in 1912 was worth maybe ten times as much as it is today. By today's standards, I was probably asking about five hundred pounds per pill. It was a ridiculous price, but these were wealthy men. They were also sex-crazy men, and as any sensible woman will tell you, a man who is very wealthy and grossly sex-crazy both at the same time is the easiest touch in the world. I trotted downstairs again and handed the letters back to their respective carriers and told them to deliver them to their masters. As I was doing this, two more messengers arrived, one from the Quai d'Orsay (the foreign minister) and one from the general at the Ministry of War or whatever it is called. And while I was scribbling the same statement about the price on these last two letters, who should turn up in a very fine hansom cab but Mr. Mitsouko himself. His appearance shocked me. The previous night he had been a bouncy, dapper, bright-eyed little Jap. This morning he hardly had the strength to get out of his cab, and as he came tottering toward me, his legs began to buckle. I grabbed hold of him just in time.

"My dear sir!" he gasped, putting both hands on my shoulders for support. "My dear, dear sir! It's a miracle! It's a wonder pill! It's . . . it's the greatest invention of all time!"

"Hang on," I said. "Are you feeling all right?"

"Of course I am all right," he gasped. "I am a little bit jiggered, that's all." He started to giggle, and there he stood, this tiny Oriental person dressed in a top-hat and tails, clinging to my shoulders and giggling quite uncontrollably now. He was so small that the top of his top-hat came no higher than my lowest rib. "I am a little bit jiggered and a little bit pokered," he said, "but who would not be, my dear boy, who would not be?"

"What happened, sir?" I asked him.

"I molested *seven women*!" he cried. "And these were not our dinky-tinky little Japanese women! No, no, no! They were enormous strong French wenchies! I took them in rotation, *bang bang bang*! And every one of them was screaming out *camarade camarade camarade*! I was a giant among these women, do you understand that, my dear young sir? I was a giant and I swung my giant club and I sent them all squiggling in every direction!"

I led him inside and sat him down in Madame Boisvain's parlour. I found him a glass of brandy. He gulped it down and a faint yellowish colour began returning to his white cheeks. I noticed that there was a leather satchel suspended by a cord around his right wrist, and when he took it off and dumped it on the table, there was the clinking of coins inside it.

"You must be careful, sir," I said to him. "You are a small man and these are large pills. I think it would be safer if you took only half the normal dose each time. Just half a pill instead of one."

"Bunkum, sir!" he cried. "Bunkum and horseradish sauce, as we say in Japan! Tonight I propose to take not one pill but three!"

"Have you read what it says on the label?" I asked him

anxiously. The last thing I wanted was a dead Jap around the place. Think of the outcry, the autopsy, the enquiries, and the pill-boxes with my name on them in his house.

"I examine the label," he said, holding his glass out for more of Madame Boisvain's brandy. "And I ignore it. We Japanese, we may be small in body but our organs are of gigantic size. That is why we walk bow-legged."

I decided I would try to discourage him by doubling the price. "I'm afraid they are terrifically expensive, these pills," I said.

"Money no object," he said, pointing to the leather satchel on the table. "I pay in gold coins."

"But Mr. Mitsouko," I said, "each pill is going to cost you *two thousand* francs! They are very difficult to manufacture. That's an awful lot of money for one pill."

"I take twenty," he said without even blinking.

My God, I thought, he *is* going to kill himself. "I cannot allow you to have them," I told him, "unless you give me your word you will never take more than one at a time."

"Do not lecture me, young buckeroo," he said. "Just get me the pills."

I went upstairs and counted out twenty pills and put them in a plain bottle. I wasn't going to risk having my name and address on this lot.

"Ten I shall send to the Emperor in Tokyo," Mr. Mitsouko said when I handed them to him. "It will put me in a very hot position with His Royal Highness."

"It'll put the Empress in some pretty hot positions, too," I said.

He grinned and took up the leather satchel and emptied a vast pile of gold coins onto the table. They were all one-hundred-franc pieces. "Twenty coins for each pill," he said, starting to count them out. "That is four hundred coins altogether. And well worth it, you young magician."

When he had gone, I scooped up the coins and carried them up to my room.

My God, I thought. I am rich already.

But before the day was done, I was a lot richer. One by one, the messengers started trickling back from their respective embassies and ministries. They all carried precise orders and exact amounts of money, most of it in gold twenty-franc pieces. This is how it went:

Sir Charles Makepiece, 4 pills	=	4,000 francs
The German ambassador, 8 pills	=	8,000 francs
The Russian ambassador, 10 pills	=	10,000 francs
The Hungarian ambassador, 3 pills	=	3,000 francs
The Peruvian ambassador, 2 pills	=	2,000 francs
The Mexican ambassador, 6 pills	=	6,000 francs
The Italian ambassador, 4 pills	=	4,000 francs
The French foreign minister, 6 pills	=	6,000 francs
The Army general, 3 pills	=	3,000 francs
		46,000 francs
Mr. Mitsouko, 20 pills (double price)		40,000 francs
Grand Total		86,000 francs

Eighty-six thousand francs! At the exchange rate of one hundred francs to five pounds, I was all of a sudden worth four thousand three hundred English pounds! It was incredible. One could buy a good house for money like that, with a carriage and a pair of horses thrown in, as well as one of those dashing newfangled automobiles!

For supper that night, Madame Boisvain served oxtail stew, and it wasn't at all bad except that the sloshiness of it all encouraged Monsieur B to suck and swig and gulp in the most disgusting fashion. At one point, he picked up his plate and tipped the gravy straight into his mouth, together with a couple of carrots and a large onion. "My wife tells me that you had a lot of peculiar visitors today," he said. His face was plastered with brown fluid and strands of meat were hanging from his moustache. "Who were these men?"

"They were friends of the British ambassador," I answered. "I am doing a little business for Sir Charles Makepiece."

"I cannot have my house turned into a market-place," Monsieur B said, speaking with his mouth full of fat. "These activities must cease."

"Don't worry," I said. "Tomorrow I am finding alternative accommodation."

"You mean you're leaving?" he cried.

"I'm afraid I must. But you may keep the advance rent my father has paid you."

There was a bit of an uproar around the table about all this, much of it from Mademoiselle Nicole, but I stuck to my guns. And the next morning I went out and found myself a quite grand ground-floor apartment with three large rooms and a kitchen. It was on the avenue Jena. I packed all my possessions and loaded them into a hackney coach. Madame Boisvain was at the front door to see me off. "Madame," I said, "I have a small favour to ask of you."

"Yes?"

"And in return I want you to take this." I held out five gold twenty-franc pieces. She nearly fell over. "From time to time," I said, "people will call at your house asking for me. All you have to do is tell them I have moved and redirect them to this address." I gave her a piece of paper with my new address written on it.

"But that is too much money, Monsieur Oswald!"

"Take it," I said, pushing the coins into her hand. "Keep it for yourself. Don't tell your husband. But it is very important that you inform everyone who calls where I am living."

She promised to do this, and I drove away to my new quarters.

6

MY BUSINESS FLOURISHED. My ten original clients all whispered the great news to their own friends and those friends whispered it to other friends and in a month or so a large snowball had been created. I spent half of each day making pills. I thanked heaven I had had the foresight to bring such a large quantity of powder from the Sudan in the first place. But I did have to reduce my price. Not everyone was an ambassador or a foreign minister, and I found early on that a lot of people simply couldn't afford to pay my absurd original fee of one thousand francs per pill. So I made it two hundred and fifty instead.

The money gushed in.

I started buying fine clothes and going out into Paris society.

I purchased a motor car and learnt to drive it. It was De Dion Bouton's brand-new model, the Sports DK, a marvellous little monobloc four with a three-speed gearbox and a pull-on handbrake. Top speed, believe it or not, was as much as 50 mph, and more than once I took her to the limit up the Champs Elysées.

But above all, I rolicked and frolicked with women to my heart's content. Paris in those days was an exceptionally cosmopolitan city. It was filled with ladies of quality from practically every country in the world, and it was during this period that a curious truth began to dawn upon me. We all know that people of different nations have different national characteristics and different temperaments. What is not quite so well recognized is the fact that these different national characteristics become even more marked during sexual, as opposed to merely social, intercourse. I became an expert on national sexual characteristics. It was extraordinary how the women of one nation or another ran true to form. You could take, for example, half a dozen Serbian ladies (and don't think I didn't) and you would find, if you were paying close attention, that every one of them possessed a number of very definite common eccentricities, common skills, and common preferences. Polish women also, because of certain habits they all had in common, were easily recognizable. So were the Basques, the Moroccans, the Ecuadorians, the Norwegians, the Dutch, the Guatemalans, the Belgians, the Russians, the Chinese, and all the rest of them. Toward the end of my stay in Paris, you could have put me on a couch blindfolded with any lady from any country, and within five minutes, though she never uttered a word, I would have told you her nationality.

Now for the obvious question. Which country produced the most exhilarating females?

I myself became rather partial to Bulgarian ladies of aristocratic stamp. They had, amongst other things, the most unusual tongues. Not only were these tongues of theirs exceptionally muscular and vibrant, but they had a roughness about them, a kind of abrasive quality that one normally finds only in cats' tongues. Get a cat to lick your finger sometime and you will see exactly what I mean.

Turkish ladies (I think I've mentioned them before) were also high on my list. They were like water-wheels. They never stopped turning until the river dried up. But by gad, you had to be fit before you challenged a Turkish lady, and I personally never allowed one into my house until after I'd had a good breakfast.

Hawaiian women interested me because they had prehensile toes, and in almost any situation you care to mention, they used their feet rather than their hands.

As far as Chinese women went, I learned by experience to tamper only with those that came from Peking and the neighbouring province of Shantung. And even then, it was essential that they were from noble families. In those days, it was the custom among the nobility of Peking and Shantung to put their girls into the hands of wise old women as soon as they reached the age of fifteen. For two years thereafter, these girls were subjected to a rigorous course of instruction designed to teach them only one thing— the art of giving physical pleasure to their future husbands. And at the end of it all, after a severe practical examination, certificates were issued indicating a pass or a failure. If the girl was exceptionally dexterous and inventive, she might get what was called Pass with Distinction, and most prized of all was the Diploma of Merit. A young lady with a Diploma could virtually pick her own husband. Unfortunately though, at least half the Diploma girls were whisked away at once into the Emperor's palace. I discovered only one Chinese lady in Paris who had earned a Diploma of Merit. She was the wife of an opium millionaire and she had come over to select a wardrobe. She selected me as well, and I must admit it was a memorable experience. She had developed into a sublime art the practice of what she called *so-far-and-no-further*. Nothing ever quite finished. She didn't allow it to. She took one to the brink. Two hundred times she took me to the brink of the golden threshold, and for three and a half hours, which was the duration of my suffering, it felt as though a long live nerve was being drawn very very slowly and with exquisite patience out of my burning body. I hung onto the edge of the cliff with my fingertips, screaming for succour or release, but the blissful torture went on and on and on. It was an amazing demonstration of skill and I have never forgotten it.

I could describe if I wished the curious feminine habits of at least fifty other nationalities, but I am not going to do so. Not here anyway, because I really must proceed with the main theme of this story, which is how I made money.

During my seventh month in Paris, a lucky incident took place that doubled my income. This is what happened. One afternoon, I had a Russian lady in my apartment who was some sort of a relation to the Tsar. She was a slim, white-skinned little herring, rather cool and casual, almost off-hand she was, and I had to stoke her up pretty vigorously before I succeeded in raising a good head of steam in her boilers. That sort of blasé attitude only makes me more determined than ever, and I can promise you that by the time I'd finished with her, she'd had a fair old roasting.

When it was over, I lay back on the couch sipping a glass of champagne as a cooler. The Russian was languidly dressing herself and wandering round my room looking at this and that.

"What are all these red pills in this bottle?" she asked me.

"They're none of your business," I said.

"When am I going to see you again?"

"Never," I said. "I told you my rules."

"You are being disagreeable," she said, pouting. "Tell me what these pills are for or I also will become disagreeable. I will throw them all out the window." She picked up the bottle that contained five hundred of my precious Blister Beetle pills just made that morning and she opened the window.

"Don't," I said.

"Then tell me."

"They are tonic pills for men," I said. "Pick-me-ups, that's all."

"Why not for women also?"

"They're only for men."

"I shall try one," she said, unscrewing the bottle top and tipping out a pill. She popped it into her mouth and washed it down with champagne. Then she continued putting on her clothes.

She was fully dressed and was adjusting her hat in front of the looking-glass when suddenly she froze. She turned and faced me. I lay where I was, sipping my drink, but I was now watching her closely and with some trepidation.

She remained frozen for maybe thirty seconds, staring at me with a cold hard dangerous stare. Then all at once, she reached both hands up to her neckline and ripped her silk dress clean off her body. She tore off her underclothes. She flung her hat across the room. She crouched. She began to move forward. She came softly across the room toward me with the slow deliberate tread of a tigress stalking an antelope.

"What's up?" I said. But by now I knew very well what was up. Nine minutes had gone by and the pill had hit her.

"Steady on," I said.

She kept coming.

"Go away," I said.

Still she kept coming.

Then she sprang, and all I could see in those first few moments was a blurred flurry of legs and arms and mouth and hands and fingers. She went quite mad. She was wild with lust. I hauled in my canvas and lay there trying to ride out the storm. That wasn't good enough for her. She began to throw me around all over the place, snorting and grunting as she did so. I didn't like it. I'd had my fill. This must stop, I decided. But I still had a terrific job pinning her down. In the end, I got her wrists locked behind her back and I carried her kicking and screaming into my bathroom and held her under the cold shower. She tried to bite me but I gave her an uppercut to the chin with my elbow. I held her under that freezing shower for at least twenty minutes while she went on yelling and swearing in Russian all the time.

"Had enough?" I said at last. She was half-drowned and pretty cold.

"I want you!" she spluttered.

"No," I said. "I'm going to keep you here until you cool down."

Finally she gave in. I let her go. Poor girl, she was shivering terribly and she looked a sight. I got a towel and gave her a good rub down. Then a glass of brandy.

"It was that red pill," she said.

"I know it was."

"I want some of them to take home."

"Those are too strong for ladies," I said. "I will make you some that are just right."

"Now?"

"No. Come back tomorrow and they'll be ready."

Because her dress was ruined, I wrapped her in my over-coat and drove her home in the De Dion. Actually, she had done me a good turn. She had demonstrated that my pill worked just as well on the female as it did on the male. Probably better. I immediately set about making some ladies' pills. I made them half the strength of the men's pills, and I turned out one hundred of them, anticipating a ready market. But the market was even more ready than I had anticipated. When the Russian woman came back the next afternoon, she demanded five hundred of them on the spot!

"But they cost two hundred and fifty francs each."

"I don't care about that. All my girl friends want them. I told them what happened to me yesterday and now they all want them."

"I can give you a hundred, that's all. The rest later. Do you have money?"

"Of course I have money."

"May I make a suggestion, madame?"

"What is it?"

"If a lady takes one of these pills on her own, I fear she may appear unduly aggressive. Men don't like that. I didn't like it yesterday."

"What is your suggestion?"

"I suggest that any lady who intends taking one of these pills should persuade her partner also to take one. And at exactly the same time. Then they'll be all square."

"That makes good sense," she said.

It not only made good sense, it would also double the sales.

"The partner," I said, "could take a larger pill. It's called the men's pill. That's simply because men are bigger than women and need a bigger dose."

"Always assuming," she said, smiling a little, "that the partner is a male."

"Whatever you like," I said.

She shrugged her shoulders and said, "Very well, then, give me also one hundred of these men's pills."

By gum, I thought, there's going to be some fun and frolics around the boudoirs of Paris tonight. Things were hot enough with just the man getting himself all pilled up, but I shuddered to think what was going to happen when both parties took the medicine.

It was a howling success. Sales doubled. They trebled. By the time my twelve months in Paris were up, I had around two million francs in the bank! That was one hundred thousand pounds! I was now nearly eighteen. I was rich. But I was not rich enough. My year in France had shown me very clearly the path I wanted to follow in my life. I was a sybarite. I wished to lead a life of luxury and leisure. I would never get bored. That was not my style. But I would never be completely satisfied unless the luxury was intensely luxurious and the leisure was unlimited. One hundred thousand pounds was not enough for that. I needed more. I needed a million pounds at least. I felt sure I would find a way to earn it. Meanwhile, I had not made a bad start.

I had enough sense to realize that first of all I must continue my education. Education is everything. I have a horror of uneducated people. And so, in the summer of 1913, I transferred my money to a London bank and returned to the land of my fathers. In September, I went up to Cambridge to begin my undergraduate studies. I was a scholar remember, a scholar of Trinity College, and as such, I had a number of privileges and was well treated by those in authority.

It was here at Cambridge that the second and final phase of my fortune-making began. Bear with me a little longer and you shall hear all about it in the pages to come.

7

MY CHEMISTRY TUTOR at Cambridge was called A. R. Woresley. He was a middle-aged, shortish man, paunchy, untidily dressed, and with a grey moustache whose edges were stained yellow ochre by the nicotine from his pipe. In appearance, therefore, a typical university don. But he struck me as being exceptionally able. His lectures were never routine. His mind was always darting about in search of the unusual. Once he said to us, "And now we need as it were a tompion to protect the contents of this flask from invading bacteria. I presume you know what a tompion is, Cornelius?"

"I can't say I do, sir," I said.

"Can anyone give me a definition of that common English noun?" A. R. Woresley said.

Nobody could.

"Then you'd better look it up," he said. "It is not my business to teach you elementary English."

"Oh, come on, sir," someone said. "Tell us what it means."

"A tompion," A. R. Woresley said, "is a small pellet

made out of mud and saliva which a bear inserts into his anus before hibernating for the winter, to stop the ants getting in."

A strange fellow, A. R. Woresley, a mixture of many attitudes, occasionally witty, more often pompous and sombre, but underneath everything there was a curiously complex mind. I began to like him very much after that little tompion episode. We struck up a pleasant student-tutor relationship. I was invited to his house for sherry. He was a bachelor. He lived with his sister, who was called Emmaline of all names. She was dumpy and frowsy and seemed to have something greenish on her teeth that looked like verdigris. She had a kind of surgery in the house where she did things to people's feet. A pedicurist, I think she called herself.

Then the Great War broke out. It was 1914 and I was nineteen years old. I joined the army. I had to, and for the next four years I concentrated all my efforts on trying to survive. I am not going to talk about my wartime experiences. Trenches, mud, mutilation, and death have no place in these journals. I did my bit. Actually, I did well, and by November 1918, when it all came to an end, I was a twenty-three-year-old captain in the infantry with a Military Cross. I had survived.

At once, I returned to Cambridge to resume my education. The survivors were allowed to do that, though heaven knows there weren't many of us. A. R. Woresley had also survived. He had remained in Cambridge doing some sort of wartime scientific work and had had a fairly quiet war. Now he was back at his old job of teaching chemistry to undergraduates, and we were pleased to see one another again. Our friendship picked up where it had left off four years before.

One evening in February 1919, in the middle of the
Lent term, A. R. Woresley invited me to supper at his
house. The meal was not good. We had cheap food and
cheap wine, and we had his pedicurist sister with verdigris
on her teeth. I would have thought they could have lived
in slightly better style than they did, but when I broached
this delicate subject rather cautiously to my host, he told
me that they were still struggling to pay off the mortgage
on the house. After supper, A. R. Woresley and I retired
to his study to drink a good bottle of port that I had
brought him as a present. It was a Croft 1890, if I remember rightly.

"Don't often taste stuff like this," he said. He was very
comfortable in an old armchair with his pipe lit and a
glass of port in his hand. What a thoroughly decent man
he was, I thought. And what a terribly dull life he leads.
I decided to liven things up a bit by telling him about my
time in Paris six years before in 1913 when I had made one
hundred thousand pounds out of Blister Beetle pills. I
started at the beginning. Very quickly I got caught up in
the fun of story-telling. I remembered everything, but in
deference to my tutor, I left out the more salacious details.
It took me nearly an hour to tell.

A. R. Woresley was enraptured by the whole escapade.
"By gad, Cornelius!" he cried. "What a nerve you've got!
What a splendid nerve! And now you are a very wealthy
young man!"

"Not wealthy enough," I said. "I want to make a million
pounds before I'm thirty."

"And I believe you will," he said. "I believe you will.
You have a flair for the outrageous. You have a nose for
the successful stunt. You have the courage to act swiftly.
And what's more, you are totally unscrupulous. In other

words, you have all the qualities of the nouveau riche millionaire."

"Thank you," I said.

"Yes, but how many boys of seventeen would have gone all the way out to Khartoum on their own to look for a powder that might not even have existed? Precious few."

"I wasn't going to miss a chance like that," I said.

"You have a great flair, Cornelius. A very great flair. I am envious of you."

We sat there drinking our port. I was enjoying a small Havana cigar. I had offered one to my host but he preferred his stinking pipe. That pipe of his made more smoke than any other pipe I had ever seen. It was like a miniature warship laying a smokescreen in front of his face. And behind the smokescreen, A. R. Woresley was brooding on my Paris story. He kept snorting and grunting and mumbling things like "Remarkable exploit! . . . What a nerve! . . . What panache! . . . Good chemistry, too, making those pills."

Then there was silence. The smoke billowed around his head. The glass of port disappeared through the smokescreen as he put it to his lips. Then it reappeared, empty. I had talked enough, so I kept my peace.

"Well, Cornelius," A. R. Woresley said at last. "You have just given me your confidence. Perhaps I had better give you mine in return."

He paused. I waited. What's coming, I wondered.

"You see," he said. "I myself have also had a little bit of a coup in the last few years."

"You have?"

"I'm going to write a paper on it when I get the time. And I might even be successful in getting it published."

"Chemistry?" I asked.

"A bit of chemistry," he said. "And a good deal of bio-chemistry. It's a mixture."

"I'd love to hear about it."

"Would you really?" He was longing to tell it.

"Of course." I poured him another glass of port. "You've got plenty of time," I said, "because we're going to finish this bottle tonight."

"Good," he said. Then he began his story.

"Exactly fourteen years ago," he said, "in the winter of 1905, I observed a goldfish frozen solid in the ice in my garden pond. Nine days later there was a thaw. The ice melted and the goldfish swam away, apparently none the worse. That set me thinking. A fish is cold-blooded. So what other forms of cold-blooded life could be preserved at low temperatures? Quite a few, I guessed. And from there, I began speculating about preserving *bloodless* life at low temperatures. By bloodless I mean bacteria, et cetera. Then I said to myself, 'Who wants to preserve bacteria? Not me.' So then I asked myself another question. 'What living organism above all others would you like to see kept alive for very long periods?' And the answer came back, spermatozoa!"

"Why spermatozoa?" I asked.

"I'm not quite sure why," he said, "especially as I'm a chemist, not a bio man. But I had a feeling that somehow it would be a valuable contribution. So I started my experiments."

"What with?" I asked.

"With sperm, of course. Living sperm."

"Whose?"

"My own."

In the little silence that followed, I felt a twinge of embarrassment. Whenever someone tells me he has done something, no matter what it is, I simply cannot help conjuring up a vivid picture of the scene. It's only a flash, but it always happens and I was doing it now. I was looking at scruffy old A. R. Woresley in his lab as he did what he had to do for the sake of his experiments, and I felt embarrassed.

"In the cause of science everything is permissible," he said, sensing my discomfort.

"Oh, I agree. I absolutely agree."

"I worked alone," he said, "and mostly late at night. Nobody knew what I was up to."

His face disappeared again behind the smokescreen, then swam back into view.

"I won't recite the hundreds of failed experiments I did," he said. "I shall speak instead of my successes. I think you may find them interesting. For example, the first important thing I discovered was that exceedingly low temperatures were required to keep spermatozoa alive for any length of time. I kept freezing the semen to lower and still lower temperatures, and with each lowering of the temp I got a longer and longer life span. By using solid carbon dioxide, I was able to freeze my semen down to $-97°$ Centigrade. But even that wasn't enough. At minus ninety-seven the sperm lived for about a month but no more. 'I must go lower,' I told myself. But how could I do that? Then I hit upon a way to freeze the stuff all the way down to $-197°$ Centigrade."

"Impossible," I said.

"What do you think I used?"

"I haven't the foggiest."

"I used liquid nitrogen. That did it."

"But liquid nitrogen is tremendously volatile," I said.

"How could you prevent it from vapourizing? What did you store it in?"

"I devised special containers," he said. "Very strong and rather elaborate vacuum flasks. In these, the nitrogen remained liquid at minus one nine seven degrees virtually forever. A little topping up was required now and again, but that was all."

"Not forever, surely."

"Oh, yes," he said. "You are forgetting that nitrogen is a gas. If you liquefy a gas, it will stay liquid for a thousand years if you don't allow it to vapourize. And you do this simply by making sure that the flask is completely sealed and efficiently insulated."

"I see. And the sperm stayed alive?"

"Yes and no," he said. "They stayed alive long enough to tell me I'd got the right temperature. But they did not stay alive indefinitely. There was still something wrong. I pondered this and in the end I decided that what the sperm needed was some sort of a buffer, an overcoat if you like, to cushion them from the intense cold. And after experimenting with about eighty different substances, I at last hit on the perfect one."

"What was it?"

"Glycerol."

"Just plain glycerol?"

"Yes. But even that didn't work at first. It didn't work properly until I also discovered that the cooling process must be done very gradually. Spermatozoa are delicate little fellows. They don't like shocks. You cause them distress if you subject them straightaway to minus one nine seven degrees."

"So you cooled them gradually?"

"Exactly. Here is what you must do. You mix the sperm with the glycerol and put it in a small rubber container. A test tube is no good. It would crack at low temperatures. And by the way, you must do all this as soon as the sperm has been obtained. You must hurry. You cannot hang about or it will die. So first you put your precious package on ordinary ice to reduce the temperature to freezing point. Next, you put it into nitrogen vapour to freeze it deeper. Finally you pop it into the deepest freeze of all, liquid nitrogen. It's a step by step process. You acclimatize the sperm gradually to coldness."

"And it works?"

"Oh, it works all right. I am quite certain that sperm which has been protected with glycerol and then frozen slowly will stay alive at minus one nine seven for as long as you like."

"For a hundred years?"

"Absolutely, provided you keep it at minus one nine seven degrees."

"And you could thaw it out after that time and it would fertilize a woman?"

"I'm quite sure of it. But having got that far I began to lose interest in the human aspect. I wanted to go a lot further. I had many more experiments to do. But one cannot experiment with men and women, not in the way I wanted to."

"How did you want to experiment?"

"I wanted to find out how much sperm wastage there was in a single ejaculation."

"I'm not with you. What d'you mean by sperm wastage?"

"The average ejaculation from a large animal such as a bull or a horse produces five cc's of semen. Each cc contains one thousand million separate spermatozoa. This means five thousand million sperm all together."

"Not five thousand *million*! Not in one go!"

"That's what I said."

"It's unbelievable."

"It's true."

"How much does a human produce?"

"About half that. About two cc's and two thousand million."

"You mean to tell me," I said, "that every time I pleasure a young lady, I shoot into her two thousand million spermatozoa?"

"Absolutely."

"All squiggling and squirming and thrashing about?"

"Of course."

"No wonder it gives her a charge," I said.

A. R. Woresley was not interested in that aspect. "The point is this," he said. "A bull, for example, definitely does *not* need five thousand million spermatozoa in order to achieve fertilization with a cow. Ultimately, he needs only a single sperm. But in order to make sure of hitting the target, he has to use a few million at least. But how many million? That was my next question."

"Why?" I asked.

"Because, my dear fellow, I wanted to find out just how many females, whether they were cows, mares, humans, or whatever, could ultimately be fertilized by a single ejaculation. I was assuming, of course, that all those millions of sperm could be divided up and shared among them. Do you see what I'm driving at?"

"Perfectly. What animals did you use for these experiments?"

"Bulls and cows," A. R. Woresley said. "I have a brother

who owns a small dairy farm over at Steeple Bumpstead not far from here. He had a bull and about eighty cows. We had always been good friends, my brother and I. So I confided in him, and he agreed to let me use his animals. After all, I wasn't going to hurt them. I might even do him a favour."

"How could you do him a favour?"

"My brother has never been well off. His own bull, the only one he could afford, was of moderate quality. He would dearly love to have had his whole herd of cows bear calves by a splendid prize bull from very high milk-yielding stock."

"You mean someone else's bull?"

"Yes, I do."

"How would you go about obtaining semen from someone else's valuable bull?"

"I would steal it."

"Ah-ha."

"I would steal one ejaculation, and then, provided of course that I was successful with my experiments, I would share out that single ejaculation, those five thousand million sperm, among all of my brother's eighty cows."

"How would you share it out?" I asked.

"By what I call hypodermic insemination. By injecting the sperm into the cow with a syringe."

"I suppose that's possible."

"Of course it's possible," he said. "After all, the male sexual organ is itself really nothing more than a syringe for injecting semen."

"Steady on," I said. "Mine's a bit more than that."

"I don't doubt it, Cornelius, I don't doubt it," he answered dryly. "But shall we stick to the point?"

"Sorry."

"So I started experimenting with bulls' semen."

I picked up the bottle of port and refilled his glass. I had the feeling now that old Woresley was onto something pretty interesting and I wanted to keep him going.

"I've told you," he said, "that the average bull produces about five cc's of fluid each time. That's not much. Even when mixed with glycerol there wouldn't be enough there for me to start dividing it up into a great many parts and then expect to be able to inject each of those tiny parts into separate cows. So I had to find a dilutant, something to increase the volume."

"Why not add more glycerol?"

"I tried it. It didn't work. Altogether too viscous. I won't bore you with a list of all the curious substances I experimented with. I will simply tell you the one that works. Skimmed milk works. Eighty per cent skimmed milk, ten per cent egg yolk, and ten per cent glycerol. That's the magic mixture. The sperm love it. You simply mix the whole cocktail thoroughly, and that, as you can see, gave me a practical volume of fluid to experiment with. So for several years, I worked with my brother's cows, and finally I arrived at the optimum dose."

"What was it?"

"The optimum dose was no more than twenty million spermatozoa per cow. When I injected that into a cow at the right time, I got eighty per cent pregnancies. And don't forget, Cornelius," he went on excitedly, "that each bull's ejaculation contains five thousand million sperm. Divided up into doses of twenty million, that gives two hundred and fifty separate doses! It was amazing! I was flabbergasted!"

"Does that mean," I said, "that with just one of my own ejaculations I could make two hundred and fifty women pregnant?"

"You are not a bull, Cornelius, much as you may like to think you are."

"How many females could one of my ejaculations do?"

"About a hundred. But I am not about to help you."

By God, I thought, I could knock up about seven hundred women a week at that rate! "Have you actually proved this with your brother's bull?" I asked.

"Many times," A. R. Woresley said. "It works. I collect one ejaculation, then I quickly mix it up with skimmed milk, egg yolk, and glycerol, then I measure it into single doses before freezing."

"What volume of fluid in each dose?" I asked.

"Very small. Just half a cc."

"Is that all you inject into the cow, just half a cc of fluid?"

"That's all. But don't forget there's twenty million living spermatozoa in that half cc."

"Ah, yes."

"I put these little doses separately into small rubber tubes," he said. "I call them straws. I seal both ends, then I freeze. Just think of it, Cornelius! Two hundred and fifty highly potent straws of spermatozoa from a single ejaculation!"

"I *am* thinking about it," I said. "It's a bloody miracle."

"And I can store them for as long as I like, deep frozen. All I have to do when a cow starts bulling is take out one straw from the liquid nitrogen flask, thaw it, which doesn't take a minute, transfer the contents to a syringe, and shoot it into the cow."

The bottle of port was three-quarters empty now and

A. R. Woresley was getting a bit tipsy. I refilled his glass again.

"What about this prize bull you were talking about?" I said.

"I'm coming to that, my boy. That's the lovely part of the whole thing. That's the dividend."

"Tell me."

"Of course I'll tell you. So I said to my brother—this was three years ago, right in the middle of the war; my brother was exempt from the army, you see, because he was a farmer—so I said to Ernest, 'Ernest,' I said, 'if you had the choice of any bull in England to service your entire herd, which one would you choose?'

" 'I don't know about in England,' Ernest said, 'but the finest bull in these parts is Champion Glory of Friesland, owned by Lord Somerton. He's a purebred Friesian, and those Friesians are the best milk producers in the world. My God, Arthur,' he said, 'you should see that bull! He's a giant! He cost ten thousand pounds and every calf he gets turns out to be a tremendous milker!'

" 'Where is this bull kept?' I asked my brother.

" 'On Lord Somerton's estate. That's over in Birdbrook.'

" 'Birdbrook? That's quite close, isn't it?'

" 'Three miles away,' my brother said. 'They've got around two hundred pedigree Friesian dairy cattle and the bull runs with the herd. He's beautiful, Arthur, he really is.'

" 'Right,' I said. 'In the next twelve months, eighty per cent of your cows are going to have calves by that bull. Would you like that?'

" 'Like it!' my brother said. 'It would double my milk yield.' Could I trouble you, my dear Cornelius, for one last glass of your excellent port?"

I gave him what there was. I even gave him the lees in the bottom of the bottle. "Tell me what you did," I said.

"We waited until one of my brother's cows was bulling good and proper. Then, in the dead of night—this took courage, Cornelius, it took a lot of courage . . ."

"I'm sure it did."

"In the dead of night, Ernest put a halter on the cow and he led her along the country lanes to Lord Somerton's place three miles away."

"Didn't you go with them?"

"I went beside them on a bicycle."

"Why the bicycle?"

"You'll see in a moment. It was the month of May, nice and warm, and the time was around one in the morning. There was a bit of a moon shining, which made it more dangerous, but we had to have some light to do what we were going to do. The journey took us an hour.

" 'There you are,' my brother said. 'Over there. Can you see them?'

"We were by a gate leading into a twenty-acre field and in the moonlight I could see the great herd of Friesians grazing all over the field. To one side, not far away, was the big house itself, Somerton Hall. There was a single light in one of the upstairs windows. 'Where's the bull?' I said.

" 'He'll be in there somewhere,' my brother said. 'He's with the herd.'

"Our cow," A. R. Woresley said to me, "was mooing away like mad. They always do when they're bulling. They're calling the bull, you see. The gate into the field was padlocked with a chain, but my brother was ready for that. He pulled out a hacksaw and sawed through the chain. He opened the gate. I leaned my bike against the hedge and we went into the field, leading the cow. The field was milky white in the moonlight. Our cow, sensing the presence of other animals, began mooing louder than ever."

"Were you frightened?" I asked.

"Terrified," A. R. Woresley said. "I am a quiet man, Cornelius. I lead a quiet life. I am not cut out for escapades like this. Every second I expected to see his lordship's bailiff come running toward us with a shotgun in his hands. But I forced myself to keep going because this thing we were doing was in the cause of science. Also, I had an obligation to my brother. He had helped me greatly. Now I must help him."

The pipe had gone out. A. R. Woresley began to refill it from a tin of cheap tobacco.

"Go on," I said.

"The bull must have heard our cow calling to him. 'There he is!' my brother cried. 'Here he comes!'

"A massive white and black creature had detached himself from the herd and was trotting our way. He had a pair of short sharp horns on his head. Lethal, they looked. 'Get ready!' my brother snapped. 'He won't wait! He'll go right at her! Give me the rubber bag! Quick!' "

"What rubber bag?" I said to Woresley.

"The semen collector, my dear boy. My own invention, an elongated bag with thick rubber lips, a kind of false vagina. Very effective too. But let me go on."

"Go on," I said.

" 'Where's the bag?' my brother shouted. 'Hurry up, man!' I was carrying the thing in a knapsack. I got it out and handed it to my brother. He took up his station near the cow's rear and to one side. I stood on the other side, ready to do my bit. I was so frightened, Cornelius, I was sweating all over and I kept wanting to urinate. I was frightened of the bull and I was frightened of that light in the window of Somerton Hall behind me, but I stood my ground.

"The bull came trotting up, snorting and dribbling. I could see a brass ring in his nose, and by God, Cornelius, he was a dangerous-looking brute. He didn't hesitate. He knew his business. He took one sniff at our cow, then he reared up and thrust his front legs onto the cow's back. I crouched alongside him. His pizzle was coming out now. He had a gigantic scrotum and just above it this incredible pizzle was getting longer and longer. It was like a telescope. It started quite short and very quickly it got longer and longer until it was as long as my arm. But not very thick. About as thick as a walking-stick, I'd say. I made a grab for it but in my excitement I missed it. 'Quick!' my brother said. 'Where is it? Get hold of it quick!' But it was too late. The old bull was an expert marksman. He'd hit the target first time and the end of his pizzle was already inside the cow. It was halfway in. 'Get it!' my brother shouted. I grabbed for it again. There was still quite a bit of it showing. I got both hands on it and pulled. It was alive and throbbing and slightly slimy. It was like pulling on a snake. The bull was thrusting it in and I was pulling it out. I pulled so hard on it I felt it bend. But I kept my head and started synchronizing my pulls with the animal's backward movements. Do you see what I mean? He would thrust forward, then he would have to arch his back before going forward again. Each time he arched his back, I gave a pull and gained a few inches. Then the bull thrust forward and in it went once more. But I was gaining on him and in the end, using both hands, I managed to bend it almost double and flip it out. The end of it whacked me across the cheek.

That hurt. But quickly I jammed it into the bag my brother was holding. The bull was still bashing away. He was totally absorbed in his work. Thank God he was. He didn't even seem to be aware of our presence. But the pizzle was in the bag now and my brother was holding it and in less than a minute it was all over. The bull lurched backwards off the cow. And then suddenly he saw us. He stood there staring at us. He seemed a bit perplexed, and who could blame him. He gave a deep bellow and started pawing the ground with his front legs. He was going to charge. But my brother, who knew about bulls, walked straight up to him and slapped him across the nose. 'Git away!' he said. The bull turned and ambled back toward the herd. We hurried out through the gate, closing it behind us. I took the rubber bag from my brother and jumped onto the bicycle and rode hell for leather back to the farm. I made it in fifteen minutes.

"At the farm I had everything ready. I scooped out the bull's semen from the bag and mixed it with my special solution of milk, egg yolk, and glycerol. I filled two hundred and fifty of my little rubber straws with half a cc each. This was not as difficult as it sounds. I always have the straws lined up in rows on a metal rack and I use an eye dropper. I transferred the rack of filled straws onto ice for half an hour. Then I lifted it into a container of nitrogen vapour for ten minutes. Finally, I lowered it into a second vacuum container of liquid nitrogen. The whole process was finished before my brother arrived back with the cow. I now had enough semen from a prize Friesian bull to fertilize two hundred and fifty cows. At least I hoped I had."

"Did it work?" I asked.

"It worked fantastically," A. R. Woresley said. "The

following year my brother's Hereford cattle began producing calves that were one-half Friesian. I had taught him
how to do the hypodermic insemination himself, and I left
the canister of frozen "straws" with him on the farm. Today, my dear Cornelius, three years later, nearly every
cow in his herd is a cross between a Hereford and a prize
Friesian. His milk yield is up by something like sixty per
cent and he has sold his bull. The only trouble is that he's
running out of straws. He wants me to go with him on
another of those dangerous journeys to Lord Somerton's
bull. Quite frankly, I dread it."

"I'll go," I said. "I'll take your place."

"You wouldn't know what to do."

"Just grab the old pizzle and bung it in the bag," I said.
"You can be waiting back at the farm all ready to freeze
the semen."

"Can you manage a bicycle?"

"I'll take my car," I said. "Twice as quick."

I had just bought a brand new Continental Morris
Cowley, a machine superior in every way to the 1912 De
Dion of my Paris days. The body was chocolate brown.
The upholstery was leather. It had nickel fittings, ma-
hogany cappings, and a driver's door. I was very proud
of it. "I'll get the semen back to you in no time," I said.

"What a splendid idea," he said. "Would you really do
that for me, Cornelius?"

"I'd love to," I said.

I left him soon after that and drove back to Trinity. My
brain was humming with all the things A. R. Woresley
had told me. There was little doubt he had made a tremendous discovery, and when he published his findings
he would be hailed all over the world as a great man. He
was probably a genius.

But that didn't bother me one way or the other. What did concern me was this: How could I myself make a million pounds out of it all? I had no objection to A. R. Woresley's getting rich at the same time. He discovered it. But yours truly came first. The more I thought about it, the more convinced I became that there was a fortune waiting for me just around the corner. But I doubted it was from bulls and cows.

I lay awake in bed that night and applied my mind assiduously to this problem. I may seem, to a reader of these diaries, like a pretty casual sort of fellow where most things are concerned, but I promise you that when my own most important interests are at stake I am capable of some very concentrated thinking. Somewhere around midnight an idea came to me and began whizzing around in my head. It appealed to me at once, this idea, for the simple reason that it involved the two things in life that I found most entertaining—seduction and copulation. It appealed to me even more when I realized that it involved a *tremendous amount* of seduction and copulation.

I got out of bed and put on my dressing-gown. I began making notes. I examined the problems that would arise. I thought up ways of overcoming them. And at the end of it all I came to the very definite conclusion that the scheme would work. It was bound to work.

There was only one snag. A. R. Woresley had to be persuaded to go along with it.

8

THE NEXT DAY, I sought him out in college and invited him to dine with me that evening.

"I never dine out," he said. "My sister expects me home for dinner."

"It's business," I said. "It's your whole future. Tell her it's vital, which it is. I am about to make you a rich man." Eventually he agreed to come.

At seven p.m., I took him to the Blue Boar in Trinity Street and I ordered for both of us. A dozen oysters each and a bottle of Clos Vougeot Blanc, a very rare wine. Then a dish of roast beef and a good Volnay.

"I must say you do yourself well, Cornelius," he said.

"I wouldn't do myself any other way," I told him. "You do like oysters, don't you?"

"Very much."

A man opened the oysters at the bar of the restaurant and we watched him doing it. They were Colchesters, medium-sized, plump. A waiter brought them to us. The wine waiter opened the Clos Vougeot Blanc. We began the meal.

"I see you are chewing your oysters," I said.

"What do you expect me to do?"

"Swallow them whole."

"That's ridiculous."

"On the contrary," I said. "When eating oysters, the

primary pleasure comes from the sensation you get as they slide down your throat."

"I can't believe that."

"And then again, the knowledge that they are actually alive as you swallow them adds enormously to that pleasure."

"I prefer not to think about it."

"Oh, but you must. If you concentrate hard enough, you can sometimes feel the living oyster wriggling in your stomach."

A. R. Woresley's nicotine moustache began twitching about. It looked like a bristly nervous little animal clinging to his upper lip.

"If you examine very closely a certain part of the oyster," I said, "just here . . . you can see a tiny pulse beating. There it is. D'you see it? And when you stick your fork in . . . like this . . . the flesh moves. It makes a shrinking movement. It does the same if you squeeze lemon juice onto it. Oysters don't like lemon juice. They don't like forks being stuck into them either. They shrink away. The flesh quivers. I shall now swallow this one—isn't he a beauty? . . . There, down he goes . . . and now I shall sit very still for a few seconds so as to experience the sensation of him moving about gently in my stomach. . . ."

The little bristly brown animal on A. R. Woresley's upper lip began jumping around more than ever and his cheeks had become visibly paler. Slowly, he pushed his plate of oysters to one side.

"I'll get you some smoked salmon."

"Thank you."

I ordered the salmon and took the rest of his oysters onto my plate. He watched me eating them as he waited for the waiter to bring the salmon. He was silent now, subdued, and this was how I wanted him to be. Dash it, the man was twice my age, and all I was trying to do was soften him up a trifle before dumping my big proposition in his lap. I simply had to unsettle him first and try to dominate him if I was to have the slightest chance of getting him to go along with my plan. I decided to soften him up a bit more. "Did I ever tell you about my old nanny?" I asked.

"I thought we came here to talk about my discovery," he said. The waiter put a plate of smoked salmon in front of him. "Ah," he said. "That looks good."

"When I went away to boarding-school at the age of nine," I said, "my dear old nanny was pensioned off by my parents. They bought her a small cottage in the country and there she lived. She was about eighty-five and a marvellously tough old bird. She never complained about anything. But one day, when my mother went down to see her, she found her looking very ill. She questioned her closely and Nanny at last admitted that she had the most awful pains in her stomach. Had she had them for long, my mother asked her. Well, as a matter of fact, yes, she had had pains in her stomach, she finally admitted, for many years. But never as bad as they were now. My mother got a doctor. The doctor sent her to hospital. They X-rayed her and the X-ray showed something quite unusual. There were two smallish opaque objects about three inches apart in the middle of her stomach. They looked like marbles. Nobody at the hospital had any idea what these two objects might be, so it was decided to perform an exploratory operation."

"I hope this is not another of your unpleasant anecdotes," A. R. Woresley said, chewing his salmon.

"It's fascinating," I said. "It'll interest you enormously."

"Go on, then."

"When the surgeon opened her up," I said, "what do you think he found these two round objects to be?"

"I haven't the faintest idea."

"They were eyes."

"What do you mean, eyes?"

"The surgeon found himself staring straight into a pair of alert unblinking round eyes. And the eyes were staring back at him."

"Ridiculous."

"Not at all," I said. "And who did they belong to, those eyes?"

"Who?"

"They belonged to a *rather large octopus*."

"You're being facetious."

"It's the gospel truth. This enormous octopus was actually living in dear old Nanny's stomach as a parasite. It was sharing her food, eating well—"

"I think that'll do, Cornelius."

"—and all of its eight beastly long tentacles were twined inextricably around her guts. They couldn't untangle them. She died on the table."

A. R. Woresley had stopped chewing his salmon.

"Now what's so interesting about all this is how the octopus got there in the first place. I mean after all, how *does* an old lady come to find herself with a fully grown octopus in her stomach? It was far too big to have gone down her throat. It was like the problem of the ship in the bottle. How on earth did it get in?"

"I prefer not to know," A. R. Woresley said.

"I'll tell you how," I said. "Every summer, my parents used to take Nanny and me to Beaulieu, in the south of

France. And twice a day we used to go swimming in the sea. So obviously what happened was that Nanny, many years before, must have swallowed a tiny new-born baby octopus, and this little creature had somehow managed to fasten itself onto the wall of her stomach with its suckers. Nanny ate well, so the little octopus ate well. Nanny always ate with the family. Sometimes it would be liver and bacon for dinner, sometimes roast lamb or pork. And believe it or not, she was particularly fond of smoked salmon."

A. R. Woresley put down his fork. There was one thin slice of salmon left on his plate. He let it stay there.

"So the little octopus grew and grew. It became a gourmet octopus. I can just see it, can't you, down there in the dark caverns of the tummy, saying to itself, 'Now I wonder what we're going to have for supper tonight. I do hope it's coq au vin. I feel like a bit of coq au vin tonight. And some crusty bread to go with it.'"

"You have an unsavoury predilection for the obscene, Cornelius."

"That case made medical history," I said.

"I find it repugnant," A. R. Woresley said.

"I'm sorry about that. I'm only trying to make conversation."

"I didn't come here just to make conversation."

"I'm going to turn you into a rich man," I said.

"Then get on with it and tell me how."

"I thought I'd leave that until the port is on the table. No good plans are ever made without a bottle of port."

"Have you had enough, sir?" the waiter asked him, eyeing the rest of the smoked salmon.

"Take it away," A. R. Woresley said.

We sat in silence for a while. The waiter brought the

roast beef. The Volnay was opened. This was the month of March, so we had roast parsnips with our beef as well as roast potatoes and Yorkshire pudding. A. R. Woresley perked up a bit when he saw the beef. He drew his chair closer to the table and began to tuck in.

"Did you know my father was a keen student of naval history?" I asked.

"No, I didn't."

"He told me a stirring story once," I said, "about the English captain who was mortally wounded on the deck of his ship in the American War of Independence. Would you like some horseradish with your beef?"

"Yes, I would."

"Waiter," I called. "Bring us a little fresh shredded horseradish. Now, as he lay dying, the captain—"

"Cornelius," A. R. Woresley said, "I have had enough of your stories."

"This isn't *my* story. It's my father's. It's not like the others. You'll love it."

He was attacking his roast beef and didn't answer.

"So as he lay dying," I said, "the captain extracted from his second-in-command a promise that his body would be taken home and buried in English soil. This created a bit of a problem because the ship was somewhere off the coast of Virginia at the time. It would take at least five weeks to sail back to Britain. So it was decided that the only way to get the body home in fair condition was to pickle it in a barrel of rum, and this was done. The barrel was lashed to the foremast and the ship set sail for England. Five weeks later, she dropped anchor in Plymouth Hoe, and the entire ship's company was lined up to pay a last tribute to their captain as his body was lifted from the barrel into the coffin. But when the lid of the barrel was prized off, there came out a stench so appalling that strong men were seen rushing to the ship's rail. Others fainted.

"Now this was a puzzler, for one can normally pickle anything in navy rum. So why, oh, why the appalling stench? You may well ask that question."

"I don't ask it," A. R. Woresley snapped. His moustache was jumping about more than ever now.

"Let me tell you what had happened."

"Don't."

"I must," I said. "During the long voyage, some of the sailors had surreptitiously drilled a hole in the bottom of the barrel and had put a bung in it. Then over the weeks, they had drunk up all the rum."

A. R. Woresley said nothing. He was not looking at all well.

" 'Finest rum I ever tasted,' one of the sailors was heard to remark afterwards. Now what shall we have for dessert?"

"No dessert," A. R. Woresley said.

I ordered the best bottle of port in the house and some Stilton cheese. There was absolute silence between us as we waited for the port to be decanted. It was a Cockburn and a good one, though I've forgotten the year.

The port was served and the splendid crumbly green Stilton was on our plates. "Now," I said, "let me tell you how I am going to make you a million pounds."

He was watchful and a shade truculent now, but he was not aggressive. He was definitely softened up.

9

"You ARE virtually broke," I said. "You have crippling mortgage interests to pay. You have a meagre salary from the university. You have no savings. You live, if you'll forgive me for saying so, on slops."

"We live very well."

"No, you don't. And you never will, unless you let me help you."

"So what is your plan?"

"You, sir," I said, "have made a great scientific discovery. There's no doubt about that."

"You agree it's important?" he said, perking up.

"Very important. But if you publish your findings, just look what will happen. Every Tom, Dick, and Harry all over the world will steal your process for their own use. You won't be able to stop them. It's been the same all through the history of science. Look at pasteurization. Pasteur published. Everyone stole his process. And where did that leave old Pasteur?"

"He became a famous man," A. R. Woresley said.

"If that's all you want to be, then by all means go ahead and publish. I shall retire gracefully from the scene."

"With your scheme," A. R. Woresley said, "would I ever be able to publish?"

"Of course. As soon as you've got the million in your pocket."

"How long would that be?"

"I don't know. I'd say five or ten years at the most. After that, you would be free to become famous."

"Come on, then," he said. "Let's hear about this brilliant scheme."

The port was very good. The Stilton was good, too, but I only nibbled it to clear my palate. I called for an apple. A hard apple, thinly sliced, is the best partner for port.

"I propose that we deal only with *human* spermatozoa," I said. "I propose that we select only the truly great and famous men alive in the world today and that we establish a sperm vault for these men. We will store two hundred and fifty straws of sperm from each man."

"What is the point of that?" A. R. Woresley said.

"Go back just sixty years," I said, "to around 1860, and pretend that you and I were living then and that we had the knowledge and the ability to store sperm indefinitely. So which living geniuses, in 1860, would you have chosen as donors?"

"Dickens," he said.

"Go on."

"And Ruskin . . . and Mark Twain."

"And Brahms," I said, "and Wagner and Tschaikovsky and Dvořák. The list is very long. Authentic geniuses every one of them. Go back further in the century, if you like, to Balzac, to Beethoven, to Napoleon, to Goya, to Chopin. Wouldn't it be exciting if we had in our liquid nitrogen bank a couple of hundred straws of the living sperm of Beethoven?"

"What would you do with them?"

"Sell them, of course."

"To whom?"

"To women. To very rich women who wanted babies by one of the greatest geniuses of all time."

"Now wait a minute, Cornelius. Women, rich or not, aren't going to allow themselves to be inseminated with the sperm of some long dead stranger just because he was a genius."

"That's what you think. Listen, I could take you to any Beethoven concert you like and I'd guarantee to find half a dozen females there who'd give almost anything to have a baby today by the great man."

"You mean spinsters?"

"No. Married women."

"What would their husbands say?"

"Their husbands wouldn't know. Only the mother would know that she was pregnant by Beethoven."

"That's knavery, Cornelius."

"Can't you see her," I said, "this rich unhappy woman who is married to some incredibly ugly, coarse, ignorant, unpleasant industrialist from Birmingham, and all at once she has something to live for. As she goes strolling through the beautifully kept garden of her husband's enormous country house, she is humming the slow movement of Beethoven's *Eroica* and thinking to herself, 'My God, isn't it wonderful! I am pregnant by the man who wrote that music a hundred years ago!'"

"We don't have Beethoven's sperm."

"There are plenty of others," I said. "There are great men in every country, in every decade. It's our job to get them. And listen," I went on, "there's one tremendous thing in our favour. You will find that very rich men are nearly always ugly, coarse, ignorant, and unpleasant. They are robber bandits, monsters. Just think of the mentality of men who spend their lives amassing million after million—Rockefeller, Carnegie, Mellon, Krupp. Those are the old-timers. Today's batch are just as unattractive. Industrialists, war profiteers. All horrible fellows. Invariably, they marry women for their beauty and the women marry them for their money. The beauties have ugly, useless children by their ugly, grasping husbands. They get to hate their husbands. They get bored. They take up culture. They buy paintings by the Impressionists and go to Wagner concerts. And at that stage, my dear sir, these women are ripe for the picking. So in steps Oswald Cornelius offering to impregnate them with guaranteed genuine Wagner sperm."

"Wagner's dead, too."

"I am simply trying to show you what our sperm vault will look like in forty years' time if we start it now, in 1919."

"Whom would we put in it?" A. R. Woresley said.

"Whom would you suggest? Who are the geniuses of today?"

"Albert Einstein."

"Good," I said. "Who else?"

"Sibelius."

"Splendid. And what about Rachmaninoff?"

"And Debussy," he said.

"Who else?"

"Sigmund Freud in Vienna."

"Is he great?"

"He's going to be," A. R. Woresley said. "He is already world famous in medical circles."

"I'll take your word for it. Go on."

"Igor Stravinsky," he said.

"I didn't know you knew music."

"Of course."

"I'd like to propose the painter Picasso in Paris," I said.

"Is he a genius?"

"Yes," I said.

"Would you accept Henry Ford in America?"

"Oh, yes," I said. "That's a good one. And our own King George the Fifth."

"*King George the Fifth!*" he cried. "What's he got to do with it?"

"He's royal blood. Just imagine what some women would pay for a child by the King of England!"

"You're being ridiculous, Cornelius. You can't go crashing into Buckingham Palace and start asking His Majesty the King if he would be good enough to provide you with an ejaculation of semen."

"You wait," I said. "You haven't heard the half of it yet. And we won't stop at George the Fifth. We must have a very comprehensive stock indeed of royal sperm. All the kings in Europe. Let's see. There's Haakon of Norway. There's Gustav of Sweden. Christian of Denmark. Albert of Belgium. Alfonso of Spain. Carol of Rumania. Boris of Bulgaria. Victor Emmanuel of Italy."

"You're being silly."

"No, I'm not. Wealthy Spanish ladies of aristocratic blood would crave for a baby by Alfonso. It'll be the same in every country. The aristocracy worships the monarchy. It is essential that we have a good stock of royal sperm in our vault. And I'll get it. Don't you worry. I'll get it."

"It's a hare-brained and impracticable stunt," A. R. Woresley said. He put a lump of Stilton in his mouth and swilled it round with port. Thus he ruined both the cheese and the wine.

"I am prepared," I said slowly, "to invest every penny of my one hundred thousand pounds into our partnership. That's how hare-brained I think it is."

"You're mad."

"You'd have told me I was mad if you'd seen me setting off for the Sudan at the age of seventeen in search of Blister Beetle powder. You would, wouldn't you?"

That pulled him up a little. "What would you charge for this sperm?" he asked.

"A fortune," I said. "Nobody is going to get a baby Einstein cheap. Or a baby Sibelius. Or a baby King Albert of the Belgians. Hey! I've just had a thought. Would a king's baby be in line for the throne?"

"He'd be a bastard."

"He'd be in line for something. Royal bastards always are. We must charge a packet for king's sperm."

"How much would you charge?"

"I think about twenty thousand pounds a shot. Commoners would be slightly cheaper. We would have a price list and a range of prices. But kings would be the most expensive."

"H. G. Wells!" he said suddenly. "He's around."

"Yes. We might put him on the list."

A. R. Woresley leaned back in his chair and sipped his port. "Assuming," he said, "just assuming we did have this remarkable sperm vault, who would go out and find the rich women buyers?"

"I would."

"And who would inseminate them?"

"I would."

"You don't know how to do it."

"I could soon learn. It might be rather fun."

"There is a flaw in this scheme of yours," A. R. Woresley said. "A serious flaw."

"What is it?"

"The really valuable sperm is not Einstein's or Stravinsky's. It's Einstein's father's. Or Stravinsky's father's. Those are the men who actually sired the geniuses."

"Agreed," I said. "But by the time a man becomes a recognized genius, his father is dead."

"So your scheme is fraudulent."

"We're out to make money," I said, "not to breed geniuses. These women aren't going to want Sibelius's father's sperm anyway. What they'll be after is a nice hot injection of twenty million living spermatozoa from the great man himself."

A. R. Woresley had his awful pipe going now and clouds of smoke enveloped his head. "I will admit," he said, "yes, I am prepared to grant you that you could find wealthy female buyers for the sperm of geniuses and royalty. But your entire bizarre scheme is unfortunately doomed to failure for the simple reason that you will be unable to obtain your supplies of sperm. You don't seriously believe that great men and kings will be prepared to go through the . . . the extremely embarrassing motions of producing an ejaculation of sperm for some totally unknown young man."

"That's not the way I'll do it."

"How will you do it?"

"The way I'll do it, not a single one of them will be able to resist becoming a donor."

"Rubbish. I'd resist it."

"No, you wouldn't." I put a thin slice of apple in my mouth and ate it. I raised the glass of port to my nose. It had a bouquet of mushrooms. I took a sip and rolled it on my tongue. The flavour filled my mouth. It reminded me of *pot-pourri*. For a few moments I was captivated by the loveliness of the wine I was tasting. And what a remarkable follow-through it had after the swallow. The flavour lingered in the back of the nose for a long time. "Give me three days," I said, "and I guarantee that I'll have in my possession one complete and genuine ejaculation of your own sperm together with a statement signed by you certifying it is yours."

"Don't be so foolish, Cornelius. You can't make me do something I don't want to do."

"That's all I'm prepared to say."

He squinted at me through the pipe smoke. "You wouldn't threaten me in some way, would you?" he said. "Or torture me?"

"Of course not. The act would be of your own free will. Would you like to bet me that I won't succeed?"

"Of my own free will, you say?"

"Yes."

"Then I'll bet you anything you like."

"Right," I said. "The bet is that if you lose, you promise the following: firstly, to withhold publication until we've each made a million. Secondly, to become a full and enthusiastic partner. Thirdly, to supply all the technical knowledge necessary for me to set up the sperm vault."

"I don't mind making a promise I'll never have to keep," he said.

"Then you promise?"

"I promise," he said.

I paid the bill and offered to drive A. R. Woresley home in my motor car. "Thank you," he said, "but I have my bicycle. We poor dons are not as affluent as some."

"You soon will be," I said.

I stood on Trinity Street and watched him pedalling away into the night. It was still only about nine thirty p.m.

I decided to make my next move immediately. I got into the motor car and headed straight for Girton.

IO

GIRTON, in case you don't know it, was and still is a ladies' college and a part of the university. Within those sombre walls there dwelt in 1919 a cluster of young ladies so physically repulsive, so thick-necked and long-snouted I could hardly bring myself to look at them. They reminded me of crocodiles. They sent shivers down the back of my neck as I passed them in the street. They seldom washed and the lenses of their spectacles were smudged with greasy fingermarks. Brainy they certainly were. Many were brilliant. To my mind, that was small compensation.

But wait.

Only one week before, I had discovered among these zoological specimens a creature of such dazzling loveliness I refused to believe she was a Girton girl. Yet she was. I had discovered her in a bunshop at lunchtime. She was eating a doughnut. I asked if I might sit at her table. She nodded and went on eating. And there I sat, gaping and goggling at her as though she were Cleopatra herself reincarnated. Never in my short life had I seen a girl or a woman with such a stench of salacity about her. She was absolutely soaked in sex. It made no difference that there was sugar and doughnut all over her face. She was wearing a mackintosh and a woolly scarf but she might just as well have been stark naked. Only once or twice in a lifetime does one meet a girl like that. The face was beautiful beyond words, but there was a flare to the nostrils and a curious little twist of the upper lip that had me wriggling all over my chair. Not even in Paris had I met a female who inspired such instant lust. She went on eating her doughnut. I went on goggling at her. Once, but only once, her eyes rose slowly to my face and there they rested, cool and shrewd, as if calculating something, then they fell again. She finished her doughnut and pushed back her chair.

"Hang on," I said.

She paused, and for a second time those calculating brown eyes came up and rested on my face.

"What did you say?"

"I said hang on. Don't go. Have another doughnut . . . or a Bath bun or something."

"If you want to talk to me, why don't you say so?"

"I want to talk to you."

She folded her hands in her lap and waited. I began to talk. Soon she joined in. She was a biology student at Girton and, like me, she had a scholarship. Her father was English, her mother Persian. Her name was Yasmin Howcomely. What we said to one another is irrelevant. We went straight from the bunshop to my rooms and stayed there until the next morning. Eighteen hours we stayed together and at the end of it all I felt like a piece of pemmican, a strip of desiccated dehydrated meat. She was electric, that girl, and wicked beyond belief. Had she been Chinese and living in Peking, she could have gotten her Diploma of Merit with her hands tied behind her back and iron shackles on her feet.

I went so dotty about her that I broke the golden rule and saw her a second time.

And now it was twenty to ten in the evening and A. R. Woresley was bicycling home and I myself was in the porter's lodge at Girton asking the old porter kindly to inform Miss Yasmin Howcomely that Mr. Oswald Cornelius wished to see her on a matter of the most urgent nature.

She came down at once. "Hop in the car," I said. "We have things to talk about." She hopped in and I drove her back to Trinity where I gave the Trinity porter half a sovereign to look the other way as she slid past him to my rooms.

"Keep your clothes on," I said to her. "This is business. How would you like to get rich?"

"I'd like it very much," she said.

"Can I trust you completely?"

"Yes," she said.

"You won't tell a soul?"

"Go on," she said. "It sounds like fun already."

I then proceeded to tell her the entire story of A. R. Woresley's discovery.

"My God!" she said when I had finished. "This is a great scientific discovery! Who the hell is A. R. Woresley? He's going to be world famous! I'd like to meet him!"

"You soon will," I said.

"When?" Being herself a bright young scientist, she was genuinely excited.

"Wait," I said. "Here's the next installment." I then told her about my plans for exploiting the discovery and making a fortune by starting a sperm vault for the great geniuses of the world and all the kings.

When I had finished, she asked me if I had any wine. I opened a bottle of claret and poured a glass for each of us. I found some good dry biscuits to go with it.

"It's sort of a funny idea, this sperm vault of yours," she said. "But I'm afraid it's not going to work." She proceeded to put forward all the same old reasons that A. R. Woresley had given me earlier in the evening. I allowed her to spout on. Then I played my ace of spades.

"Last time we met I told you the story of my Parisian caper," I said. "You remember that?"

"The splendid Blister Beetle," she said. "I keep wishing you'd brought some back with you."

"I did."

"You're not serious!"

"When you use only a pinhead at a time, five pounds of powder goes an awful long way. I've got about a pound left."

"Then that's the answer!" she cried, clapping her hands.

"I know."

"Slip them a powder and they'll give us a thousand million of their little squigglers every time!"

"Using you as the teaser."

"Oh, I'll be the teaser all right," she said. "I'll tease them to death. Even the ancient ones will be able to deliver! Show me this magic stuff."

I fetched the famous biscuit tin and opened it. The powder lay an inch deep in the tin. Yasmin dipped a finger in it and started to put it to her mouth. I grabbed her wrist. "Are you mad?" I shouted. "You've got about six full doses sticking to the skin of that finger!" I hung onto her wrist and dragged her to the bathroom and held her finger under the tap.

"I want to try it," she said. "Come on, darling. Just give me a tiny bit."

"My God, woman," I said, "have you any idea what it does to you!"

"You already told me."

"If you want to see it working, just watch what it does to A. R. Woresley when you give it to him tomorrow."

"Tomorrow?"

"Absolutely," I said.

"Whoopee! When tomorrow?"

"You get old Woresley to deliver and I win my bet," I said. "That means he's got to join us. Woresley, you, and me. We'll make a great team."

"I like it," she said. "We'll rock the world."

"We'll rock more than that," I said. "We'll rock all the crowned heads of Europe. But we must rock Woresley first."

"He has to be alone."

"No problem," I said. "He's alone in the lab every evening between five thirty and six thirty. Then he goes home to his supper."

"How am I going to feed it to him?" she asked. "The powder?"

"In a chocolate," I said. "In a delicious little chocolate. It has to be small so that he'll pop the whole thing in his mouth in one go."

"And where pray do we get delicious little chocolates these days?" she asked. "You forget there's been a war on."

"That's the whole point," I said. "A. R. Woresley won't have had a decent bit of chocolate since 1914. He'll gobble it up."

"But do you have any?"

"Right here," I said. "Money can buy anything." I opened a drawer and produced a box of chocolate truffles. Each was identical. Each was the size of a small marble. They were supplied to me by Prestat, the great chocolateers of Oxford Street, London. I took one of them and made a hole in it with a pin. I enlarged the hole a bit. I then used the head of the same pin to measure out one dose of Blister Beetle powder. I tipped this into the hole. I measured a second dose and tipped that in also.

"Hey!" Yasmin cried. "That's two doses!"

"I know. I want to make absolutely sure Mr. Woresley delivers."

"It'll drive him round the twist."

"He'll get over it."

"What about me?"

"I think you can take care of yourself," I said. I pressed the soft chocolate together to seal up the hole. I then stuck a matchstick into the chocolate. "I'm giving you two chocolates," I said. "One for you and one for him. His is the one with the match in it." I put the chocolates in a paper bag and passed them over. We discussed at some length the plan of battle.

"Will he become violent?" she asked.

"Just a tiny bit."

"And where do I get that thing you were talking about?"

I produced the thing in question. She examined it to make sure it was in good condition, then put it in her handbag.

"All set?"

"Yes," she said.

"Don't forget this one will be a dress rehearsal for all the others you'll be doing later on. So learn all you can."

"I wish I knew judo," she said.

"You'll be all right."

I drove her back to Girton and saw her safely in through the gates of the college.

II

WE NOW MOVE FORWARD to five thirty in the afternoon of
the following day. I myself was lying quite comfortably
on the floor behind a row of wooden filing cabinets in
A. R. Woresley's laboratory. I had spent much of the day
wandering casually in and out of the lab, reconnoitring the
terrain and gradually easing the cabinets twenty inches
away from the wall so that I could squeeze in behind them.
I had also left a one-inch gap between two of the cabinets
so that by looking through it I was able to get an excellent
view along the whole length of the lab. A. R. Woresley
always worked at the far end of the room, about twenty
feet from where I was stationed. He was there now. He
was fooling about with a rack of test tubes and a pipette
and some blue liquid. He was not wearing his usual white
coat today. He was in shirt-sleeves and a pair of grey
flannels. There was a knock on the door.

"Come in!" he called out, not looking up.

Yasmin entered. I had not told her I was going to be
watching. Why should I? But a general must always keep
an eye on his troops during battle. My girl looked ravishing in a cotton print dress that fitted tightly around her
superstructure, and as she came into the room there came
with her that elusive aura of lust and lechery that followed
her like a shadow wherever she went.

"Mr. Woresley?"

"Yes, I'm Woresley," he said, still not looking up. "What do you want?"

"Please forgive me for barging in on you like this, Mr. Woresley," she said. "I'm not a chemist. I'm actually a biology student. But I've run up against a rather difficult problem which is more chemical than biological. I've asked around all over the place but no one seems able to give me the answer. They all referred me to you."

"They did, did they," A. R. Woresley said, sounding pleased. He went on carefully measuring out blue liquid from a beaker into the test tubes with his pipette. "Just let me finish this," he added. Yasmin stood still, waiting, sizing up the victim.

"Now, my dear," A. R. Woresley said, laying down the pipette and turning round for the first time. "What was it you—" He stopped dead in mid-sentence. His mouth dropped open and his eyes became as large and round as half-crowns. Then the tip of his red tongue appeared underneath the bristles of his nicotine moustache and began sliding wetly over his lips. For a man who had seen little else but Girton girls and his own diabolic sister for years on end, Yasmin must have appeared before him like the creation, the first morning, the spirit moving over the waters. But he recovered quickly.

"You had something to ask me, my dear?"

Yasmin had prepared her question brilliantly. I have forgotten precisely how it went, but it dealt with a situation where chemistry (his subject) and biology (her subject) became intertwined in a most complex manner, and where a deep knowledge of chemistry was required in order to unravel the problem. The answer, as she had so shrewdly calculated, would take at least nine minutes to deliver, probably more.

"A fascinating question," A. R. Woresley said. "Let me see how best to answer it for you." He crossed to a long blackboard fixed to the wall of the lab. He picked up a piece of chalk.

"Would you like a chocolate?" Yasmin said. She had the paper bag in her hand and when A. R. Woresley turned round, she popped one into her own mouth. She took the second chocolate from the bag and held it toward him in her fingertips.

"My goodness gracious me!" he burbled. "What a treat!"

"Delicious," she said. "Try it."

A. R. Woresley took it and sucked it and rolled it round in his mouth and chewed it and finally swallowed it. "Glorious," he said. "How very kind of you."

At the moment when the chocolate went down his gullet, I noted the time on my watch. I saw Yasmin doing exactly the same thing. Such a sensible girl. A. R. Woresley was standing at the blackboard giving a long exposition with many splendid chemical formulae written in chalk. I didn't listen to it. I was counting the minutes passing by. So was Yasmin. She hardly took her eyes from the watch on her wrist.

Seven minutes gone by . . .

Eight minutes . . .

Eight minutes and fifty seconds . . .

Nine minutes! And dead on time, the hand that held the chalk against the blackboard suddenly stopped writing. A. R. Woresley went rigid.

"Mr. Woresley," Yasmin said brightly, timing it to

perfection, "I wonder if you'd mind giving me your autograph. You are the only science lecturer whose autograph I still don't have for my collection." She was holding out a pen and a sheet of chemistry department notepaper.

"What's that?" he stammered, putting one hand into his trouser pocket before turning round to face her.

"Just there," Yasmin said, placing a finger halfway down the sheet as I had instructed her. "Your autograph. I collect them. I shall treasure yours more than any of the others."

In order to take the pen, A. R. Woresley had to remove his hand from the pocket. It was a comical sight. The poor man looked as though he had a live snake in his trousers. And now he was beginning to bounce up and down on his toes.

"Just there," Yasmin said, keeping her finger on the notepaper. "Then I shall paste it in my autograph book along with all the others."

With his mind fogged by gathering passions, A. R. Woresley signed. Yasmin folded the paper and put it in her purse. A. R. Woresley clutched the edge of the wooden lab bench with both hands. He started rocking about all over the place as if the whole building were in a storm at sea. His forehead was damp with sweat. I reminded myself that he had had a double dose. I think Yasmin was reminding herself of the same thing. She took a couple of paces backwards and braced herself for the coming onslaught.

Slowly, A. R. Woresley turned his head and stared at her. The powder was hitting him hard and there was a glimmer of madness in his eyes.

"I . . . er . . . I . . . I . . ."

"Is something wrong, Mr. Woresley?" Yasmin said sweetly. "Are you feeling all right?"

He went on clutching the bench and staring at her. The sweat was all over his face now and running onto his moustache.

"Can I do something to help?" Yasmin said.

A funny gurgling noise came out of his throat.

"Can I get you a glass of water?" she asked. "Or some smelling-salts perhaps?"

And still he stood there, clutching the bench and waggling his head and making those queer gurgling noises. He reminded me of a man who'd got a fishbone stuck in his throat.

Suddenly he let out a great bellow and made a rush at the girl. He grasped her by the shoulders with both hands and tried to push her to the floor but she skipped back out of his reach.

"Ah-ha!" she said. "So that's what's bothering you, is it? Well, it's nothing to be ashamed about, my darling man." Her voice as she spoke to him was as cool as a thousand cucumbers.

He came at her again with hands outstretched, pawing at her, but she was too nimble for him. "Hold on a sec," she said, flipping open her purse and taking out the rubbery thing I had given her the night before. "I'm perfectly willing to have a bit of fun with you, Mr. W, but we don't want anyone around here to get preggers, now do we? So be a good boy and stand still for a moment while I put your little mackintosh on."

But A. R. Woresley didn't care about the little mackintosh. He had no intention of standing still. I don't think he *could* have stood still if he'd wanted to. From my own point of view, it was instructive to observe the curious effect a double dose had upon the subject. Above all, it made him hop. He kept hopping up and down as though he were doing calisthenics. And he kept making these absurd bellowing noises. And he kept waving his arms round and round windmill fashion. And the sweat kept trickling down his face. And there was Yasmin, dancing around him and holding out the ridiculous rubbery thing with both hands and shouting, "Oh, do keep *still*, Mr. Woresley! I'm not letting you come *near* me till I get this on!"

I don't think he even heard her. And although he was clearly going mad with lust, he also gave the impression of a man who was in great discomfort. He was hopping, it appeared, because excessive irritation was taking place. Something was *stinging* him. It was stinging him so much he couldn't stand still. In greyhound racing, to make a dog run faster, they frequently insert a piece of ginger up its rectum, and the dog runs flat out in an effort to get away from the terrible sting in its backside. With A. R. Woresley, the sting was in a rather different part of his body, and the pain of it was making him hop, skip, and jump all over the lab, and at the same time he was telling himself, or so it seemed, that only a woman could help him to get rid of that terrible sting. But the wretched woman was being too quick for him. He couldn't catch her. And the stinging feeling kept getting worse all the time.

Suddenly, using both hands, he ripped the front of his trousers and half a dozen buttons scattered across the room with little tinkling sounds. He dropped the trousers. They fell around his ankles. He tried to kick them off, but couldn't do so because he still had his shoes on.

With the trousers now around his ankles, A. R. Woresley was temporarily but effectively hobbled. He couldn't run. He couldn't even walk. He could only hop. Yasmin saw her chance and took it. She made a dive for the erect and quivering rod that was sticking out through the slit in his underpants. She grabbed it in her right hand and held onto it as tightly as if it were the handle of a tennis racquet. She had him now. He began to bellow even louder.

"For God's sake, shut up," she said, "or you'll have the whole university in here! And keep *still* so I can get this damn thing on you!"

But A. R. Woresley was deaf to everything except his fierce and fundamental desires. He simply could *not* stand still. Hobbled as he was by the trousers round his ankles, he went on hopping about and waving his arms and bellowing like a bull. For Yasmin, it must have been like trying to thread a needle on a sewing machine while the machine was still in motion.

Finally, she lost patience and I saw her right hand, the one which was grasping, as it were, the handle of the tennis racquet, I saw it give a wicked little flick. It was as though she were making a sharp backhand return to a half volley with a quick roll of the wrist at the end of the shot to impart topspin. A vicious wristy little flick it was, and it was certainly a winner, because the victim let out a howl that rattled every test tube in the lab. It stopped him cold for five seconds, which gave her just enough time to get the rubbery thing on and then to jump back out of reach.

"Couldn't we calm down just a teeny weeny little bit?" she said. "This isn't a bullfight."

He was tearing off his shoes now and throwing them across the room, and when he kicked off his trousers and became fully mobile again, Yasmin must have known that the moment of truth had arrived at last.

It had indeed. But there is no profit in describing the coarse rough and tumble that followed. There were no intermissions, no pauses, no half-time. The vigour that my double dose of Blister Beetle had imparted to that man was astounding. He went at her as though she were an uneven road surface and he was trying to flatten out the bumps. He raked her from stem to stern. He raked her fore and aft, and still he kept reloading and firing away although his cannon must by then have been scorching hot. They say that the ancient Britons used to make fire by rotating the point of a wooden stick very fast and for a long time on a wooden block. Well, if that made fire then A. R. Woresley was about to start a raging conflagration any moment, wood or no wood. It wouldn't have surprised me in the least to see a puff of smoke come up from the wrestlers on the floor.

While all this was going on, I took the opportunity of making a few notes with pad and pencil for future reference.

Note one: Endeavour always to arrange for Yasmin to confront the subject in a room where there is a couch or an armchair or at the very least a carpet on the floor. She is undoubtedly a strong and resilient girl, but having to work on a hard wooden surface in exceptionally severe circumstances as she is doing now is asking rather a lot. The way things are going, she could easily suffer severe damage to her lumbar region or even a pelvic fracture. And where would our clever little scheme be then, tra-la-la?

Note two: Never again prescribe a double dose for any man. Too much powder causes excessive irritation in the vital regions and gives the victim a sort of St. Vitus's dance. This makes it almost impossible for Yasmin to roll on the sperm collector without resorting to foul play. An overdose also makes the victim bellow, which could be embarrassing if the wife of the victim, the Queen of Denmark, for example, or Mrs. Bernard Shaw, happened to be sitting quietly in the next room doing needlepoint.

Note three: Try to think of a way of helping Yasmin to get out from under and to do a bunk with the precious sperm as soon as possible after the stuff is in the bag. The devilish powder, even when sparingly administered, might easily keep a ninety-year-old genius bashing away for a couple of hours or more. And quite apart from any discomfort Yasmin might be suffering, it is vital to get the little squigglers into the freezer quickly, while they are still fresh. Look, for example, at old Woresley right now and how he's still grinding away although he's obviously delivered the goods at least six times in succession. Perhaps a sharp jab in the buttocks with a hatpin would do the trick in the future.

Out there on the floor of the lab Yasmin had no hatpin to help her, and to this day I do not know precisely what it was she did to A. R. Woresley that caused him to let out yet another of those horrendous howls and to freeze so suddenly in his tracks. Nor do I wish to know, because it's none of my business. But whatever it was, I was quite certain a nice girl like her would never have done it to a nice man like him if it had not been absolutely necessary. The next thing I knew, Yasmin was up and away and dashing for the door with the spoils of victory in her hand. I nearly stood up and clapped for her as she left the stage. What a performance! What a splendid exit! The door slammed shut and she was gone.

All at once, the laboratory became silent. I saw A. R. Woresley picking himself up slowly off the floor. He stood there dazed and wobbly. He looked like a man who had been struck on the head with a cricket bat. He staggered over to the sink and began splashing water onto his face, and while he was doing this, I myself crept from my hiding place and tiptoed out of the room, closing the door softly behind me.

There was no sign of Yasmin in the corridor. I had told her I would be sitting in my rooms at Trinity throughout the operation, so she was probably making her way there now. I hurried outside and jumped into my motor car and drove from the Science Building to the College by a roundabout route so as not to pass her on the way. I parked the car and went up to my rooms and waited.

A few minutes later, in she came.

"Give me a drink," she said, crossing to an armchair. I noticed she was walking sort of bow-legged and treating herself tenderly.

"You look as though you've just brought the good news from Ghent to Aix riding bareback," I said.

She didn't answer me. I poured her two inches of gin and added a cubic centimetre of lime juice. She took a good gulp of the splendid stuff and said, "Ah-h-h, that's better."

"How did it go?"

"We gave him a little bit too much."

"I thought we might have done," I said.

She opened her purse and took out the repulsive rubbery thing which she had very sensibly knotted at the open end. Also the sheet of notepaper with A. R. Woresley's signature on it.

"Tremendous!" I cried. "You did it! It all worked! Did you enjoy it?"

Her answer astonished me. "As a matter of fact I rather did," she said.

"You *did*? You mean he wasn't too rough?"

"He made every other man I've ever met look like a eunuch," she said.

I laughed at that.

"Including you," she said.

I stopped laughing.

"That," she said softly, taking another gulp of gin, "is exactly how I want my men to be from now on."

"But you said we gave him too much."

"Just a teensy bit," she said. "I couldn't stop him. He was absolutely tireless."

"How *did* you stop him?"

"Never you mind."

"Would a hatpin be helpful next time?"

"That's a good idea," she said. "I shall carry a hatpin. But I'd much rather get the dose exactly right so I don't have to use it."

"We'll get it right."

"I really would prefer not to go sticking hatpins into the King of Spain's bum, if you see what I mean."

"Oh, I do, I do."

"I like to part company on friendly terms."

"And didn't you?"

"Not exactly, no," she said, smiling slightly.

"Well done, anyway," I said. "You pulled it off."

"He was funny," she said. "I wish you could have seen him. He kept hopping up and down."

I took the sheet of notepaper with A. R. Woresley's signature on it and placed it in my typewriter. I sat down and typed the following legend directly above the signature:

I hereby certify that I have on this day, the 27th of March, 1919, delivered personally a quantity of my own

*semen to Oswald Cornelius Esquire, President of The
International Semen's Home of Cambridge, England. It
is my wish that this semen shall be stored indefinitely,
using the revolutionary and recently discovered Woresley
Technique, and I further agree that the aforementioned
Oswald Cornelius may at any time use portions of that
semen to fertilize selected females of high quality in
order to disseminate my own bloodline throughout the
world for the benefit of future generations.*

(Signed) *A. R. Woresley
Lecturer in Chemistry,
Cambridge University*

I showed it to Yasmin. "Obviously it doesn't apply to
Woresley," I said, "because his stuff isn't going into the
freezer. But what do you think of it otherwise? Will it look
all right over the signature of kings and geniuses?"

She read it through carefully. "It's good," she said. "It'll
do nicely."

"I've won my bet," I said. "Woresley will have to capit-
ulate now."

She sat sipping her gin. She was relaxed and amazingly
cool. "I have a strange feeling," she said, "that this whole
thing's actually going to work. At first it sounded ridiculous. But now I can't see what's to stop us."

"Nothing can stop us," I said. "You'll win every time
so long as you can always reach your man and feed him the
powder."

"It really is fantastic stuff."

"I found that out in Paris."

"You don't think it might give some of the very old ones
a heart attack, do you?"

"Of course not," I said, although I had been wondering the same thing myself.

"I don't want to leave a trail of corpses around the world," she said. "Especially the corpses of great and famous men."

"You won't," I said. "Don't worry about it."

"Take for example Alexander Graham Bell," she said. "According to you, he is now seventy-two years old. Do you think *he* could stand up to it?"

"Tough as nuts," I said. "All the great men are. But I'll tell you what we might do if it'll make you feel a bit easier. We'll regulate the dose according to age. The older they are, the less they'll get."

"I'll buy that," she said. "It's a good idea."

I took Yasmin out and treated her to a superb dinner at the Blue Boar. She deserved it. Then I delivered her safely back to Girton.

12

THE NEXT MORNING, carrying the rubbery thing and the signed letter in my pocket, I went looking for A. R. Woresley. They told me in the Science Building that he had not shown up that morning. So I drove out to his house and rang the bell. The diabolic sister came to the door.

"Arthur's a bit under the weather," she said.

"What happened?"

"He fell off his bike."

"Oh dear."

"He was cycling home in the dark and he collided with a pillar-box."

"I *am* sorry. Is he much hurt?"

"He's bruised all over," she said.

"Nothing broken, I hope?"

"Well," she said, and there was an edge of bitterness to her voice, "not *bones*."

Oh God, I thought. Oh, Yasmin. What have you done to him?

"Please offer him my sincere condolences," I said. Then I left.

The following day, a very fragile A. R. Woresley reported for duty.

I waited until I had him alone in the lab, then I placed before him the sheet of chemistry department notepaper containing the legend I had typed out over his own signature. I also dumped about a thousand million of his very own spermatozoa (by now dead) on the bench and said, "I've won my bet."

He stared at the obscene rubbery thing. He read the letter and recognized his signature.

"You bounder!" he cried. "You tricked me!"

"You assaulted a lady."

"Who typed this?"

"I did."

He stood there taking it all in.

"All right," he said. "But what *happened* to me? I went absolutely crazy. What in God's name did you do?"

"You had a double dose of *Cantharis vesicatoria sudanii*," I said. "The old Blister Beetle. Powerful stuff that."

He stared at me, comprehension dawning on his face. "So *that's* what it was," he said. "Inside the bloody chocolate, I suppose."

"Naturally. And if *you* swallowed it, then so will the King of the Belgians and the Prince of Wales and Mr. Joseph Conrad and all the rest of them."

He started pacing up and down the lab, albeit a trifle gingerly. "I told you once before, Cornelius," he said, "that you are a totally unscrupulous fellow."

"Absolutely," I said, grinning.

"Do you *know* what that woman did to me?"

"I can make a pretty good guess."

"She's a witch! She's a—a vampire! She's disgusting!"

"*You* seemed to like her well enough," I said, pointing to the thing on the bench.

"I was drugged!"

"You raped her. You raped her like an animal. *You* were the disgusting one."

"That was the Blister Beetle."

"Of course it was," I said. "But when Mr. Marcel Proust rapes her like an animal, or King Alfonso of Spain, will *they* know they've had the Blister Beetle?"

He didn't answer me.

"They most certainly will not," I said. "They may well wonder what the hell came over them, just as you did. But they'll never know the answer, and in the end they'll simply have to put it down to the incredible attractiveness of the girl. That's all they *can* put it down to. Right?"

"Well . . . yes."

"They will be embarrassed at having raped her, just as you are. They will be very contrite, just as you are. They will want to hush the whole thing up, just as you do. In other words, they will give us no more trouble. We skidaddle with the signed notepaper and the precious sperm and that will be the end of it."

"You are a rapscallion of the first water, Cornelius. You are an unmitigated scoundrel."

"I know," I said, grinning again. But the logic of my argument was irrefutable. The plan was watertight. A. R. Woresley, who was certainly no fool, was beginning to realize this. I could see him weakening.

"What about that girl?" he said. "Who was she?"

"She's the third member of our organization. She's our official teaser."

"Some teaser," he said.

"That's why I chose her."

"I shall be embarrassed, Cornelius, if I have to meet her again."

"No, you won't," I said. "She's a great girl. You'll like her very much. She happens to like you, too."

"Rubbish. What makes you think that?"

"She said you were absolutely and positively the greatest. She said that from now on she wants all her men to be like you."

"She said that? Did she actually say that, Cornelius?"

"Word for word."

A. R. Woresley beamed.

"She said you made all other men look like eunuchs," I said, ramming it home.

A. R. Woresley's whole face began to glow with pleasure. "You are not pulling my leg, are you, Cornelius?"

"Ask her yourself when you see her."

"Well well well," he said, beaming away and preening his horrible moustache lightly with the back of his fingers.

"Well well well," he said again. "And may I ask what her name is, this remarkable young lady?"

"Yasmin Howcomely. She's half Persian."

"How interesting."

"You must have been terrific," I said.

"I have my moments, Cornelius," he said. "Ah yes indeed, I certainly have my moments." He seemed to have forgotten about the Blister Beetle. He wanted all the credit himself now and I let him have it.

"She can't wait to meet you again."

"Splendid," he said, rubbing his hands. "And she's going to be a part of our little organization, you say?"

"Absolutely. You'll be seeing a lot of her from now on."

"Good," he said. "Goody good."

And thus A. R. Woresley joined the firm. It was as easy as that. What's more, he was a man of his word.

He agreed to withhold publication of his discovery.

He agreed to assist Yasmin and me in every possible way.

He agreed to construct for us a portable container for liquid nitrogen which we could take with us on our travels.

He agreed to instruct me in the exact procedure for diluting the collected semen and measuring it out into straws for freezing.

Yasmin and I would be the travellers and the collectors.

A. R. Woresley would remain at his post in Cambridge but would establish at the same time in a convenient and secret place a large central freezer, The Semen's Home.

From time to time, the travellers, Yasmin and I, would return with our spoils and transfer them from the portable suitcase freezer to The Semen's Home.

I would provide ample funds for everything. I would

pay all travelling expenses, hotels, etc., while Yasmin and I were on the road. I would give Yasmin a generous dress allowance so that she might buy herself a superb wardrobe.

It was all straightforward and simple.

I resigned from the university and so did Yasmin.

I found and bought a house not far from where A. R. Woresley lived. It was a plain red-brick affair with four bedrooms and two fairly large living-rooms. Some retired empire builder in years gone by had christened it, of all things, Dunroamin. Dunroamin would be the headquarters of the Home. It would be where Yasmin and I lived during the preparatory period, and it would also be a secret laboratory for A. R. Woresley. I spent a lot of money equipping that lab with apparatus for making liquid nitrogen, with mixers, microscopes, and everything else we needed. I furnished the house. Yasmin and I moved in. But from then on, ours was a business relationship only.

Within a month, A. R. Woresley had constructed our portable liquid nitrogen container. It had double vacuum walls of aluminium and all manner of neat little trays and other contraptions to hold the tiny straws of sperm. It was the size of a large suitcase and what's more it looked like a suitcase because the outside was sheathed in leather.

A second smaller travelling case contained compartments for ice and a hand-mill and bottles for carrying glycerol, egg yolk, and skimmed milk. Also a microscope for testing the potency of newly collected sperm in the field. Everything was got ready with meticulous care.

Finally, A. R. Woresley set about building The Semen's Home in the cellar of the house.

13

BY EARLY JUNE 1919, we were almost ready to go. I say almost because we still had not yet agreed upon the list of names. Who would be the great men in the world to be honoured by a visit from Yasmin—and lurking in the background, me? The three of us had many meetings in Dunroamin to discuss this knotty problem. The kings were easy. We wanted all the kings. We wrote them down first:

KING ALBERT OF THE BELGIANS	present age	44
KING BORIS OF BULGARIA	" "	25
KING CHRISTIAN OF DENMARK	" "	49
KING ALEXANDER OF THE HELLENES	" "	26
KING VITTORIO EMANUELE OF ITALY	" "	50
KING HAAKON OF NORWAY	" "	47
KING FERDINAND OF RUMANIA	" "	54
KING ALFONSO OF SPAIN	" "	75
KING GUSTAV OF SWEDEN	" "	61
KING PETER OF SERBIA	" "	33

The Netherlands was out because it had only a queen. Portugal was out because the monarchy had been overthrown in the revolution of 1910. And Monaco was not worth fooling with. There remained only our King George V. After much debate, we decided to leave the old boy alone. It was all just a little bit too much on our own doorstep for comfort, and in any event I had plans for using this particular gentleman in quite another way, as you will see in a moment. We decided, though, to put Edward, Prince of Wales, on the list as a possible extra. Yasmin plus Blister Beetle could roll him over anytime she wished. What's more, she could hardly wait.

The list of great men and geniuses was more difficult to compile. A few of them like Puccini and Joseph Conrad and Richard Strauss were obvious. So were Renoir and Monet, two rather ancient candidates who must clearly be visited pretty soon. But there was more to it than that. We had to decide which of the present-day (1919) great and famous men would still be great and famous ten, twenty, and even fifty years thence. There was also a more difficult group, the younger ones who were at present only moderately famous but who looked as though they might well become great and famous later on. This part of it was a bit of a gamble. It was also a matter of flair and judgement. Would the young James Joyce, for example, who was only thirty-seven years old, come to be regarded as a genius by later generations? I voted yes. So did A. R. Woresley. Yasmin had never heard of him. By a vote of two to one we put him on the list.

In the end, we decided to make two separate lists. The first would have top priority. The second would contain the possibles. We would get round to the possibles only after we had polished off the top priority boys. We would also pay attention to age. The older ones should, whenever possible, be attended to first in case they expired before we got to them.

We agreed that lists should be updated each year to include any new possibles who might suddenly have shot into prominence.

Our priority list, compiled in June 1919, was as follows, in alphabetical order:

BELL, ALEXANDER GRAHAM	present age	72
BONNARD, PIERRE	" "	52
CHURCHILL, WINSTON	" "	45
CONRAD, JOSEPH	" "	62
DOYLE, ARTHUR CONAN	" "	60
EINSTEIN, ALBERT	" "	40
FORD, HENRY	" "	56
FREUD, SIGMUND	" "	63
KIPLING, RUDYARD	" "	54
LAWRENCE, DAVID HERBERT	" "	34
LAWRENCE, THOMAS EDWARD	" "	31
LENIN, VLADIMIR ILYICH	" "	49
MARCONI, GUGLIELMO	" "	45
MATISSE, HENRI	" "	50
MONET, CLAUDE	" "	79
MUNCH, EDVARD	" "	56
PROUST, MARCEL	" "	48
PUCCINI, GIACOMO	" "	61
RACHMANINOFF, SERGEI	" "	46
RENOIR, AUGUSTE	" "	78
SHAW, GEORGE BERNARD	" "	63
SIBELIUS, JEAN	" "	54
STRAUSS, RICHARD	" "	55
STRAVINSKY, IGOR	" "	37
YEATS, WILLIAM BUTLER	" "	54

And here was our second list, comprising some fairly speculative younger men as well as a few borderline cases:

AMUNDSEN, ROALD	present age	47
BRAQUE, GEORGES	" "	37
CARUSO, ENRICO	" "	46
CASALS, PABLO	" "	43
CLEMENCEAU, GEORGES	" "	78
DELIUS, FREDERICK	" "	57
FOCH, MARÉCHAL FERDINAND	" "	68
GANDHI, MOHANDAS	" "	50
HAIG, GENERAL SIR DOUGLAS	" "	58
JOYCE, JAMES	" "	37
KANDINSKY, WASSILY	" "	53
LLOYD GEORGE, DAVID	" "	56
MANN, THOMAS	" "	44
NIJINSKY, VASLAV	" "	29
PERSHING, GENERAL JOHN J.	" "	59
PICASSO, PABLO	" "	38
RAVEL, MAURICE	" "	44
RUSSELL, BERTRAND	" "	47
SCHOENBERG, ARNOLD	" "	45
TAGORE, RABINDRANATH	" "	58
TROTSKY, LEV DAVIDOVICH	" "	40
VALENTINO, RUDOLPH	" "	24
WILSON, WOODROW	" "	63

Of course there were errors and omissions in these lists. There is no more difficult game than to try spotting an authentic and enduring genius during his lifetime. Fifty years after he's dead it becomes easier. But dead men were no use to us. One more point. Rudolph Valentino was included not because we thought he was a genius. It was a commercial decision. We were guessing that the semen of a man who had such an immense and fanatical band of followers might well be a good seller in days to come. Nor did we think Woodrow Wilson was a genius, or Caruso. But they were world-famous figures, and we had to take that into consideration.

Europe, of course, must be covered first. The long trip to America would have to wait. So onto one wall of the living-room we fixed an enormous map of Europe and covered it with little flags. Each flag pinpointed the precise whereabouts of a candidate—red flags for the priorities, yellow for the second group, with a name and address on each flag. Thus, Yasmin and I would be able to plan our visits geographically, area by area, instead of rushing from one end of the continent to the other and back again. France had the most flags of all, and the Paris region was literally cluttered with them.

"What a pity both Degas and Rodin died two years ago," I said.

"I want to do the kings first," Yasmin said. The three of us were sitting in the living-room of Dunroamin discussing the next move.

"Why the kings?"

"Because I have a terrific urge to be ravished by royalty," she said.

"You are being flippant," A. R. Woresley said.

"Why shouldn't I choose," she said. "I'm the one at the receiving end, not you. I'd like to do the King of Spain first. Then we can nip over to Italy and do old Vittorio Emanuele, then Serbia, then Greece, and so on. We'll polish off the whole lot of them in a couple of weeks."

"May I ask how you intend to gain access to all these royal palaces?" A. R. Woresley said to me. "Yasmin can't just go knocking on the front door and expect to be received in private by the king. And don't forget it's got to be in private or it's no good."

"That part shouldn't be too difficult," I said.

"It's going to be impossible," Woresley said. "We shall probably have to forget about the kings."

I had been working on this problem for several weeks and I had my answer ready. "Easy as pie," I said. "We shall use King George the Fifth as a decoy. He'll get her in."

"Don't be ridiculous, Cornelius."

I went to a drawer and took out some sheets of note-paper. "Let's assume you want to do the King of Spain first," I said, riffling through the sheets. "Ah yes, here we are. 'My dear Alfonso . . .' " I handed the notepaper to Woresley. Yasmin got up from her chair to look at it over his shoulder.

"What in God's name is this?" he cried.

"It's an extremely personal letter from King George the Fifth to King Alfonso," I said. And indeed it was.

The notepaper had a heavily embossed royal coat of arms in red at the top centre, and on the top right, also embossed in red, it said simply BUCKINGHAM PALACE, LONDON. Below, in a reasonable imitation of the King's flowing handwriting, I had written the following:

My Dear Alfonso,

This will introduce to you a dear friend of mine, Lady Victoria Nottingham. She is travelling alone to Madrid to clear up a small matter that has to do with an estate that has come to her through her Spanish maternal grandmother.

My request is that you see Lady Victoria briefly and in <u>absolute privacy</u>. She is having some trouble with the local authorities over title deeds and I am sure that if you yourself, after she has explained her problem, will drop

*a hint with the right people, then everything will go
smoothly for her.*

*I am taking you, my dear Alfonso, very deeply into
my confidence when I tell you that Lady Victoria is an
especially close personal friend of mine. Let us leave it
at that and say no more. But I know I can rely upon you
to keep this intelligence entirely to yourself.*

*When you receive this note, the lady in question will
be at the Ritz Hotel, Madrid. Do please send her a message as soon as possible granting her a private audience.*

Burn this letter when read, and make no reply to me.

I am at your service at all times.

With warmest personal regards,

George RI

Both A. R. Woresley and Yasmin looked up at me with
eyes popping.

"Where did you get this notepaper?" Woresley said.

"I had it printed."

"Did you write this yourself?"

"I did and I'm rather proud of it. It's a very fair imitation of the King's handwriting. And the signature is almost
perfect. I practiced it for days."

"You'll be had up for forgery! You'll be sent to prison!"

"No, I won't," I said. "Alfonso won't dare tell a soul.
Don't you see the beauty of it? Our great and noble King
is hinting that he is having a backstairs affair with Yasmin.
That, my dear sir, is very confidential and dangerous
material. And don't forget, European royalty is the most
tightly knit and exclusive club in the world. They work
together. Every ruddy one of them is related to the other

in some crazy way. They're tangled up like spaghetti. No—there is not the slightest chance of Alfonso letting the King of England down. He'll see Yasmin at once. He'll be dying to see her. He'll want to take a good look at this woman who is the secret mistress of old George Five. Remember also that right now our King is the most respected of all the royals. He's just won the war."

"Cornelius," A. R. Woresley said, "you frighten me to death. You'll have us all behind bars."

"I think it's terrific," Yasmin said. "It's brilliant. It's bound to work."

"What if a secretary opens the envelope?" Woresley said.

"That won't happen," I said. I took a bunch of envelopes from the drawer and found the right one and gave it to Woresley. It was a long high-quality white envelope with the red royal coat of arms top left, and BUCKINGHAM PALACE top right. In the King's handwriting, I had written on it:

His Royal Highness, King Alfonso XIII.
Personal and Confidential.
To be opened only by HRH himself.

"That should do it," I said. "The envelope will be delivered to the Oriente Palace in Madrid by my own hand."

A. R. Woresley opened his mouth to say something, then closed it again.

"I have a roughly similar letter for each of the other nine kings," I said. "Obviously there are small changes. Each message is tailored to the individual. Haakon of Norway, for instance, is married to King George's sister Maud—I'll bet you didn't know that—and so there we finish up with 'Give my love to Maud, but I trust you absolutely to make no mention to her of this private little piece of business.' And so on and so on. It's foolproof, my dear Arthur." I was calling him by his first name now.

"You appear to have done your homework, Cornelius." He himself, in the manner of all dons and schoolmasters, refused to use my given name. "But how do you propose to get in to see all the others, the non-kings?"

"There will be no problem," I said. "Not many men will refuse to see a girl like Yasmin when she knocks on the door. *You* certainly didn't. I'll bet you began dribbling with excitement as soon as she came into the lab."

That shut him up.

"So can we do the King of Spain first?" Yasmin asked. "He's only thirty-three and from his photograph he's rather dishy."

"Very well," I said. "Madrid first stop. But then we must move into France. Renoir and Monet are top priority. One's seventy-eight and the other seventy-nine. I want to nobble them both before it's too late."

"With Blister Beetle it'll be heart attack time for those old boys," Yasmin said.

"We'll reduce the dose," I said.

"Now see here, Cornelius," A. R. Woresley said. "I won't be a party to the murder of Mr. Renoir or Mr. Monet. I don't want blood on my hands."

"You'll have a lot of valuable sperm on your hands and that's all," I said. "Leave it to us."

14

THE STAGE WAS SET. Yasmin and I packed our bags and left for Madrid. We had with us the vital liquid nitrogen suitcase, the smaller case containing glycerol, etc., a supply of Prestat's best chocolate truffles, and four ounces of Blister Beetle powder. I must again mention that in those days the examination of luggage by customs was virtually non-existent. There would be no trouble with our curious suitcases. We crossed the Channel and travelled to Madrid via Paris by *wagon-lits*. The whole trip took only nineteen hours. In Madrid, we registered at the Ritz, where we had booked separate rooms by telegram, one for Oswald Cornelius Esquire and one for Lady Victoria Nottingham, using the name and title I had recently conferred on Yasmin.

The next morning I went to the Oriente Palace where I was stopped at the gates by a couple of soldiers on guard duty. Waving my envelope and shouting, "This is for the King!" in Spanish, I reached the big main entrance. I pulled the bell knob. A flunkey opened one of the doors. I then spoke a Spanish sentence that I had committed to memory, which said, "This is for His Majesty King Alfonso from King George of Great Britain. It is most urgent." I walked away.

Back at the hotel, I settled down with a book in Yasmin's room to await developments.

"What if he's out of town?" she said.

"He isn't," I said. "The flag was flying over the palace."

"What if he doesn't answer?"

"He'll answer. He wouldn't dare not to, after reading that letter on that notepaper."

"But can he read English?"

"All kings can read English," I said. "It's a part of their education. Alfonso speaks perfect English."

Just before lunchtime, there was a knock on the door. Yasmin opened it and there stood the manager of the hotel himself with a look of importance on his face. He had a silver tray in his hand on which lay a white envelope. "An urgent message, my lady," he said, bowing. Yasmin took the envelope, thanked him, and closed the door.

"Rip it open!" I said.

She ripped it open and took out a letter handwritten on magnificent palace notepaper.

My Dear Lady Victoria, it said. *We shall be pleased to see you at four o'clock this afternoon. If you will give your name at the gates you will be admitted immediately.*
Alfonso R.

"Simple, isn't it?" I said.

"What does he mean *we?*"

"All monarchs refer to themselves as we. You have three hours to get ready and be at the palace gates," I said. "Let's fix the chocolate."

I had obtained from Prestat a number of very small and elegant boxes, each holding no more than six truffles. Yasmin was to give one box to the King as a small present. She was to say to him, "I have brought you, sire, a little present of chocolates. They're delicious. George has them specially made for me." She was then to open the box and say with a most disarming smile, "Do you mind if I steal one? I simply can't resist them." She pops one into her mouth, then she picks up the marked chocolate and holds it out to the King delicately between forefinger and thumb, saying, "Try one." The poor man will be charmed. He will eat the choc just as A. R. Woresley did in the lab. And that will be that. Thereafter, Yasmin will simply have to carry on nine minutes of flirtatious small talk without getting entangled in any complicated reason for her visit.

I got out the Blister Beetle powder and we prepared the fatal truffle. "No double doses this time," Yasmin said. "I don't want to have to use the hatpin." I agreed. She herself marked the truffle with small scratches on the surface of the chocolate.

It was June and very hot in Madrid. Yasmin dressed with great care but wore the lightest possible clothes. I gave her a rubbery thing from my large stock and she put it in her purse.

"For God's sake don't fail to get it on him," I said. "That's what it's all about. And hurry back here with it quickly afterwards. Come straight to my room next door." I wished her good luck and off she went.

In my own room I made careful preparations for dealing with the sperm as soon as it arrived. This was my very first time under actual field conditions and I wanted to get everything just right. I will admit I felt nervous. Yasmin was at the palace. She was giving Blister Beetle to the King of Spain and after that there would be a good old wrestling match and I only hoped she would handle things properly.

The time went slowly. I finished my preparations. I leaned out of the window and watched the carriages in the street below. Once or twice a motor car came by, but there were not so many here as in London. I looked at my watch.

It was after six o'clock. I made myself a whiskey and soda. I carried it to the open window and sipped it there. I was hoping to see Yasmin stepping out of a carriage at the hotel entrance. I didn't see her. I got myself a second whiskey. I sat down and tried to read a book. It was now six thirty. She had been gone two and a half hours. Suddenly there was a loud knocking on my door. I got up and opened it. Yasmin, with cheeks afire, swept into the room.

"I did it!" she cried, waving her handbag at me like a flag. "I've got it! It's in here!"

"Give it to me quick," I said.

There were at least three cc's of royal semen in the knotted rubbery thing Yasmin handed to me. I put a drop under the microscope to test it for potency. The tiny royal squigglers were squiggling madly all over the place, supremely active. "First rate stuff," I said. "Let me get this into the straws and frozen up before you say a word. After that, I want to hear exactly what happened."

Yasmin went to her room to bathe and change. I set about the business in hand. A. R. Woresley and I had agreed that we would make exactly fifty straws of semen for each person. More than that would take too much room in our travelling sperm freezer. I set about diluting the semen with egg yolk, skimmed milk, and glycerol. I mixed it. I measured it out with a graduated eye dropper into the little rubber straws. I sealed the straws. I put them on ice for half an hour. I exposed them to nitrogen vapour for a few minutes. Then finally I lowered them gently into the liquid nitrogen and closed the container. It was done. We now had fifty doses of the King of Spain's semen and strong doses at that. The equation was simple. He gave us three cc's originally. Three cc's would contain approximately three thousand million sperm and those three thousand million, when divided up into fifty doses, would produce a potency of sixty million sperm per dose. This was exactly three times A. R. Woresley's optimum figure of twenty million per dose. In other words, the Spanish royal straws were of prime potency. I was elated. I rang the bell for service and ordered a bottle of Krug on ice.

Yasmin came in looking cool and clean. The champagne arrived at the same time. We waited until the servant had opened the bottle and filled the glasses and left the room. "Now," I said, "tell me all."

"It was amazing," she said. "The preliminaries went exactly as you said they would. I was ushered into an enormous room with Goyas and El Grecos all over the walls. The King was at the far end sitting behind a huge desk. He was dressed in a plain suit. He stood up and came forward to greet me. He had a moustache and was not a bad-looking little fellow. He kissed my hand. And my God, Oswald, you should have seen the way he fawned all over me because he thought I was the King of England's mistress. 'Madame,' he said, 'I am enchanted to meet you. And how is our mutual friend?'

" 'He has a slight touch of gout,' I said, 'but otherwise he's in splendid condition.' Then I went through the chocolate routine and he ate his little truffle like a lamb and with a good deal of relish. 'These are magnificent,' he said, chewing away. 'I must have my ambassador send me a few pounds.' As he swallowed the last bit of chocolate, I noted the time on my watch. 'Pray be seated,' he said.

"There were four big sofa things in the room and before sitting down I examined them carefully. I wanted to choose the softest and most practical of the four. I knew that in nine minutes' time the one I selected would become a battle-field."

"Good thinking," I said.

"I chose an enormous sort of chaise longue covered in plum-colored velvet. The King remained standing, and as we talked he strolled about the room with his hands clasped behind his back, trying to look regal.

"I said, 'Our mutual friend has asked me to tell you, sire, that if you yourself should ever require any confidential assistance in his country, you could rely upon him absolutely.'

" 'I shall bear it in mind,' he said.

" 'He sent you another message as well, your Majesty.'

" 'What was that?'

" 'You promise you won't be cross if I tell you?'

" 'Certainly not, madame. Tell me what else he said.'

" 'He said, "You tell that good-looking Alfonso to keep his hands off my girl." That's word for word what he said, your Majesty.' Little Alfonso laughed and clapped his hands and said, 'Dear lady, I shall respect his wishes but only with the greatest difficulty.' "

"Yasmin," I said, "you're a clever little bitch."

"Oh, it was such fun," she said. "I loved twisting him around. He was madly curious about my so-called affair, but he didn't quite dare to mention it. He kept putting leading questions to me. He said, 'I presume you have a house in London?'

" 'Of course,' I said. 'I have my own London house where I entertain in normal fashion. Then I have a small, very private place in Windsor Great Park where a certain person can call on me when he is out riding. And I have a cottage on the Sandringham estate where again that certain person can pop in for a cup of tea when he is out shooting pheasants. As you probably know, he adores shooting.'

" 'I know that,' Alfonso said. 'And I hear he is the best shot in England.'

" 'Yes,' I said. 'And in more ways than one, your Majesty.'

" 'Ha!' he said. 'I see you are a funny lady.' "

"Were you watching the time?" I said to Yasmin.

"You bet I was. I've forgotten exactly what he was saying when the moment arrived, but the interesting thing is that he froze right in the middle of a sentence just as old Woresley had done in the lab. Here it comes, I told myself. Put on the boxing gloves."

"Did he jump you?"

"No, he didn't. Don't forget Woresley had had a double dose."

"Ah yes."

"Anyway, he was standing in front of me when he froze and he was wearing tight trousers so I could see very clearly what was going on around there. At precisely that moment, I told him I collected the autographs of great men and asked him if he would give me his signature on palace notepaper. I got up and went to his desk myself and found the paper and told him where to sign. It was too easy. The wretched man hardly knew what he was doing. He signed and I put the paper in my purse and sat down again. You know, Oswald, you can make them do just about anything you want if you catch them right at the very moment when the powder first hits them. They're so astonished and embarrassed by the suddenness of it all they'll do absolutely anything. We're never going to have any trouble getting their signatures. Anyway, I was back again on the sofa now and Alfonso was standing there goggling at me and he kept swallowing, which made his Adam's apple jump up and down. Red in the face he was, too, and then he started taking deep breaths. 'Come and sit down, your Majesty,' I said, patting the place beside me. He came and sat down. The swallowing and the goggling and the fidgeting went on for about a minute and I could see this absolutely terrific letch building up inside him as the powder got to work. It was like steam building up in a boiler with nowhere to escape except through the safety valve. And the safety valve was little me. If he didn't get little me he was going to explode. Suddenly he said in a choky and rather prim sort of voice, 'I wish you to remove your clothes, madame.'

" 'Oh, sire!' I cried, putting both hands on my breast. 'What are you saying!'

" 'Take them off,' he said, gulping.

" 'But then you will ravish me, your Majesty!' I cried.

" 'Please don't keep me waiting,' he said, gulping some more.

" 'If you ravish me, sire, I will become pregnant and our mutual friend will know something has happened between us. He will be so angry he will send warships to bombard your cities.'

" 'You must tell him it was he who got you pregnant. Come along now, I cannot wait!'

" 'He'll know it wasn't he, your Majesty, because he and I always take precautions.'

" 'Then take precautions now!' he snapped. 'And please do not argue with me, madame!' "

"You handled it beautifully," I said to Yasmin. "So you put the thing on him."

"No problem," she said. "It was easy. With Woresley I had had the most awful fight, but this time it was as easy as putting a tea-cosy on a teapot."

"Then what?"

"They're pretty odd, these royals," Yasmin said. "They know a few tricks we ordinary mortals have never heard of."

"Such as what?"

"Well," she said, "for one thing he doesn't move. I suppose the theory is that kings don't do any manual labour."

"So he made you do all the work?"

"I wasn't allowed to move either."

"Now don't be silly, Yasmin. You can't have static copulation."

"Kings can," she said. "Wait till you hear this. You won't believe it. You simply won't believe this sort of thing could happen."

"What sort of thing?" I said.

"I told you I had chosen a chaise longue covered in purple velvet," Yasmin said.

"Yes."

"Well, it turned out I'd picked exactly the right one. This damn sofa was some sort of specially constructed royal romping ground. It was the most fantastic experience I've ever had. It had something underneath it—God knows what, but it was some sort of an engine, and when the King pulled a lever the whole sofa began to joggle up and down."

"You're having me on."

"I am *not* having you on!" she cried. "I couldn't make that up even if I wanted to, and you jolly well know it."

"You really mean there was an *engine* under the sofa? Did you see it?"

"Of course not. But I heard it all right. It made the most godawful grinding noise."

"You mean a *petrol* engine?"

"No, it wasn't a petrol engine."

"What was it then?"

"Clockwork," she said.

"*Clockwork!* It's not possible! How did you know it was clockwork?"

"Because when it started to run down, he had to roll off and wind the thing up again with a handle."

"I don't believe a word of this," I said. "What sort of a handle?"

"A big handle," she said, "like the starting handle of a motor car, and when he was winding it up it went *clickety-click*. That's how I knew it was clockwork. You always get that clicking noise when you wind up clockwork."

"Jesus," I said. "I still don't believe it."

"You don't know much about kings," Yasmin said. "Kings are different. They get very bored, therefore they are always trying to think up ways of amusing themselves. Look at that mad King of Bavaria who had a hole drilled in the middle of the seat of each chair around his dining-room table. And halfway through dinner, when all the guests were sitting there in their wonderful, expensive clothes, he would turn on a secret tap and jets of water would squirt up through the holes. Very powerful jets of cold water right up their backsides. Kings are crazy."

"Go on with the clockwork sofa," I said. "Was it amazing and terrific?"

Yasmin sipped her champagne and didn't answer me at once.

"Did it have the maker's name on it?" I said. "Where can I get one?"

"I wouldn't get one," she said.

"Why not?"

"It's not worth it. It's only a toy. It's a toy for silly

kings. It has a kind of shock value but that's all. When it
first started up I got the shock of my life. 'Hey!' I shouted.
'What the hell's going on?'

" 'Silence!' the King said. 'Talking is forbidden!'

"There was a loud whirring noise coming from underneath the damn sofa and the thing was vibrating most
terribly. And at the same time it was jogging up and down.
Honestly, Oswald, it was like riding a horse on the deck
of a boat in a rough sea. Oh God, I thought, I'm going
to be seasick. But I wasn't and after he'd wound it up a
second time I began to get the hang of it. You see, it *was*
rather like riding a horse. You had to go along with it. You
had to get the rhythm."

"So you began to enjoy it?"

"I wouldn't say that. But it does have its advantages. For
one thing, you never get tired. It would be great for old
people."

"Alfonso's only thirty-three."

"Alfonso's crazy," Yasmin said. "Once when he was
winding up the motor, he said, 'I usually have a servant
doing this.' Christ, I thought, the silly sod really is crazy."

"How did you get away?"

"It wasn't easy," Yasmin said. "You see, with him not
having to do any work except winding the thing up now
and again, he never got puffed. After about an hour, I'd
had enough. 'Switch off,' I said. 'I've had enough.'

" 'We go on till I give the order,' he said.

" 'Don't be like that,' I said. 'Come on, pack it in.'

" 'Nobody gives orders here except me,' he said.

"Oh well, I thought. I suppose it'll have to be the hatpin."

"Did you use it? Did you actually stick him?" I asked.

"You're damn right I did," she said. "It went in about two inches!"

"What happened?"

"He nearly hit the ceiling. He gave a piercing yell and bounced off onto the floor. 'You stuck me!' he shrieked, clutching his backside. I was up in a flash and starting to put my clothes on and he was jumping up and down stark naked and shrieking, 'You stuck me! You stuck me! How dare you do that to me!' "

"Terrific," I said to Yasmin. "Marvellous. Wonderful. I wish I'd seen it. Did he bleed?"

"I don't know and I don't care, but I was really fed up with him by then and I got a bit ratty and I said, 'Listen to me, you, and listen carefully. Our mutual friend would have you by the balls if he ever heard about this. You raped me—you do realize that, don't you?' That shut him up. 'What on earth came over you?' I said. I was getting dressed as fast as I could and stalling for time. 'Whatever made you do a thing like that to me?' I shouted. I had to shout because the damn sofa was still rattling away behind me.

" 'I don't know,' he said. Suddenly he had become all meek and mild. When I was ready to go, I went up to him and kissed him on the cheek and said, 'Let's just forget it ever happened, shall we?' At the same time, I quickly removed the sticky rubbery thing from his royal knob and marched grandly out of the room."

"Did anyone try to stop you?" I asked.

"Not a soul."

"Full marks," I said. "You did a great job. You better

give me that notepaper." She gave me the sheet of palace notepaper with the signature on it and I filed it carefully away. "Now go pack your bags," I said. "We're leaving town on the next train."

15

WITHIN HALF AN HOUR we had packed our bags and checked out of the hotel and were heading for the railway station. Paris next stop.

And so it was. We went to Paris on the night sleeper and arrived there on a sparkling June morning. We got rooms at the Ritz. "Wherever you are," my father used to say, "when in doubt, stay at the Ritz." Wise words. Yasmin came into my room to discuss strategy over an early lunch—a cold lobster for each of us and a bottle of Chablis. I had the list of priority candidates in front of me on the table.

"Whatever happens, Renoir and Monet come first," I said. "In that order."

"Where do we find them?" Yasmin asked.

It is never difficult to discover the whereabouts of famous men. "Renoir is at Essoyes," I said. "That's a small town about one hundred and twenty miles south-east of Paris, between Champagne and Burgundy. He is now seventy-eight, and I'm told he's in a wheel-chair."

"Jesus Christ, Oswald, I'm not going to feed Blister Beetle to some poor old bastard in a wheel-chair!" Yasmin said.

"He'll love it," I told her. "There's nothing wrong with him except a bit of arthritis. He's still painting. He is easily the most celebrated painter alive today, and I'll tell you another thing. No living painter in the history of art has ever received such high prices for his pictures during his lifetime as Renoir. He's a giant. In ten years' time we'll be selling his straws for a fortune."

"Where's his wife?"

"Dead. He's a lonely old man. You'll cheer him up no end. When he sees you, he'll probably want to paint you in the nude on the spot."

"I'd like that."

"On the other hand, he has a model called Dedée he's absolutely mad about."

"I'll soon fix her," Yasmin said.

"Play your cards right and he might even give you a picture."

"Hey, I'd like that, too."

"Work on it," I said.

"What about Monet?" she asked.

"He is also a lonely old man. He's seventy-nine, a year older than Renoir, and he's living the life of a recluse at Giverny. That's not far from here. Just outside Paris. Very few people visit him now. Clemenceau drops in occasionally, so I'm told, but almost no one else. You'll be a little sunbeam in his life. And another canvas perhaps? A Monet landscape? Those things are going to be worth hundreds of thousands later on. They're worth thousands already."

The possibility of getting a picture from one or both of these great artists excited Yasmin a good deal. "You'll be visiting lots of other painters before we're finished," I said. "You could form a collection."

"That's a pretty good idea," she said. "Renoir, Monet,

Matisse, Bonnard, Munch, Braque, and all the rest of them.
Yes, it's a *very* good idea. I must remember that."

The lobsters were huge and delicious, with enormous
claws. The Chablis was good, too—a *Grand Cru* Bourgros.
I have a passion for fine Chablis, not only for the steely-dry
Grands Crus but also for some of the *Premiers Crus*, where
the fruit is a little closer to the surface. This particular
Bourgros was as steely as any I had ever tasted. Yasmin and
I discussed strategy while we ate and drank. It was my
contention that no man was going to turn away a young
lady who possessed the charm and the devastating beauty
of Yasmin. No male, however ancient, was capable of
treating her with indifference. Wherever we went I kept
seeing evidence of this. Even the suave, marble-faced recep-
tionist downstairs had gone all over queer when he caught
sight of Yasmin standing before him. I had been watching
him closely and I had seen that famous old spark flashing
in the very centre of the pupil of each of his jet-black eyes,
and then his tongue had poked out and had begun sliding
over his upper lip, and his fingers had fumbled inanely
with our registration forms, and at the end of it all he had
given us the wrong keys. A scintillating and sex-soaked
creature our Yasmin was, a kind of human Blister Beetle all
on her own, and as I say, no man on earth was going to
send her packing.

But none of this sexual chemistry was going to help us
one bit unless the girl was able actually to present herself
to the customer. Formidable housekeepers and equally
formidable wives could well be a problem. My optimism,
however, was based on the fact that the fellows we were
after were nearly all painters or musicians or writers. They
were artists. And artists are probably the most approach-
able people you can find. Even the very great ones are

never guarded, as businessmen are, by iron-mouthed secretaries and amateur gangsters in black suits. Big businessmen and their like live in caves that can be reached only by passing through long tunnels and many rooms with a Cerberus around every corner. Artists are loners, and more often than not they open the front door themselves when you ring the bell.

But why would Yasmin be ringing the bell in the first place?

Ah well, she was a young English girl, a student of art (or music or literature, whichever was applicable) who had such a massive admiration for the work of Monsieur Renoir or Monet or Stravinsky or whomever, that she had come all the way from England to pay homage to the great man, to say hello to him, to give him a little present and then to go away again. *Nunc dimittis.*

"That," I said to Yasmin as I polished off the last succulent lobster claw—and by the way, don't you love it when you are able to draw the flesh of the claw out of the shell whole and pinky-red in one piece? There is some kind of tiny personal triumph in that. I may be childish, but I experience a similar triumph when I succeed in getting a walnut out of its shell without breaking it in two. As a matter of fact, I never approach a walnut without this particular ambition in mind. Life is more fun if you play games. But back to Yasmin—"that," I said to her, "will get you invited right into the house or the studio ninety-nine times out of a hundred. With your smile and your lascivious looks, I cannot see any of these lads turning you away."

"What about their watchdogs or their wives?"

"I think you'll get past them, too. Occasionally they may tell you the man's busy painting or writing and to come back at six o'clock. But you're always going to win in the end. Don't forget, you've travelled a long way just to pay homage. And make a point of saying you won't stay more than a few minutes."

"Nine," Yasmin said, grinning. "Just nine minutes. When do we start?"

"Tomorrow," I said. "I shall buy a motor car this afternoon. We're going to need it for our French and other European operations. And tomorrow we will drive to Essoyes and you will meet Monsieur Renoir."

"You never waste time, do you, Oswald?"

"My darling," I said, "as soon as I have made a fortune, I propose to spend the rest of my life wasting time. But until the money is in the bank, I shall work very hard indeed. And so must you."

"How long do you think it will take?"

"To make our fortunes? About seven or eight years. No more. That's not such a long stretch when it means you can laze about doing nothing forever after."

"No," she said, "it isn't. And anyway, I'm rather enjoying this."

"I know you are."

"What I'm enjoying," she said, "is the thought of being ravished by all the greatest men in the world. And all the kings. It tickles my fancy."

"Let's go out and buy a French motor car," I said. So out we went and this time I bought a splendid little 10 hp Citroën *torpédo*, a four-seater, a brand-new model only just out. It cost me the equivalent of three hundred fifty pounds in French money, and it was exactly what I wanted. Although it had no luggage compartment, there was plenty of room on the back seats for all my equipment and suitcases. It was an open tourer, and it had a canvas roof that could be put up in less than a minute if it started to rain. The body was dark blue, the colour of royal blood, and its top speed was an exhilarating 55 mph.

The next morning we set off for Essoyes with my travelling laboratory packed away in the back of the Citroën. We stopped at Troyes for lunch where we ate trout from the Seine (I had two, they were so good) and drank a bottle of white *vin du pays*. We got to Essoyes at four in the afternoon and booked into a small hotel whose name I have forgotten. My bedroom again became my laboratory, and as soon as everything had been laid out in readiness for the immediate testing and mixing and freezing of semen, Yasmin and I went out to find Monsieur Renoir. This was not difficult. The woman at the desk gave us precise instructions. A large white house, she said, on the right-hand side, three hundred metres beyond the church or some such thing.

I spoke fluent French after my year in Paris. Yasmin spoke just enough of it to get along. She had had a French governess sometime or other during her childhood and that had been a help.

We found the house without any trouble. It was a medium-sized white wooden building standing on its own in a pleasant garden. It was not, I knew, the great man's main residence. That was down south in Cagnes-sur-Mer, but he probably found it cooler up here in the summer months.

"Good luck," I said to Yasmin. "I'll be waiting about a hundred yards down the road."

She got out of the car and went toward the gates. I watched her going. She wore flat-heeled shoes and a creamy-coloured linen dress, no hat. Cool and demure, she passed through the gates and moved on up the drive swinging her arms as she went. There was a lilt in her walk, a little shadow attending her, and she looked more like a young postulant going in to see the mother superior than someone who was about to cause a saucy explosion within the mind and body of one of the great painters of the world.

It was a warm sunshiny evening. Sitting there in the open motor car I dozed off and did not wake up until two hours later when I found Yasmin getting into the seat beside me.

"What happened?" I said. "Tell me quick! Was everything all right? Did you see him? Have you got the stuff?"

She had a small brown-paper parcel in one hand, her purse in the other. She opened the purse and took out the signed notepaper and the all-important rubbery thing. She handed them to me without speaking. She had a funny look on her face, a mixture of ecstasy and awe, and when I spoke to her she didn't appear to hear me. Miles away she seemed, miles and miles away.

"What's the matter?" I said. "Why the great silence?"

She gazed straight ahead through the windscreen, not hearing me. Her eyes were very bright, her face serene, beatific almost, with a queer radiance.

"Christ, Yasmin," I said. "What the hell's the matter with you? You look like you've seen a vision."

"Just get going," she said, "and leave me alone."

We drove back to the hotel without talking and went to our separate rooms. I made an immediate microscopic examination of the semen. The sperm were alive but the count was low, very low. I was able to make no more than ten straws. But they were ten sound straws with a count of about twenty million sperm in each. By God, I thought,

these are going to cost somebody a lot of money in years
to come. They'll be as rare as the First Folio of Shakespeare. I ordered champagne and a plate of foie-gras and
toast, and I sent a message to Yasmin's room telling her I
hoped she would come in and join me.

She arrived half an hour later and she had with her the
little brown-paper parcel. I poured her a glass of champagne and put a slice of foie-gras on toast for her. She accepted the champagne, ignored the foie-gras, and remained
silent.

"Come on," I said, "what's bothering you?"

She emptied her glass in one long swallow and held it out
for more. I refilled the glass. She drank half of it, then
put it down. "For God's sake, Yasmin!" I cried. "What
happened?"

She looked at me very straight and said simply, "He
smote me."

"You mean he *hit* you? Good God, I am sorry! You
mean he actually struck you?"

"Don't be an ass, Oswald."

"What *do* you mean then?"

"I mean I was smitten by him. He's the first man who's
ever bowled me completely over."

"Oh, I *see* what you mean! Good heavens!"

"He is a wonder, that man," she said. "He is a genius."

"Of course he's a genius. That's why we chose him."

"Yes, but he's a beautiful genius. He is so beautiful, Oswald, and so gentle and wonderful. I've never met anyone
like him."

"He smote you all right."

"He certainly did."

"So what's your problem?" I said. "Are you feeling
guilty about it?"

"Oh no," she said. "I don't feel in the least guilty. I'm just overwhelmed."

"You're going to be a hell of a lot more overwhelmed before we've finished," I said. "He's not the only genius you're going to call on."

"I know that."

"You're not running out, are you?"

"Certainly not. Give me some more drink."

I filled her glass for the third time in as many minutes. She sat sipping it. Then she said, "Listen, Oswald . . ."

"I'm listening."

"We've been pretty jokey about this whole thing up to now, haven't we? It's all been a bit of a lark, right?"

"Rubbish! I take it very seriously."

"What about Alfonso?"

"You were the one who joked about him," I said.

"I know that," she said. "But he deserved it. He's a joker."

"I can't quite see what you're getting at," I said.

"Renoir was different," she said. "That's what I'm getting at. He's a giant. His work is going to live through the ages."

"So will his sperm."

"Stop it and hear me out," she said. "What I'm saying is this. Some people are jokers. Some are not. Alfonso is a joker. All the kings are jokers. We have a few other jokers on our list, too."

"Who?"

"Henry Ford's a joker," she said. "I think that fellow Freud in Vienna is a joker. And the wireless boy, Marconi. He's a joker."

"What's the point of all this?"

"The point is," Yasmin said, "I don't in the least mind

being jokey about jokers. I don't mind treating them a little rough either if I have to. But I'll be damned if I'm going to start sticking hatpins into men like Renoir and Conrad and Stravinsky. Not after what I saw today."

"What did you see today?"

"I told you, I saw a really great and wonderful old man."

"And he smote you."

"You're damn right he did."

"Let me ask you this, did *he* have a good time?"

"Amazing," she said. "He had an amazing time."

"Tell me what happened."

"No," she said. "I don't mind telling you about the jokers. But the non-jokers are private."

"Was he in a wheel-chair?"

"Yes. And now he has to strap the paint-brush to his wrist because he can't hold it in his fingers."

"Because of arthritis?"

"Yes."

"And you gave him the Blister Beetle?"

"Of course."

"It wasn't too much for him?"

"No," she said. "When you're that age you have to have it."

"And he gave you a picture," I said, pointing to the brown-paper parcel.

She unwrapped it now and held it up for me to see. It was a small unframed canvas of a young rosy-cheeked girl with long golden hair and blue eyes, a wondrous little picture, a magic thing, a marvel to look at. A warm glow came out of it and filled the entire room. "I didn't ask him for it," Yasmin said. "He made me take it. Isn't it beautiful?"

"Yes," I said. "It is beautiful."

16

THE EFFECT that Renoir had upon Yasmin during that dramatic visit to Essoyes did not, thank heavens, take all the fun out of our future operations. I myself have always found it difficult to treat anything too seriously and I believe the world would be a better place if everyone followed my example. I am completely without ambition. My motto—"It is better to incur a mild rebuke than to perform an onerous task"—should be well known to you by now. All I want out of life is to enjoy myself. But before one can achieve this happy end one must obviously get hold of a lot of money. Money is essential to a sybarite. It is the key of the kingdom. To which the carping reader will almost certainly reply, "You say you are without ambition, but do you not realize that the desire for wealth is in itself one of the most obnoxious ambitions of them all?" This is not necessarily true. It is the *manner* in which one acquires wealth that determines whether or not it is obnoxious. I myself am scrupulous about the methods I employ. I refuse to have anything to do with money-making unless the process obeys two golden rules. First, it must amuse me tremendously. Second, it must give a great deal of pleasure to those from whom I extract the loot. This is a simple philosophy and I recommend it wholeheartedly to all business tycoons, casino operators, chancellors of the Exchequer, and budget directors everywhere.

Two things stood out vividly during this period. First,

the unusual sense of fulfillment Yasmin was getting from each artist she visited. She would emerge from house or studio with eyes shining like stars and a bright red rose on each cheek. All of which caused me to ruminate many times upon the sexual dexterity of men of outstanding creative genius. Did this prodigious creativity of theirs spill over into other fields? And if so, did they know deep secrets and magic methods of exciting a lady that were beyond the reach of ordinary mortals like me? The red roses upon Yasmin's cheeks and the shine in her eyes made me suspect, a trifle reluctantly let me say, that this was so.

The second surprising facet of the whole operation was its extraordinary simplicity. Yasmin never seemed to have the slightest trouble in getting her man to deliver the goods. Mind you, the more one thinks about this, the more obvious it becomes that she never *was* going to have any trouble in the first place. Men are by nature polygamous creatures. Add to that the well-substantiated fact that supreme creative artists tend to be more viripotent than their fellows (just as they also tend to be heavier drinkers) and you can begin to see why no one was going to give Yasmin much of an argument. So what do you have? You have a bunch of supremely gifted and therefore hyperactive artists, loaded with the very finest Sudanese Blister Beetle, who find themselves staring goggle-eyed at a young female of indescribable beauty. They were jiggered. They were scrambled and dished up on buttered toast from the moment they swallowed the fatal chocolate. I am positive that the Pope in Rome himself, in the same situation, would have had his cassock off in nine minutes flat just like the rest of them.

But I must go back for a moment to where we left off. After Renoir, we returned to our headquarters at the

Ritz in Paris. From there we went after old Monet. We drove out to his splendid house at Giverny and I dropped Yasmin off at the gates in the approved fashion. She was inside for over three hours, but I didn't mind that. Knowing there would be lots of other long waits like this coming along, I had installed a small library in the back of the car—a complete Shakespeare, some Jane Austen, some Dickens, some Balzac, and the latest Kipling.

Yasmin emerged at last and I saw she had a large canvas under one arm. She was walking slowly, just sauntering along the sidewalk in a dreamy sort of way, but when she came closer, the first thing I noticed was that old glint of ecstasy in her eyes and the brilliant roses on her cheeks. She looked like a nice tame tigress who had just swallowed the Emperor of India and had liked the taste.

"Everything all right?"

"Fine," she murmured.

"Let's see the picture."

It was a shimmering study of water-lilies on the lake in Monet's Giverny garden, a real beauty.

"He said I was a miracle worker."

"He's right."

"He said I was the most beautiful woman he'd ever seen in his life. He asked me to stay."

Monet's semen, as it turned out, had a better count than Renoir's in spite of his being a year older, and I was fortunate in being able to make twenty-five straws. Admittedly, each straw had the minimum count of only twenty million sperm, but they would do. They would do very well. They would be worth hundreds of thousands, I reckoned, those Monet straws, in the years to come.

17

THEN WE HAD a stroke of luck. In Paris at this time there was a dynamic and extraordinary producer of ballets called Diaghilev. Diaghilev had a talent for spotting great artists, and in 1919 he was regrouping his company after the war and preparing a new repertory of ballets. He had gathered around him for this purpose a group of remarkably gifted men. For example, at that very moment:

Igor Stravinsky had come up from Switzerland to write the music for Diaghilev's *Pulcinella*.

Pablo Picasso was designing the sets.

Picasso was also doing the sets for *Three-Cornered Hat*.

Henri Matisse had been hired to design the costumes and the decor for *Le Chant de Rossignol*.

And another painter we had not heard of called André Derain was busy preparing the sets for *La Boutique Fantasque*.

Stravinsky, Picasso, and Matisse were all on our list. On the theory that Monsieur Diaghilev's judgement was probably sounder than ours, we decided to put Derain's name on as well. All of these men were in Paris.

We took Stravinsky first. Yasmin walked right in on him while he was working at the piano on *Pulcinella*. He was more surprised than angry. "Hello," he said. "Who are you?"

"I have come all the way from England to offer you a chocolate," she said.

This absurd remark, which Yasmin was to use on many other occasions, disarmed completely this kind and friendly man. The rest was simple, and although I longed for salacious details, Yasmin remained mute.

"You might at least tell me what he was like as a person."

"Sparkling bright," she said. "Oh, he was so sparkling bright and so quick and clever. He has a huge head and a nose like a boiled egg."

"Is he a genius?"

"Yes," she said, "he's a genius. He's got the spark, the same as Monet and Renoir."

"What is this spark?" I said. "Where is it? Is it in the eyes?"

"No," she said. "It isn't anywhere special. It's just *there*. You know it's there. It's like an invisible halo."

I made fifty straws from Stravinsky.

Next it was Picasso's turn. He had a studio at that time in the rue de la Boétie and I dropped Yasmin off in front of a rickety-looking door with brown paint peeling off it. There was no bell or knocker so Yasmin simply pushed it open and went in. Outside in the car I settled down with *La Cousine Bette*, which I still think is the best thing the old French master ever wrote.

I don't believe I had read more than four pages when the car door was flung open and Yasmin tumbled in and flopped onto the seat beside me. Her hair was all over the place and she was blowing like a sperm whale.

"Christ, Yasmin! What happened?"

"My God!" she gasped. "Oh, my God!"

"Did he throw you out?" I cried. "Did he hurt you?"

She was too out of breath to answer me at once. A trickle of sweat was running down the side of her forehead.

She looked as though she'd been chased around the block four times by a maniac with a carving knife. I waited for her to simmer down.

"Don't worry," I said. "We're bound to have one or two washouts."

"He's a demon!" she said.

"What did he do to you?"

"He's a bull! He's like a little brown bull!"

"Go on."

"He was painting on a huge canvassy thing when I went in and he turned round and his eyes opened so wide they became circles and they were black and he shouted '*Olé*' or something like that and then came towards me very slowly and sort of crouching as though he was going to spring..."

"And did he spring?"

"Yes," she said. "He sprang."

"Good Lord."

"He didn't even put his paint-brush down."

"So you had no chance to get the mackintosh on?"

"Afraid not. Didn't even have time to open my purse."

"Hell."

"I was hit by a hurricane, Oswald."

"Couldn't you have slowed him down a bit? You remember what you did to old Woresley to make him keep still?"

"Nothing would have stopped this one."

"Were you on the floor?"

"No. He threw me onto a filthy sofa thing. There were tubes of paint everywhere."

"It's all over you now. Look at your dress."

"I know."

One couldn't blame Yasmin for the failure, I knew that.

But I felt pretty ratty all the same. It was our first miss. I only hoped there wouldn't be many more.

"Do you know what he did afterwards?" Yasmin said. "He just buttoned up his trousers and said, 'Thank you, mademoiselle. That was very refreshing. Now I must get back to my work.' And he turned away, Oswald! He just turned away and started painting again!"

"He's Spanish," I said, "like Alfonso." I stepped out of the car and cranked the starting handle and when I got back in again, Yasmin was tidying her hair in the car mirror. "I hate to say it," she said, "but I rather enjoyed that one."

"I know you did."

"Phenomenal vitality."

"Tell me," I said, "is Monsieur Picasso a genius?"

"Yes," she said. "It was very strong. He will be wildly famous one day."

"Damn."

"We can't win them all, Oswald."

"I suppose not."

Matisse was next.

Yasmin was with Monsieur Matisse for about two hours and blow me if the little thief didn't come out with yet another painting. It was sheer magic, that canvas, a Fauve landscape with trees that were blue and green and scarlet, signed and dated 1905.

"Terrific picture," I said.

"Terrific man," she said. And that was all she would say about Henri Matisse. Not a word more.

Fifty straws.

18

My travelling container of liquid nitrogen was beginning to fill up with straws. We now had King Alfonso, Renoir, Monet, Stravinsky, and Matisse. But there was room for a few more. Each straw held only one-quarter cc of fluid, and the straw itself was only slightly thicker than a matchstick and about half as long. Fifty straws stacked neatly in a metal rack took up very little room. I decided we could accommodate three more batches on this trip, and I told Yasmin we would be visiting Marcel Proust, Maurice Ravel, and James Joyce. All of them were living in the Paris area.

If I have given the impression that Yasmin and I were paying our visits more or less on consecutive days, that is wrong. We were, in fact, moving slowly and carefully. Usually about a week went between visits. This gave me time to investigate thoroughly the next victim before we moved in on him. We never drove up to a house and rang the bell and hoped for the best. Before we made a call, I knew all about the man's habits and his working hours, about his family and his servants if he had any, and we would choose our time with care. But even then Yasmin would occasionally have to wait outside in the motor car until a wife or a servant came out to go shopping.

Monsieur Proust was our next choice. He was forty-eight years old, and six years back, in 1913, he had published *Du Côté de chez Swann*. Now he had just brought out

A l'Ombre des jeunes filles en fleurs. This book had been received with much enthusiasm by the reviewers and had won him the Goncourt Prize. But I was a bit nervous about Monsieur Proust. My enquiries showed him to be a very queer duck indeed. He was independently wealthy. He was a snob. He was anti-Semitic. He was vain. He was a hypochondriac who suffered from asthma. He slept until four in the afternoon and stayed awake all night. He lived with a faithful watchdog servant called Céleste and his present address was an apartment at No. 8 bis rue Laurent-Pichet. The house belonged to the celebrated actress Réjane, and Réjane's son lived in the flat immediately below Proust, while Réjane herself occupied the rest of the place.

I learned that Monsieur Proust was, from a literary point of view, totally unscrupulous and would use both persuasion and money to inspire rave articles about his books in newspapers and magazines. And on top of all this, he was completely homosexual. No woman, other than the faithful Céleste, was ever permitted into his bedroom. In order to study the man more closely, I got myself invited to a dinner at the house of his close friend Princess Soutzo. And there I discovered that Monsieur Proust was nothing to look at. With his black moustache, his round bulging eyes, and his baggy little figure, he bore an astonishing resemblance to an actor on the cinematograph screen called Charlie Chaplin. At Princess Soutzo's, he complained a lot about draughts in the dining-room and he held court among the guests and expected everyone to be silent when he spoke. I can remember two incredible pronouncements he made that evening. Of a man who preferred women, he said, "I can answer for him. He is completely abnormal."

And another time I heard him say, "Fondness for men leads to virility." In short, he was a tricky fellow.

"Now wait just a minute," Yasmin had said to me when I told her all this. "I'll be damned if I'm going to take on a bugger."

"Why not?"

"Don't be so stupid, Oswald. If he's a raging hundred per cent fairy—"

"He calls it an invert."

"I don't care what he calls it."

"It's a very Proustian word," I said. "Look up 'to invert' in the dictionary and you'll find the definition is 'to turn upside down.' "

"He's not turning me upside down, thank you very much," Yasmin said.

"Now don't get excited."

"Anyway, it's a waste of time," she said. "He wouldn't even look at me."

"I think he would."

"What d'you want me to do, dress up as a choirboy?"

"We'll give him a double dose of Blister Beetle."

"That's not going to change his habits."

"No," I said, "but it'll make him so bloody horny he won't care what sex you are."

"He'll invert me."

"No, he won't."

"He'll invert me like a comma."

"Take a hatpin with you."

"It's still not going to work," she said. "If he's a genuine twenty-four carat homo, then all women are physically repulsive to him."

"It's essential we get him," I said. "Our collection won't be complete without fifty Proust straws."

"Is he really so important?"

"He's going to be," I said. "I'm sure of it. There'll be a strong demand for Proust children in the years to come."

Yasmin gazed out of the Ritz windows at the cloudy-grey summer sky over Paris. "If that's the case, then there's only one thing for it," she said.

"What's that?"

"You do it yourself."

I was so shocked I jumped.

"Steady on," I said.

"He wants a man," she said. "Well, you're a man. You're perfect. You're young, you're beautiful, and you're lecherous."

"Yes, but I am not a catamite."

"You don't have the guts?"

"Of course I've got the guts. But field work is your province, not mine."

"Who said so?"

"I can't cope with a man, Yasmin, you know that."

"This isn't a man. It's a fairy."

"For God's sake!" I cried. "I'll be damned if I'll let that little sod come near me! I'll have you know that even an enema gives me the shakes for a week!"

Yasmin burst into shrieks of laughter. "I suppose you're going to tell me next," she said, "that you have a small sphincter."

"Yes and I'm not having Mr. Proust enlarge it, thanks very much," I said.

"You're a coward, Oswald," she said.

It was an impasse. I sulked. Yasmin got up and poured

herself a drink. I did the same. We sat there drinking in silence. It was early evening.

"Where shall we have dinner tonight?" I said.

"I don't care," she said. "I think we ought to try to solve this Proust thing first. I'd hate to see this little bugger get away."

"Do you have any ideas?"

"I'm thinking," she said.

I finished my drink and got myself another. "You want one?" I said to her.

"No," she said. I left her to go on thinking. After a while she said, "Well now, I wonder if that will work."

"What?"

"I've just had a tiny little idea."

"Tell me."

Yasmin didn't answer. She stood up and walked over to the window and leaned out. She stayed leaning out of that window for fully five minutes, immobile, deep in thought, and I watched her but kept my mouth shut. Then all of a sudden I saw her reach behind her with her right hand, and the hand started snatching at the air as though she were catching flies. She didn't look round as she did this. She just went on hanging out of the window and snatching away at those invisible non-existent flies behind her.

"What the hell's going on?" I said.

She turned round and faced me, and now there was a big smile on her face. "It's great!" she cried. "I love it! I *am* a clever little girl!"

"Out with it then."

"It's going to be tricky," she said, "and I'm going to have to be very quick but I'm good at catching. Come to think of it, I was better than my brother at catching cricket balls."

"What the hell are you talking about?" I said.

"It would mean disguising me as a man."

"Easy," I said. "No problem."

"A beautiful young man."

"Will you give him the Beetle?"

"A double dose," she said.

"Isn't that a bit risky? Don't forget what it did to old Woresley."

"That's just how I want him," she said. "I want him out of his mind."

"Would you please tell me exactly what you propose to do?" I asked her.

"Don't ask so many questions, Oswald. Just leave that side of it to me. I regard Monsieur Proust as fair game. He's in the joker class and I shall treat him as a joker."

"Actually he's not," I said. "He's another genius. But take the hatpin by all means. The royal hatpin. The one that's been two inches into the King of Spain's bum."

"I'd feel happier with a carving-knife," she said.

We spent the next few days dressing Yasmin up as a boy. We told the couturier and the wigmaker and the shoe people that we were rigging her up for a very grand fancy-dress party, and they rallied round with enthusiasm. It is amazing what a good wig can do to a face. From the moment the wig was on and the make-up was off, Yasmin became a male. We chose slightly effeminate pale grey trousers, a blue shirt, a silk stock tie, a flowered silk waistcoat, and a fawn jacket. The shoes were brogues, white and brown. The hat was a soft felt trilby the colour of snuff, with a large brim. We took the curves out of her noble bosom by strapping it with a wide crepe bandage. I

taught her to speak in a soft whispering voice to disguise
the pitch, and I rehearsed her diligently in what she was
to say, first to Céleste when the door was opened, and then
to Monsieur Proust when she was shown into his presence.

Within a week, we were ready to go. Yasmin had still
not told me how she intended to save herself from being
inverted in true Proustian fashion and I did not press her
any further about this. I was happy enough that she had
agreed to take the man on.

We decided that she should arrive at his house at seven
p.m. By then our victim would have been up and about
for a good three hours. In her bedroom at the Ritz, I
helped Yasmin to dress. The wig was a beauty. It gave her
a head of hair that was golden-bronze in colour, slightly
curly, and a bit on the long side. The grey trousers, the
flowered waistcoat, and the fawn jacket turned her into
an effeminate but ravishingly beautiful young man.

"No bugger could resist buggering you," I said.

She smiled but made no comment.

"Hang on," I said. "There's something missing. Your
trousers look distinctly empty. It's a dead giveaway." There
was a bowl of fruit on the sideboard, a present from the
hotel management. I selected a small banana. Yasmin
lowered her trousers and we strapped the banana to the
inside of her upper thigh with sticking plaster. When she
pulled up her trousers again, the effect was electric—a
telltale and tantalizing bulge in exactly the right place.

"He'll see it," I said. "It'll drive him dotty."

19

WE WENT DOWNSTAIRS and got into the motor car. I drove to the rue Laurent-Pichet and stopped the car about twenty yards short of number eight, on the other side of the street. We examined the house. It was a large stone building with a black front door. "Off you go," I said. "And good luck. He's on the second floor."

Yasmin got out of the car. "This banana's a bit uncomfortable," she said.

"Now you know what it's like to be a man," I said.

She turned away and strode toward the house with her hands in her trouser pockets. I saw her try the door. It was unlocked, presumably because the place was divided into separate apartments. She went in.

I settled down in the motor car to await the outcome. I, the general, had done all I could to prepare for the battle. The rest was up to Yasmin, the soldier. She was well armed. She carried a double dose (we had finally decided) of Blister Beetle and a long hatpin whose sharp end still bore the crusted traces of Spanish royal blood which Yasmin had refused to wipe off.

It was a warm cloudy August evening in Paris. The canvas hood of my blue Citroën *torpédo* was folded back. My seat was comfortable but I was too fidgety to concentrate on a book. I had a good view of the house and I fixed my eyes upon it with a certain fascination. I could see the large windows on the second floor where Monsieur Proust lived, and the green velvet curtains that were drawn back on either side, but I couldn't see in. Yasmin was up there now, probably in that very room, and she would be saying, as I had so carefully instructed her to say, "Pray forgive me, monsieur, but I am in love with your work. I have come all the way from England simply to pay homage to your greatness. Please accept this little box of chocolates . . . they are delicious . . . do you mind if I have one . . . and here's one for you . . ."

I waited twenty minutes. I waited thirty minutes. I was watching the clock. The way Yasmin felt about 'that little bugger' as she called him, I reckoned there would be no *tête-à-tête* and pleasant conversation afterwards, as there had been with Renoir and Monet. This, I reflected, would be a brief sharp visit and possibly a rather painful one for the great writer.

I was correct about its being brief. Thirty-three minutes after Yasmin had gone in, I saw the big black front door opening and out she came.

As she walked toward me, I looked for traces of dishevelment in her clothes. There were none. The snuff-coloured trilby was at the same saucy angle as before and altogether she looked as trim and crisp coming out as she had going in.

Or did she? Was there not a slight lack of bounce in her walk? There was indeed. And was there not a tendency to move those splendid long limbs of hers rather carefully? Unquestionably yes. She was walking, in fact, like a person who had just dismounted from a bicycle after a long ride upon an uncomfortable saddle.

These small observations comforted me. They were evidence, surely, that my gallant soldier had been engaged in fierce combat.

"Well done," I said as she got into the car.

"What makes you think it was so successful?"

She was a cool one, our Yasmin.

"Don't tell me it went wrong."

She didn't answer me. She settled herself in the seat and closed the car door.

"I have to know, Yasmin, because if you do have the loot I must rush it back quickly and freeze it up."

She had it. Of course she had it. I rushed it back to the hotel and made fifty exceptional straws. Each straw, according to my microscopic density count, contained no less than seventy-five million sperm. I know they were potent straws because at this very moment, as I write these words nineteen years after the event, I am able to state positively that there are fourteen children running around in France who have Marcel Proust as their father. Only I know who they are. Such matters are great secrets. They are secrets between me and the mothers. The husbands don't know. It's a mother's secret. But my goodness me, you should see those fourteen silly rich ambitious literary-minded mothers. Each one of them, as she gazes proudly upon her Proustian offspring, is telling herself that she has almost certainly given birth to a great writer. Well, she is wrong. All of them are wrong. There is no evidence whatsoever that great writers beget great writers. Occasionally they beget minor writers, but that's as far as it goes. There is, I think, slightly more evidence that great painters sometimes beget great painters. Look at Teniers and Bruegel and Tiepolo, and even Pissarro. And in music, the wonderful Johann Sebastian had such an overwhelming genius that it was impossible for him not to pass some of it on to his children. But writers, no. Great writers seem to spring more often than not from stony soil—the sons of coal-miners or pork butchers or impoverished teachers. But that simple truth was never going to prevent a small number of wealthy literary-snob ladies from wishing to have a baby by the brilliant Monsieur Proust or the extraordinary Mr. James Joyce. My job, anyway, was not to propagate geniuses but to make money.

By the time I had filled those fifty Proust straws and had immersed them safely in liquid nitrogen, it was nearly nine o'clock at night. Yasmin was now bathed and changed into fine feminine clothes and I took her out to Maxim's for supper to celebrate our success. She had not yet told me anything of what went on.

My diary from that date informs me that we both started the meal with a dozen escargots. It was mid-August and the grouse were just beginning to come in from Yorkshire and Scotland, so we ordered one each and I told the head-waiter we wanted them blood-rare. The wine was to be a bottle of Volnay, one of my favourite burgundies.

"Now," I said when we had given our order. "Tell me all."

"You want a blow by blow account?"

"Every tiny detail."

There was a bowl of radishes on the table and Yasmin popped one into her mouth and crunched it up. "He had a bell on his door," she said, "so I rang it. Céleste opened the door and glared at me. You should see that Céleste, Oswald. She's skinny and sharp-nosed with a mouth like a knife and two small brown eyes that looked me up and down with utter distaste. 'What is it you wish?' she said sharply, and I gave her the bit about having travelled from England to bring a present to the famous writer whom I worshipped. 'Monsieur Proust is working,' Céleste said and tried to shut the door. I put my foot in it and pushed it open and marched in. 'I have not travelled all this distance to have a door slammed in my face,' I said. 'Kindly inform your master that I am here to see him.' "

"Well done, you," I said.

"I had to bluff it out," she said. "Céleste glared at me. 'What name?' she snapped. 'Mister Bottomley,' I said, 'of London.' I was rather pleased with that name."

"Apt," I said. "Did the maid announce you?"

"Oh yes. And out he came into the hall, this funny little pop-eyed bugger, still holding a pen in his hand."

"What happened next?"

"I immediately launched into the long speech you taught me, starting with, 'Pray forgive me, monsieur . . .' but I'd hardly got half a dozen words out when he raised his hand and cried, 'Stop! I have already forgiven you!' He was goggling at me as though I were the most beautiful and desirable and spicy little lad he'd ever seen in his life, which I'll bet I was."

"Was he speaking in English or French?"

"A bit of each. His English was pretty good, about like my French, so it didn't matter."

"And he fell for you right away?"

"He couldn't take his eyes off me. 'That will be all, thank you, Céleste,' he said, licking his lips. But Céleste didn't like it. She stayed put. She scented trouble.

" 'You may *go*, Céleste,' Monsieur Proust said, raising his voice.

"But she still refused to go. 'You do not wish anything more, Monsieur Proust?'

" 'I wish to be left alone,' he snapped, and the woman stalked out of the room in a huff.

" 'Pray sit down, Monsieur Bottomley,' he said. 'May I

take your hat? I do apologize for my servant. She's a trifle overprotective.'

" 'What is she protecting you from, monsieur?'

"He smiled at me, showing horrid teeth with wide gaps. 'From you,' he said softly.

"By golly, I thought, I'm going to be inverted any moment. At this point, Oswald, I seriously considered skipping the Blister Beetle altogether. The man was drooling with lust. If I'd so much as bent down to do up a shoelace, he'd have been on me."

"But you didn't skip it?"

"No," she said. "I gave him the chocolate."

"Why?"

"Because in some ways they're easier to handle when they're under the influence. They don't quite know what they're doing."

"Did the chocolate work well?"

"It always works well," she said. "But this was a double dose so it worked better."

"How much better?"

"Buggers are different," she said.

"I believe you."

"You see," she said, "when an ordinary man is driven crazy by the Beetle, all he wants to do is to rape the woman on the spot. But when a bugger is driven crazy by the powder, his first thought is not to start buggering right away. He begins by making violent grabs for the other fellow's pizzle."

"A bit awkward, that."

"Very," Yasmin said. "I knew that if I let him come near enough to grab me, all he'd get in his hand would be a squashed banana."

"So what did you do?"

"I kept jumping out of the way," she said. "And in the end, of course, it became a chase with him chasing me all round the room and knocking things over right and left."

"Rather strenuous."

"Yes, and in the middle of it all the door opened and there stood that dreadful little maid again. 'Monsieur Proust,' she said, 'all this exercise is bad for your asthma.'

" 'Get out!' he yelled. 'Get out, you witch!' "

"I imagine she's fairly used to that sort of thing."

"I'm sure she is," Yasmin said. "Anyway, there was a round table in the middle of the room and so long as I stayed close to it I knew he couldn't catch me. Many a girl has been saved from a dirty old man by a round table. The trouble was he seemed to be enjoying this part of it, and soon I got to thinking that a good old chase around the room was probably an essential preliminary for those chaps."

"A sort of pipe-opener."

"Right," she said. "And he kept saying things to me as we circled round and round the table."

"What sort of things?"

"Dirty stuff," she said. "Not worth repeating. By the way, putting that banana in was a mistake."

"Why?"

"Too big a bulge," she said. "He noticed it at once. And all the time he was chasing me round the table, he kept pointing at it and singing its praises. I was longing to tell him it was just a silly old banana from the Ritz Hotel but that wasn't on. It was driving him up the wall, that banana, and the Blister Beetle was hitting him harder every second, and suddenly I had another problem on my hands. How in God's name, I thought, am I going to get the rubbery thing on him before he jumps me? I couldn't exactly say it was a necessary precaution, could I?"

"Not really."

"I mean after all, what earthly reason had I even to be carrying the bloody thing?"

"Tricky," I said. "Very tricky. How did you get out of it?"

"In the end I said to him, 'Do you want me, Monsieur Proust?'

" 'Yes!' he screamed. 'I want you more than anyone in my life! Stop running!'

" 'Not yet,' I said. 'First you must put this funny little thing on him to keep him warm.' I took it from my pocket and slung it across the table. He stopped chasing me and stared at it. I doubt he'd ever set eyes on one before. 'What is this?' he cried.

" 'It's called a tickler,' I said. 'It's one of our famous English ticklers invented by Mr. Oscar Wilde.'

" 'Oscar Wilde!' he cried. 'Ha, ha! A great fellow!'

" 'He invented the tickler,' I said. 'And Lord Alfred Douglas helped him.'

" 'Lord Alfred was another fine fellow!' he cried.

" 'King Edward the Seventh,' I said, laying it on, 'carried a tickler on his person wherever he went.'

" 'King Edward the Seventh!' he cried. 'My God!' He picked up the little thing lying on the table. 'It is good, yes?'

" 'It doubles the rapture,' I said. 'Put it on quickly like a good boy. I'm getting impatient.'

" 'You help me.'

" 'No,' I said. 'Do it yourself.' And while he was fiddling around with it, I—well—I absolutely had to make sure he didn't see the banana and all the rest of it, didn't I?

And yet I knew the dreaded time had come when I was going to have to take my trousers down . . ."

"A bit risky, that."

"It couldn't be helped, Oswald. So while he was fiddling around with Oscar Wilde's great invention, I turned my back on him and whipped down my trousers and assumed what I imagined was the correct position by bending over the back of the sofa . . ."

"My God, Yasmin, you don't mean you were going to allow him—"

"Of course not," she said. "But I had to hide my banana and keep it out of his reach."

"Yes, but didn't he jump you?"

"He came at me like a battering-ram."

"How did you dodge it?"

"I didn't," she said, smiling. "That's the whole point."

"I'm not with you," I said. "If he came at you like a battering-ram and you didn't dodge it, then he must have rammed you."

"He didn't ram me the way you're *thinking* he rammed me," she said. "You see, Oswald, I had remembered something. I had remembered the story about A. R. Woresley and his brother's bull and how the bull was fooled into thinking his pizzle was in one place while actually it was in another. A. R. Woresley had grabbed hold of it and directed it somewhere else."

"Is that what you did?"

"Yes."

"But surely not into a bag the way Woresley did?"

"Don't be an ass, Oswald. I don't need a bag."

"Of course not . . . no . . . I see what you mean now . . . but wasn't it a bit tricky? What I mean is . . . you facing the other way and all that . . . and him coming at you like a battering-ram . . . you had to be pretty quick, didn't you?"

"I was quick. I caught it in mid-air."

"But didn't he twig?"

"No more than the bull did," she said. "Less so, in fact, and I'll tell you why."

"Why?"

"First of all, he was going mad with the Beetle, right?"

"Right."

"He was grunting and snorting and flapping his arms, right?"

"Right."

"And his head was in the air just like the bull's, right?"

"Probably, yes."

"But most important of all, he was assuming I was a *man*. He thought he was doing it to a *man*, right?"

"Of course."

"And his pizzle was in a good place. It was having a good time, right?"

"Right."

"So in his own mind there was only one place it could be. A man doesn't *have* any other place."

I stared at her in admiration.

"Bound to fool him," she said. She twisted a snail out of its shell and popped it into her mouth.

"Brilliant," I said. "Absolutely brilliant."

"I was rather pleased with it myself."

"It's the ultimate deception."

"Thank you, Oswald."

"There's just one thing I can't fathom," I said.

"What's that?"

"When he came at you like a battering-ram, didn't he take aim?"

"Only after a fashion."

"But he's a very experienced marksman."

"My dear old frump," she said, "you can't seem to get it into your head what a man's like when he's had a double dose."

I jolly well can, I told myself. I was behind the filing cabinets when A. R. Woresley got his.

"No," I said, "I can't. What is a man like when he's had a double dose?"

"Berserk," she said. "He literally doesn't know what the other end of him's doing. I could have shoved it in a jar of pickled onions and he wouldn't have known the difference."

Over the years I have discovered a surprising but simple truth about young ladies and it is this: *The more beautiful their faces, the less delicate their thoughts.* Yasmin was no exception. There she sat now across the table from me in Maxim's wearing a gorgeous Fortuny dress and looking for all the world like Queen Semiramis on the throne of Assyria, but she was talking vulgar. "You're talking vulgar," I said.

"I'm a vulgar girl," she said, grinning.

The Volnay arrived and I tasted it. Wonderful wine. My father used to say never pass up a Volnay by a good shipper if you see one on the wine card. "How did you get away so soon?" I asked her.

"He was very rough," she said. "Rough and sort of spiky. It felt as though I had a gigantic lobster on my back."

"Beastly."

"It was horrid," she said. "He had a heavy gold watch-chain across his waistcoat which kept grinding into my spine. And a big watch in the waistcoat pocket."

"Not good for the watch."

"No," she said. "It went crunch. I heard it."

"Yes, well . . ."

"Terrific wine this, Oswald."

"I know. But how *did* you get away so quickly?"

"That's bound to be a problem with the younger ones after they've had the Beetle," she said. "How old is this fellow?"

"Forty-eight."

"In the prime of life," she said. "It's different when they're seventy-six. At that age, even with the Beetle, they soon grind to a halt."

"But not this chap?"

"God, no," she said. "Perpetual motion. A mechanical lobster."

"So what did you do?"

"What could I do? It's either me or him, I said. So as soon as he'd had his explosion and delivered the goods, I reached into my jacket pocket and got out the trusty hatpin."

"And you let him have it?"

"Yes, but don't forget it had to be a backhander this time and that wasn't so easy. It's hard to get a good swing."

"I can see that."

"Luckily my backhand's always been my strongest point."

"At tennis you mean?"

"Yes," she said.

"And you got him first time?"

"Deep to the baseline," she said. "Deeper than the King of Spain. A winner."

"Did he protest?"

"Oh my God," she said, "he squealed like a pig. And he

danced round the room clutching himself and yelling, 'Céleste! Céleste! Fetch a doctor! I have been stabbed!' The woman must have been looking through the keyhole because she came bursting in at once and rushed up to him crying, 'Where? Where? Let me see!' And while she was examining his backside, I ripped the all-important rubbery thing off him and dashed out of the room pulling up my trousers as I went."

"Bravo," I said. "What a triumph."

"Bit of a lark actually," she said. "I enjoyed it."

"You always do."

"Lovely snails," she said. "Great big juicy ones."

"The snail farms put them on sawdust for two days before they sell them for eating," I said.

"Why?"

"So the snails can purge themselves. When did you get the signed notepaper? Right at the beginning?"

"At the beginning, yes. I always do."

"But why did it say boulevard Haussmann on it, instead of rue Laurent-Pichet?"

"I asked him that myself," she said. "He told me that's where he used to live. He's only just moved."

"That's all right, then," I said.

They took the empty snail-shells away and soon afterwards they brought on the grouse. By grouse I mean red grouse. I do not mean black grouse (blackcock and greyhen) or wood grouse (capercaillie) or white grouse (ptarmigan). These others are good, especially the ptarmigan, but the red grouse is the king. And provided of course they are this year's birds, there is no meat more tender or more tasty in the entire world. Shooting starts on the twelfth of August, and every year I look forward to that date with even greater impatience than I do to the first of September, when the oysters come in from Colchester and Whitstable. Like a fine sirloin, red grouse should be eaten rare with the blood just a shade darker than scarlet, and at Maxim's they would not like you to order it any other way.

We ate our grouse slowly, slicing off one thin sliver of breast at a time, allowing it to melt on the tongue and following each mouthful with a sip of fragrant Volnay.

"Who's next on the list?" Yasmin asked me.

I had been thinking about that myself, and now I said to her, "It was going to be Mr. James Joyce, but perhaps it would be nice if we took a short trip down to Switzerland for a change of scenery."

"I'd like that," she said. "Who's in Switzerland?"

"Nijinsky."

"I thought he was up here with that Diaghilev chap."

"I wish he was," I said. "But it seems he's gone a bit dotty. He thinks he's married to God, and he walks about with a big gold cross around his neck."

"What rotten luck," Yasmin said. "Does that mean his dancing days are over?"

"Nobody knows," I said. "They say he was dancing at a hotel in St. Moritz only a few weeks ago. But that was just for fun, to amuse the guests."

"Does he live in a hotel?"

"No, he's got a villa above St. Moritz."

"Alone?"

"Unfortunately not," I said. "There's a wife and a child and a whole bunch of servants. He's a rich man. Fabulous sums he used to get. I know Diaghilev paid him twenty-five thousand francs for each performance."

"Good Lord. Did you ever see him dance?"

"Only once," I said. "The year the war broke out, 1914, at the old Palace Theatre in London. He did *Les Sylphides.* Stunning it was. He danced like a god."

"I'm crazy to meet him," Yasmin said. "When do we leave?"

"Tomorrow," I said. "We have to keep moving."

20

AT THIS POINT in my narrative, just as I was about to describe our trip to Switzerland to find Nijinsky, my pen suddenly came away from the paper and I found myself hesitating. Was I not perhaps getting into a rut? Becoming repetitious? Yasmin was going to be meeting an awful lot of fascinating people over the next twelve months, no doubt about that. But in nearly every case (there would of course be one or two exceptions) the action was going to be very much the same. There would be the giving of the Beetle powder, the ensuing cataclysm, the escape with the spoils, and all the rest of it, and that, however interesting the men themselves might be, was going to become pretty boring for the reader. Nothing would have been easier than for me to describe in great detail how the two of us met Nijinsky on a path through the pinewoods below his villa, as indeed we did, and how we gave him a chocolate, and how we held him in conversation for nine minutes until the powder hit him, and how he chased Yasmin into the dark wood, leaping from boulder to boulder and rising so high in the air with each leap he seemed to be flying. But if I did that, then it would be fitting also to describe the James Joyce encounter, Joyce in Paris, Joyce in a dark blue serge suit, a black felt hat, old tennis shoes on his feet, twirling an ashplant and talking obscenities. And after Joyce, it would be Monsieur Bonnard and Monsieur Braque and then a quick trip back to Cambridge to unload our precious spoils in The Semen's Home. A very quick trip that was because Yasmin and I were in the rhythm of it now and we wanted to push on until it was finished.

A. R. Woresley was wildly excited when I showed him our haul. We now had King Alfonso, Renoir, Monet, Matisse, Stravinsky, Proust, Nijinsky, Joyce, Bonnard, and Braque. "And you've done a fine job with the freezing," he said to me as he carefully transferred the racks of straws with their labels on them from my suitcase freezer to the big freezer in Dunroamin, our headquarters house. "Keep going, children," he said, rubbing his hands together like a grocer. "Keep going."

We kept going. When Yasmin and I returned the next day to Paris, we collected Clemenceau, Foch, and Maurice Ravel, who was living alone out at Monfort-l'Amaury with a houseful of Siamese cats. After that, and it was the beginning of October now, we drove on south into Italy, looking for D. H. Lawrence. We found him living at the Palazzo Ferraro in Capri with Frieda, and on this occasion I had to distract fat Frieda for two hours out on the rocks while Yasmin went to work on Lawrence. We got a bit of a shock with Lawrence though. When I rushed his semen back to our Capri hotel and examined it under the microscope, I found that the spermatozoa were all stone dead. There was no movement there at all.

"Jesus," I said to Yasmin. "The man's sterile."

"He didn't act like it," she said. "He was like a goat. Like a randy goat."

"We'll have to cross him off the list."

"Who's next?" she asked.

"Giacomo Puccini."

2 I

"PUCCINI IS A BIG ONE," I said. "A giant. We mustn't fail."

"Where does he live?" Yasmin asked.

"Near Lucca, about forty miles west of Florence."

"Tell me about him."

"Puccini is an enormously rich and famous man," I said. "He has built himself a huge house, the Villa Puccini, on the edge of a lake beside the tiny village where he was born, which is called Torre del Lago. Now this is the man, Yasmin, who has written *Manon*, *La Bohème*, *Tosca*, *Madame Butterfly*, and *The Girl of the Golden West*. Classics every one of them. He is probably not a Mozart or a Wagner or even a Verdi, but he's still a genius and a giant. He's a bit of a lad, too."

"In what way?"

"Terrific womanizer."

"Super."

"He is now sixty-one but that hasn't stopped him," I said. "He's a roustabout, a drinker, a crazy car driver, a mad-keen fisherman, and an even keener duck shooter. But above all, he's a lecher. Someone once said of him that he hunts women, wild-fowl, and libretti in that order."

"Sounds like a good chap."

"Splendid fellow," I said. "He's got a wife, an old bag called Elvira, and believe it or not, this Elvira was once sentenced to five months in prison for causing the death of one of Puccini's girl friends. The girl was a servant in the house, and the beastly Elvira caught Puccini out in the garden with her late one night. There was a tremendous scene, the girl was sacked, and thereafter Elvira hounded her to such an extent that the poor thing took poison and killed herself. Her family went to court and Elvira was given five months in the clink."

"Did she go?"

"No," I said. "Puccini got her off by paying twelve thousand lire to the girl's family."

"So what's the plan?" Yasmin asked me. "Do I just knock on the door and walk in?"

"That won't work," I said. "He's surrounded by faithful watchdogs and his bloody wife. You'd never get near him."

"What do you suggest then?"

"Can you sing?" I asked her.

"I'm not Melba," Yasmin said, "but I have quite a decent little voice."

"Great," I said. "Then that's it. That's what we'll do."

"What?"

"I'll tell you on the way up," I said.

We had just returned to the mainland from Capri and we were in Sorrento now. It was warm October weather in this part of Italy and the sky was blue as we loaded up the trusty Citroën *torpédo* and headed north for Lucca. We had the hood down and it was a great pleasure to be driving along the lovely coastal road from Sorrento to Naples.

"First of all, let me tell you how Puccini met Caruso," I said, "because this has a bearing on what you're going to be doing. Puccini was world famous. Caruso was virtually unknown, but he desperately wanted to get the part of Rodolfo in a forthcoming production of *La Bohème* at Livorno. So one day he turned up at the Villa Puccini and asked to see the great man. Almost every day second-rate singers were trying to get in to see Puccini, and it was necessary that he be protected from these people or he would get no peace. 'Tell him I'm busy,' Puccini said. The servant told Puccini that the man absolutely refused to go. 'He says he'll camp in your garden for a year if necessary.' 'What does he look like?' Puccini asked. 'He's a small stubby little chap with a moustache and a bowler hat on his head. He says he's a Neapolitan.' 'What kind of a singer?' Puccini asked. 'He says he's the best tenor in the world,' the servant reported. 'They all say that,' Puccini said, but something prompted him, and to this day he doesn't know what it was, to put down the book he was reading and to go into the hallway. The front door was open and little Caruso was standing just outside in the garden. 'Who the hell are you?' Puccini shouted. Caruso lifted up his full-throated magnificent voice and answered with the words of Rodolfo in *La Bohème*, '*Chi son? Sono un poeta*' . . . 'Who am I? I am a poet.' Puccini was absolutely bowled over by the quality of the voice. He'd never heard a tenor like it before. He rushed up to Caruso and embraced him and cried out, 'Rodolfo is yours!' That's a true story, Yasmin. Puccini himself loves to tell it. And now of course Caruso *is* the greatest tenor in the world, and he and Puccini are the closest of friends. Rather marvellous, don't you agree?"

"What's this got to do with me singing?" Yasmin asked. "My voice is hardly going to bowl Puccini over."

"Of course not. But the general idea is the same. Caruso wanted a part. You want three cubic centimetres of semen. The latter is easier for Puccini to give than the former, especially to someone as gorgeous as you. The singing is simply a way to attract the man's attention."

"Go on, then."

"Puccini works only at night," I said, "from about ten thirty p.m. to three or four in the morning. At that time the rest of the household will be asleep. At midnight, you and I will creep into the garden of the Villa Puccini and locate his studio, which I believe is on the ground floor. A window will certainly be open because the nights are still warm. So while I hide in the bushes, you will stand outside the open window and sing softly the gentle aria '*Un bel dì vedremo*' from *Madame Butterfly*. If everything goes right, Puccini will rush to the window and will see standing there a girl of surprising beauty—you. The rest should be easy."

"I rather like that," Yasmin said. "Italians are always singing outside each other's windows."

When we got to Lucca, we holed up in a small hotel, and there, beside an ancient piano in the hotel sitting-room, I taught Yasmin to sing the aria. She had almost no Italian but she soon learnt the words by heart, and in the end she was able to sing the complete aria very nicely indeed. Her voice was small but she had perfect pitch. I then taught her to say in Italian, "Maestro, I adore your work. I have travelled all the way from England . . ." etc., etc., and a few other useful phrases, including of course, "All I ask is to have your signature on your own notepaper."

"I don't think you're going to need the Beetle with this chap," I said.

"I don't think I am either," Yasmin said. "Let's skip it for once."

"And no hatpin," I told her. "This man is a hero of mine. I won't have him stuck."

"I won't need the hatpin if we don't use the Beetle," she said. "I'm really looking forward to this one, Oswald."

"Ought to be fun," I said.

When all was ready, we drove out one afternoon to the Villa Puccini to scout the premises. It was a massive mansion set on the edge of a large lake and completely surrounded by an eight-foot-high spiked iron fence. Not so good, that. "We'll need a small ladder," I said. So back we drove to Lucca and bought a wooden ladder, which we placed in the open car.

Just before midnight we were once again outside the Villa Puccini. We were ready to go. The night was dark and warm and silent. I placed the ladder up against the railings. I climbed up it and dropped down into the garden. Yasmin followed. I lifted the ladder over onto our side and left it there, ready for the escape.

We saw at once the one room in the entire place that was lit up. It was facing toward the lake. I took Yasmin's hand in mine and we crept closer. Although there was no moon, the light from the two big ground-floor windows reflected onto the water of the lake and cast a pale illumination over the house and garden. The garden was full of trees and bushes and shrubs and flower beds. I was enjoying this. It was what Yasmin called "a bit of a lark." As we came closer to the window, we heard the piano. One

window was open. We tiptoed right up to it and peeped
in. And there he was, the man himself, sitting in his shirt-
sleeves at an upright piano with a cigar in his mouth, tap-
tapping away, pausing to write something down and then
tapping away again. He was thickset, a bit paunchy, and he
had a black moustache. There was a pair of candlesticks in
elaborate brass holders screwed onto either side of the
piano, but the candles were not lit. There was a tall stuffed
white bird, a crane of some sort, standing on a shelf alongside the piano. And around the walls of the room there
were oil paintings of Puccini's celebrated ancestors—his
great-great-grandfather, his great-grandfather, his grand-
father, and his own father. All these men had been famous
musicians. For over two hundred years, the Puccini males
had been passing on musical gifts of a high order to their
children. Puccini straws, if only I could get them, were
going to be immensely valuable. I resolved to make one
hundred of them instead of the usual fifty.

And now there we stood, Yasmin and I, peering through
the open window at the great man. I noticed that he had a
fine head of thick black hair brushed straight back from
the forehead.

"I'm going out of sight," I whispered to Yasmin. "Wait
until he's not playing, then start to sing."

She nodded.

"I'll meet you by the ladder."

She nodded again.

"Good luck," I said, and I tiptoed away and stood behind a bush only five yards from the window. Through the
foliage of the bush not only could I still see Yasmin but I
could also see into the room where the composer was sitting, because the big window was low to the ground.

The piano tinkled. There was a pause. It tinkled again.

He was working out the melody with one finger only, and it was wonderful to be standing out there somewhere in Italy on the edge of a lake at midnight listening to Giacomo Puccini composing what was almost certainly a graceful aria for a new opera. There was another pause. He had got the phrase right this time and he was writing it down. He was leaning forward with a pen in his hand and writing on the manuscript paper in front of him. He was jotting his musical notes above the words of the librettist.

Then suddenly, in the absolute stillness that prevailed, Yasmin's small sweet voice began to sing *"Un bel dì vedremo."* The effect was stunning. In that place, in that atmosphere, in the dark night beside the lake outside Puccini's window, I was moved beyond words. I saw the composer freeze. The pen was in his hand against the paper and the hand froze and his whole body became motionless as he sat listening to the voice outside the window. He didn't look around. I don't think he dared to look round for fear of breaking the spell. Outside his window a young maiden was singing one of his favourite arias in a small clear voice in absolutely perfect pitch. His face didn't change expression. His mouth didn't move. Nothing about him moved while the aria was in progress. It was a magic moment. Then Yasmin stopped singing. For a few seconds longer Puccini remained sitting at the piano. He seemed to be waiting for more, or for a sign of some sort from outside. But Yasmin didn't move or speak either. She simply stood there with her face upturned to the window, waiting for the man to come to her.

And come to her he did. I saw him put down his pen and rise slowly from the piano stool. He walked to the window. Then he saw Yasmin. I have spoken many times of her scintillating beauty, and the sight of her standing out there so still and serene must have come as a glorious shock to Puccini. He stared. He gaped. Was this a dream? Then Yasmin smiled at him and that broke the spell. I saw him come suddenly out of his trance and I heard him say, *"Dio mio, come bella!"* Then he jumped clear out of the window and clasped Yasmin in a powerful embrace.

That was more like it, I thought. That was the real Puccini. Yasmin was not slow to respond. Then I heard him say softly to her in Italian, which I'm sure Yasmin didn't understand, "We must go back inside. If the piano stops playing for too long a time, my wife wakes up and becomes suspicious." I saw him smile at this, showing fine white teeth. Then he picked Yasmin up and hoisted her through the window and climbed in after her.

I am not a voyeur. I watched A. R. Woresley's antics with Yasmin for purely professional reasons, but I had no intention of peeping through the window at Yasmin and Puccini. The act of copulation is like that of picking the nose. It's all right to be doing it yourself but it is a singularly unattractive spectacle for the onlooker. I walked away. I climbed the ladder and dropped over the fence and went for a stroll along the edge of the lake. I was away about an hour. When I returned to the ladder there was no sign of Yasmin. When three hours had gone by, I climbed back into the garden to investigate.

I was creeping cautiously between the bushes when suddenly I heard footsteps on the gravel path, and Puccini himself with Yasmin on his arm walked past me not ten feet away. I heard him saying to her in Italian, "No gentleman is going to permit a lady to walk back to Lucca all alone at this time of night."

Was he going to walk her back to the hotel? I followed them to see where they were going. Puccini's motor car was standing in the drive in the front of the house. I saw him help Yasmin into the passenger seat. Then, with a great deal of fuss and match-striking, he got the acetylene head-lamps alight. He cranked the starting handle. The engine fired and ticked over. He unlocked the gates, jumped into the driver's seat, and off they went with the motor roaring and revving.

I ran out to my own car and got the thing started. I drove fast toward Lucca but I never caught up with Puccini. In fact, I was only halfway there when he passed me on his way home again, alone this time.

I found Yasmin at the hotel.

"Did you get the stuff?"

"Of course," she said.

"Give it to me quickly."

She handed it over and by dawn I had made one hundred Puccini straws of good quality. While I was working on them, Yasmin sat in an armchair in my room drinking red Chianti and giving her report.

"Great time," she said. "Really marvellous. I wish they were all like him."

"Good."

"He was so *jolly*," she said. "Lots of laughs. And he sang me a bit from the new opera he's doing."

"Did he say what he's calling it?"

"*Turio*," she said. "*Turidot*. Something like that."

"No trouble from the wife upstairs?"

"Not a peep," she said. "But it was so funny because even when we were plunged in passion on the sofa, he had to keep reaching out every now and again to bang the piano. Just to let her know he was working hard and not banging some woman."

"A great man, you think?"

"Terrific," Yasmin said. "Stupendous. Find me another like him."

2 2

FROM LUCCA we headed north for Vienna, and on the way we called on Sergei Rachmaninoff in his lovely house on Lake Lucerne.

"It's a funny thing," Yasmin said to me when she came back to the car after what had obviously been a fairly energetic session with the great musician, "it's a funny thing, but there's an amazing resemblance between Mr. Rachmaninoff and Mr. Stravinsky."

"You mean facially?"

"I mean everything," she said. "They've both got small bodies and great big lumpy faces. Enormous strawberry noses. Beautiful hands. Tiny feet. Thin legs. And great equipment."

"Is it your experience so far," I asked her, "that geniuses have larger pizzles than ordinary men?"

"Definitely," she said. "Much larger."

"I was afraid you'd say that."

"And they make better use of them," she said, rubbing it in. "Their swordsmanship is superb."

"Rubbish."

"It's not rubbish, Oswald. I ought to know."

"Aren't you forgetting they've all had the Beetle?"

"The Beetle helps," she said. "Of course it helps. But there's no comparison between the way a great creative genius handles his sword and the way an ordinary fellow does it. That's why I'm having such a nice time."

"Am I an ordinary fellow?"

"Don't be grumpy," she said. "We can't all be Rachmaninoff or Puccini."

I was deeply wounded. Yasmin had pricked me in my most sensitive area. I sulked all the way to Vienna, but the sight of that noble city soon restored my humour.

In Vienna, Yasmin had a hilarious encounter with Dr. Sigmund Freud in his consulting room at Berggasse 19, and I think this visit merits a brief description.

First of all, she made a proper application for an appointment with the famous man, stating that she was in urgent need of psychiatric treatment. She was told there would be four days to wait. So I arranged for her to fill in the time by calling first upon the august Mr. Richard Strauss. Mr. Strauss had just been appointed co-director of the Vienna State Opera and he was, according to Yasmin, rather pompous. But he was easy meat and I got fifty excellent straws from him.

Then it was Dr. Freud's turn. I regarded the celebrated psychiatrist as being in the semi-joker class and saw no reason why we shouldn't have a bit of fun with him. Yasmin agreed. So the two of us cooked up an interesting psychiatric malady for her to be suffering from, and in she went to the big greystone house on Berggasse at two thirty on a cool, sunny October afternoon. Here is her own description of the encounter as she told it to me later that day over a bottle of Krug after I had frozen the straws.

"He's a goosey old bird," she said. "Very severe looking and correctly dressed, like a banker or something."

"Did he speak English?"

"Quite good English, but with that dreadful German accent. He sat me down on the other side of his desk and right away I offered him a chocolate. He took it like a lamb. Isn't it odd, Oswald, how every one of them takes the chocolate without any argument?"

"I don't think it's odd," I said. "It's the natural thing to do. If a pretty girl offered me a chocolate, I'd take it."

"He was a hairy sort of fellow," Yasmin said. "He had a moustache and a thick pointed beard which looked as though it had been trimmed very carefully in front of a mirror with scissors. Whitish-grey it was. But the hair had been cut well back from his mouth above and below so that the bristles made a sort of frame for his lips. That's what I noticed above everything else, his lips. Very striking, those lips of his, and very thick. They looked like a pair of false lips made out of rubber which had been stuck on over the real ones.

" 'So now, fräulein,' he said, munching away at his chocolate, 'tell me about this so urgent problem of yours.'

" 'Oh, Doctor Freud, I do hope you can help me!' I cried, working myself up at once. 'Can I speak to you frankly?'

" 'That's vot you are here for,' he said. 'Lie down on that couch over there, please, and just let yourself go.'

"So I lay down on the goddamn couch, Oswald, and as I did so I thought well anyway I'm going to be in a reasonably comfy place for once when the fireworks start."

"I see your point."

"So I said to him, 'Something terrible is wrong with me, Doctor Freud! Something terrible and shocking!'

" 'And vot is that?' he asked, perking up. He obviously enjoyed hearing about terrible and shocking things.

" 'You won't believe it,' I said, 'but it is impossible for

me to be in the presence of a man for more than a few minutes before he tries to rape me! He becomes a wild animal! He rips off my clothes! He exposes his organ—is that the right word?'

" 'It is as good a word as any,' he said. 'Continue, fräulein.'

" 'He jumps on top of me!' I cried. 'He pins me down! He takes his pleasure of me! Every man I meet does this to me, Doctor Freud! You must help me! I am being raped to death!'

" 'Dear lady,' he said, 'this is a very common fantasy among certain types of hysterical vimmen. These vimmen are all frightened of having physical relations with men. Actually, they long to indulge in fornication and copulation and all other sexy frolics but they are terrified of the consequences. So they fantasize. They imagine they are being raped. But it never happens. They are all firgins.'

" 'No, no!' I cried. 'You are wrong, Doctor Freud! I'm not a virgin! I'm the most over-raped girl in the world!'

" 'You are hallucinating,' he said. 'Nobody has ever raped you. Vy you do not admit it and you vill feel better instamatically?'

" 'How can I admit it when it isn't true?' I cried. 'Every man I've ever met has had his way with me! And it'll be just the same with you if I stay here much longer, you see if it isn't!'

" 'Do not be ridiculous, fräulein,' he snapped.

" 'It will, it will!' I cried. 'You'll be as bad as all the rest of them before this session's over!'

"When I said that, Oswald, the old buzzard rolled his eyes up at the ceiling and smiled a thin supercilious smile. 'Fantasy, fantasy,' he said, 'all is fantasy.'

" 'What makes you think you're so right and I'm so wrong?' I asked him.

" 'Allow me to explain a little further,' he said, leaning back in his chair and clasping his hands across his tummy. 'In your subconscious mind, my dear fräulein, you believe that the masculine organ is a machine-gun—'

" 'That's just about what it is so far as I'm concerned!' I cried. 'It's a lethal weapon!'

" 'Exactly,' he said. 'Now vee are getting somewhere. And you also believe that any man who points it at you is going to pull the trigger and riddle you with bullets.'

" 'Not bullets,' I said. 'Something else.'

" 'So you run avay,' he said. 'You reject all men. You hide from them. You sit all alone through the nights—'

" 'I do not sit alone,' I said. 'I sit with my lovely old Doberman pinscher, Fritzy.'

" 'Male or female?' he snapped.

" 'Fritzy's a male.'

" 'Vorse than ever,' he said. 'Do you with this Doberman pinscher indulge in sexual relations?'

" 'Don't be so daft, Doctor Freud. Who do you think I am?'

" 'You run avay from men,' he said. 'You run avay from dogs. You run avay from anything that an organ has. . . .'

" 'I've never heard such codswallop in all my life!' I cried. 'I am not frightened of anyone's organ! I do not think it's a machine-gun! I think it's a bloody nuisance, that's all! I'm fed up with it! I've had enough!'

" 'Do you like carrots, fräulein?' he asked me suddenly.

" 'Carrots?' I said. 'Good God. Not particularly, no. If I do have them I usually dice them. I chop them up.'

" 'Vot about cucumbers, fräulein?'

" 'Pretty tasteless,' I said. 'I prefer them pickled.'

" '*Ja ja*,' he said, writing all this down on my record sheet. 'It may interest you to know, fräulein, that the carrot and the cucumber are both very powerful sexuality symbols. They represent the masculine phallic member. And you are vishing either to chop it up or to pickle it!'

"I tell you, Oswald," Yasmin said to me, "it was as much as I could do to stop myself screaming with laughter. And to think people actually believe this horseshit."

"He believes it himself," I said.

"I know he does. He sat there writing it all down on a large sheet of paper. Then he said, 'And vot also have you got to tell me, fräulein?'

" 'I can tell you what *I* think is wrong with me,' I said.

" 'Proceed, please.'

" 'I believe I have a little dynamo inside me,' I said, 'and this dynamo goes whizzing round and round and gives off a terrific charge of sexual electricity.'

" 'Very interesting,' he said, scribbling away. 'Continue, please.'

" 'This sexual electricity is of such high voltage,' I said, 'that as soon as a man comes close to me, it jumps across the gap from me to him and it jiggers him up.'

" 'Vot is meaning, please, "jiggers him up"?'

" 'It means it excites him,' I said. 'It electrifies his private parts. It makes them red hot. And that's when he starts to go crazy and he jumps on me. Don't you believe me, Doctor Freud?'

" 'This is a serious case,' the old geezer said. 'It is going to take many psychoanalytical sessions on the couch to make you normal.'

"Now all this time, Oswald," Yasmin said to me, "I was keeping an eye on my watch. And when eight minutes had gone by, I said to him, 'Please don't rape me, Doctor Freud. You ought to be above that sort of thing.'

" 'Do not be ridiculous, fräulein,' he said. 'You are hallucinating again.'

" 'But my electricity!' I cried. 'It's going to jigger you up! I know it is! It's going to jump across from me to you and electrify your private parts! Your pizzle will become red hot! You will rip my clothes off! You will have your way with me!'

" 'Stop this hysterical shoutings at once,' he snapped, and he got up from his desk and came and stood near where I was lying on the couch. 'Here I am,' he said, spreading out his arms. 'I am not harming you, am I? I am not trying to jump upon you, yes?'

"And at that very moment, Oswald," Yasmin said to me, "the Beetle suddenly hit him and his old doodly came alive and stuck out as though he had a walking-stick in his trousers."

"You timed it lovely," I said.

"Not bad, was it? So I thrust out my arm and pointed an accusing finger and shouted, 'There! It's happening to you, you old goat! My electricity has jolted you! Will you believe me now, Doctor Freud? Will you believe what I am saying?'

"You should have seen his face, Oswald. You really should have seen it. The Beetle was hitting him and the sex-crazy glint was coming into his eyes and he was beginning to flap his arms like an old crow. But I'll say this for him. He didn't jump me right away. He held off for at least a minute or so while he tried to analyze what the hell was happening. He looked down at his trousers. Then he looked up at me. Then he started muttering. 'This is incredible! . . . amazing! . . . unbelievable! . . . I must make notes, I must record every moment. Vere is my pen, for God's sake? Vere is the ink? Vere is some paper? Oh, to hell with the paper! Please remove your clothes, fräulein! I cannot vait any longer!' "

"Must have shaken him," I said.

"Shook him rigid," Yasmin said. "It was undermining one of his most famous theories."

"You didn't hatpin him, did you?"

"Of course not. He was really very decent about it all. As soon as he'd had his first explosion, and although the Beetle was still hitting him hard, he jumped away and ran back to his desk stark naked and began writing notes. He must be terrifically strong-minded. Great intellectual curiosity. But he was completely foxed and bewildered by what had happened to him.

" 'Do you believe me now, Doctor Freud?' I asked him.

" 'I have to believe you!' he cried. 'You have opened up a whole new field vith this sexual electricity of yours! This case vill make history! I must see you again, fräulein!'

" 'You'll jump me,' I said. 'You won't be able to stop yourself.'

" 'I know,' he said, smiling for the first time. 'I know that, fräulein. I know.' "

I got fifty first-class straws from Dr. Freud.

23

FROM VIENNA we drove north in the pale autumn sunshine to Berlin. The war had been over for only eleven months and the city was bleak and dreary, but we had two impor-

tant persons to visit here and I was determined to collar
them. The first was Mr. Albert Einstein, and at his house
at Haberlandstrasse 9 Yasmin had a pleasant and successful
encounter with this amazing fellow.

"How was it?" I said, asking her the usual question in
the car.

"He had a great time," she said.

"Didn't you?"

"Not really," she said. "He's all brains and no body. Give
me Puccini any day."

"Will you please try to forget that Italian Romeo?"

"Yes, Oswald, I will. But I'll tell you what's odd. The
brainy ones, the great intellects behave quite differently
from the artistic ones when the Beetle hits them."

"How?"

"The brainy ones stop and think. They try to figure out
what on earth has happened to them and why it's happened. The artists just take it for granted and plunge right
in."

"What was Einstein's reaction?"

"He couldn't believe it," she said. "In fact he smelled
a rat. He's the very first one who has ever suspected us of
jiggery-pokery. Shows how bright he is."

"What did he say?"

"He stood there and looked at me from under those
bushy eyebrows and he said, 'There is something extremely
fishy here, fräulein. This is not my normal reaction to a
pretty visitor.'

" 'Doesn't that depend on how pretty she is?' I said.

" 'No, fräulein, it does not,' he said. 'Was that an ordinary chocolate you gave me?'

" 'Perfectly ordinary,' I said, quaking a bit. 'I had one
myself.'

"The little chap was strongly hotted up by the Beetle, Oswald, but like old Freud, he managed to hold off in the beginning. He paced up and down the room muttering, 'What is happening to me? This is not natural. . . . There is something wrong. . . . I would never allow this. . . .'

"I was draped all over the sofa in a seductive attitude waiting for him to get on with it, but no, Oswald, absolutely not. For about five whole minutes his thinking processes completely blocked out his carnal desires or whatever you call them. I could almost hear the old brain whizzing round as he tried to puzzle it out.

" 'Mr. Einstein,' I said, 'relax.' "

"You were dealing with the greatest intellect in the world," I said. "The man has supernatural powers of reasoning. Try to understand what he says about relativity and you'll see what I mean."

"We'd be finished if someone twigged what we were doing."

"No one will," I said. "There's only one Einstein."

Our second important donor in Berlin was Mr. Thomas Mann. Yasmin reported that he was pleasant but uninspiring.

"Like his books," I said.

"Then why did you choose him?"

"He's done some fine work. I think his name is going to live."

My travelling liquid nitrogen suitcase was now crammed full of straws. I had Clemenceau, Foch, Ravel, Puccini, Rachmaninoff, Strauss, Freud, Einstein, and Mann. So once again we rushed back to Cambridge with our precious cargo.

A. R. Woresley was ecstatic. He knew damn well we were onto something big now. All three of us were ecstatic, but I was in no mood to waste time yet with celebrations. "While we're here," I said, "we'll polish off some of the English lads. We'll start tomorrow."

Joseph Conrad was possibly the most important of these, so we took him first. Capel House, Orlestone, Kent was his address and we drove down there in mid-November. To be precise, it was November 16th, 1919. I have already said that I am not keen to give a detailed description of too many of our visits for fear of becoming repetitious. I will not break this rule again unless something juicy or amusing comes along. Our visit to Mr. Conrad was neither juicy nor amusing. It was routine, although Yasmin did comment afterwards that he was one of the nicest men she had met so far.

From Kent we drove to Crowborough in Sussex where we nobbled Mr. H. G. Wells. "Not a bad sort of egg," Yasmin said when she came out. "Rather portly and pontif-icating, but quite pleasant. It's an odd thing about great writers," she added. "They look so ordinary. There's noth-ing about them that gives you the slightest clue to their greatness, as there is with painters. A great painter some-how *looks* like a great painter. But the great writer usually looks like the wages clerk in a cheese factory."

From Crowborough we drove on to Rottingdean, also in Sussex, to call on Mr. Rudyard Kipling. "Bristly little bugger," was Yasmin's only comment on that one. Fifty straws from Kipling.

We were very much in the rhythm now, and the next day in the same county of Sussex we picked off Sir Arthur Conan Doyle as easily as picking a cherry. Yasmin simply rang the doorbell and told the maid who answered it that she was from his publishers and had important papers to de-liver to him. She was at once shown into his study.

"What did you think of Mr. Sherlock Holmes?" I asked her.

"Nothing special," she said. "Just another writer with a thin pencil."

"Wait," I said. "The next on the list is also a writer, but I doubt you'll find this one boring."

"Who is he?"

"Mr. Bernard Shaw."

We had to drive through London to get to Ayot St. Lawrence in Hertfordshire where Shaw lived, and on the way I told Yasmin something about this smug literary clown. "First of all," I said, "he's a rabid vegetarian. He eats only raw vegetables and fruit and cereal. So I doubt he'll accept the chocolate."

"What do we do, give it to him in a carrot?"

"What about a radish?" I suggested.

"Will he eat it?"

"Probably not," I said. "So it had better be a grape. We'll get a good bunch of grapes in London and doctor one of them with the powder."

"That'll work," Yasmin said.

"It's got to work," I said. "This lad won't do it without the Beetle."

"What's wrong with him?"

"Nobody quite knows."

"Doesn't he practice the noble art?"

"No," I said. "He's not interested in sex. He appears to be a sort of capon."

"Oh hell."

"He's a lanky, garrulous old capon with an overwhelming conceit."

"Are you suggesting his machinery is out of order?" Yasmin asked.

"I'm not sure. He's sixty-three. He married at forty-two, a marriage of companionship and convenience. No sex."

"How do you know that?"

"I don't. But that's the general opinion. He himself has stated that 'I had no adventures of a sexual kind until I was twenty-nine.'"

"A bit retarded."

"I doubt he's had any at all," I said. "Many famous women have pursued him without success. Mrs. Pat Campbell, gorgeous actress, said, 'He's all hen and no cock.'"

"I like that."

"His diet," I said, "is deliberately aimed at mental efficiency. 'I flatly declare,' he once wrote, 'that a man fed on whiskey and dead bodies cannot possibly do good work.'"

"As opposed to whiskey and live bodies, I suppose."

Pretty quick our Yasmin was. "He's a Marxist Socialist," I added. "He thinks the State should run everything."

"Then he's an even bigger ass than I thought," Yasmin said. "I can't wait to see his face when the old Beetle strikes."

On the way through London, we bought a bunch of superb hothouse muscatel grapes from Jackson's in Piccadilly. They were very costly, very pale yellowish-green, and very large. North of London, we stopped on the side of the road and got out the tin of Blister Beetle powder.

"Shall we give him a double shot?" I asked.

"Triple," Yasmin said.

"D'you think that's safe?"

"If what you say about him is true, he's going to need half the tin."

"Very well, then," I said. "Triple it is."

We chose the grape that was hanging at the lowest point

of the bunch and carefully made a nick in its skin with a knife. I scooped out a little of the inside and then inserted a triple dose of powder, pushing the stuff well into the grape with a pin. Then we continued on to Ayot St. Lawrence.

"You do realize," I said, "that this will be the first time anyone's had a triple dose?"

"I'm not worried," Yasmin said. "The man's obviously wildly undersexed. I wonder if he's a eunuch. Does he have a high voice?"

"I don't know."

"Bloody writers," Yasmin said. She settled herself deeper into the seat and kept a grumpy silence for the rest of the trip.

The house, known as Shaw's Corner, was a large, unremarkable brick pile with a good garden. The time, as I pulled up outside, was four twenty in the afternoon.

"What do I do?" Yasmin asked.

"You walk round to the back of the house and all the way down to the bottom of the garden," I said. "There, you will find a small wooden shed with a sloping roof. That's where he works. He's certain to be in it now. Just barge in and give him the usual patter."

"What if the wife sees me?"

"That's a chance you'll have to take," I said. "You'll probably make it. And tell him that you're a vegetarian. He'll like that."

"What are the names of his plays?"

"*Man and Superman*," I said. "*The Doctor's Dilemma, Major Barbara, Caesar and Cleopatra, Androcles and the Lion, Pygmalion.*"

"He'll ask me which I like best."

"Say *Pygmalion.*"

"All right, I'll say *Pygmalion*."

"Flatter him. Tell him he is not only the greatest play-wright but also the greatest music critic that ever lived. You don't have to worry. He'll do the talking."

Yasmin stepped out of the car and walked with a firm step through the gate into Shaw's garden. I watched her until she had disappeared around the back of the house, then I drove up the road and booked a room in a pub called The Waggon and Horses. Up in the room, I laid out my equipment and got everything ready for the rapid con-version of Shaw's semen into frozen straws. An hour later, I returned to Shaw's Corner to wait for Yasmin. I didn't wait long, but I am not going to tell you what happened next until you have heard what happened first. Such things are better in their right order.

"I walked down the garden," Yasmin told me afterwards in the pub over an excellent steak and kidney pudding and a bottle of reasonable Beaune. "I walked down the garden and I saw the hut. I walked quickly towards it. I was ex-pecting any moment to hear Mrs. Shaw's voice behind me shouting 'Halt!' But no one saw me. I opened the door of the hut and looked in. It was empty. There was a cane armchair, a plain table covered with sheets of paper, and a Spartan atmosphere. But no Shaw. Well, that's it, I thought. Better get out. Back to Oswald. Total failure. I banged the door shut.

" 'Who is there?' shouted a voice from behind the hut. It was a male voice, but high-pitched and almost squeaky. Oh, my God, I thought, the man *is* a eunuch after all.

" 'Is that you, Charlotte?' the squeaky voice demanded.

"What effect, I wondered, would the Beetle have upon a one hundred per cent eunuch?

" 'Charlotte!' he called. 'What are you doing?'

"Then a tall bony creature with an enormous beard came round the corner of the hut holding a pair of garden clippers in one hand. 'Who, may I enquire, are *you*?' he demanded. 'This is private property.'

" 'I'm looking for the public lavatory,' I said.

" 'What is your business, young lady?' he demanded, pointing the clippers at me like a pistol. 'You went into my hut. What have you stolen?'

" 'I haven't stolen a damn thing,' I said. 'I came, if you want to know, to bring you a present.'

" 'A present, eh?' he said, softening a little.

"I lifted the fine bunch of grapes out of the bag and held it up by the stem.

" 'And what have I done to deserve such munificence?' he said.

" 'You have given me a terrific amount of pleasure at the theatre,' I said. 'So I thought it would be nice if I gave you something in return. That's all there is to it. I have no other motive. Here, try one.' I picked off the bottom grape and offered it to him. 'They're really awfully good.'

"He stepped forward and took the grape and pushed it through all those whiskers into his mouth.

" 'Excellent,' he said, chewing away. 'A muscat.' He glared at me under those beetley brows. 'It is fortunate for you, young lady, that I wasn't working or I'd have kicked you out, grapes or no grapes. As it happens, I was pruning my roses.'

" 'I apologize for barging in,' I said. 'Will you forgive me?'

" 'I will forgive you when I am convinced that your motives are pure,' he said.

" 'As pure as the Virgin Mary,' I said.

" 'I doubt it,' he said. 'A woman never pays a visit to a man unless she is seeking some advantage. I have made that point many times in my plays. The female, madam, is a predatory animal. She preys upon men.'

" 'What a damn stupid thing to say,' I told him. '*Man* is the hunter.'

" 'I have never hunted a woman in my life,' he said. 'Women hunt me. And I flee like a fox with a pack of hounds at his heels. Rapacious creatures,' he added, spitting out a seed from the grape. 'Rapacious, predatory, all-devouring animals.'

" 'Oh, come on,' I said. 'Everyone hunts a bit now and again. Women hunt men for marriage and what's wrong with that? But men hunt women because they want to get into bed with them. Where shall I put these grapes?'

" 'We'll put them in the hut,' he said, taking them from me. He went into the hut and I followed. I was praying for the nine minutes to pass quickly. He sat down in his cane armchair and stared at me under great bushy eyebrows. I quickly sat myself on the only other chair in the place.

" 'You are a spirited young lady,' he said. 'I admire spirit.'

" 'And you talk a lot of bosh about women,' I said. 'I don't believe you know the first thing about them. Have you ever fallen passionately in love?'

" 'A typical woman's question,' he said. 'For me, there is only one kind of passion. Intelligence is passion. The activity of the intellect is the keenest passion I can experience.'

" 'What about physical passion?' I asked. 'Isn't that in the running?'

" 'No, madam, it is not. Descartes got far more passion and pleasure out of life than Casanova.'

" 'What about Romeo and Juliet?'

" 'Puppy love,' he said. 'Superficial tosh.'

" 'Are you saying that your *Caesar and Cleopatra* is a greater play than *Romeo and Juliet?*'

" 'Without a doubt,' he said.

" 'Boy, you've got a nerve, Mr. Shaw.'

" 'So have you, young lady.' He picked up a sheet of paper from the table. 'Listen to this,' he said and he started to read aloud in that squeaky voice of his, '. . . the body always ends by being a bore. Nothing remains beautiful and interesting except thought, because thought is life. . . .'

" 'Of course it *ends* by being a bore,' I said. 'That's a pretty obvious remark. But it isn't a bore at my age. It's a juicy fruit. What's the play?'

" 'It's about Methuselah,' he said. 'And now I must ask you to leave me in peace. You are pert and pretty but that does not entitle you to take up my time. I thank you for the grapes.'

"I glanced at my watch. Just over a minute to go. I had to keep talking. 'I'll be off then,' I said. 'But in exchange for my grapes I'd love it if you gave me your autograph on one of your famous postcards.'

"He reached for a postcard and signed it. 'Now be off with you,' he said. 'You have wasted enough of my time.'

" 'I'm going,' I said, fumbling about and trying to string out the seconds. The nine minutes were up now. Oh Beetle, lovely Beetle, kind Beetle, where are you? Why have you deserted me?"

"A bit dicey, that," I said.

"I was desperate, Oswald. It had never happened before.

'Mr. Shaw,' I said, pausing by the door, searching for a time killer, 'I promised my dear old mother who thinks you are God the Father himself to be sure to ask you one question. . . .'

" 'You are a pest, madam!' he barked.

" 'I know I am, I know, I know, but please answer it for her. Here's the question. Is it really true that you disapprove of all artists who create works of art for purely aesthetic reasons?'

" 'I do, madam.'

" 'You mean pure beauty is not enough?'

" 'It is not,' he said. 'Art should always be didactic, serving a social purpose.'

" 'Did Beethoven serve a social purpose, or Van Gogh?'

" 'Get out of here!' he roared. 'I have no wish to bandy words—' He stopped in mid-sentence. For at that moment, Oswald, heaven be praised, the Beetle struck."

"Hooray. Did it hit him hard?"

"This was a triple dose, remember."

"I know. So what happened?"

"I don't think it's safe to give triples, Oswald. I'm not going to do it again."

"Rocked him a bit, did it?"

"Phase one was devastating," Yasmin said. "It was as if he were sitting in an electric chair and someone had pulled the switch and jolted him with a million volts."

"Bad as that?"

"Listen, his whole body rose up off the chair and there it hung, in mid-air, rigid, quivering, the eyes popping, the face all twisted."

"Oh dear."

"Rattled me."

"I'll bet."

"What do we do now, I thought. Artificial respiration, oxygen, what?"

"You're not exaggerating, are you, Yasmin?"

"God no. The man was contorted. He was paralyzed. He was garrotted. He couldn't speak."

"Was he conscious?"

"Who knows?"

"Did you think he might kick the bucket?"

"I reckoned it was about even money."

"You really thought that?"

"You only had to look at him."

"Christ, Yasmin."

"I stood there by the door and I remember thinking, well whatever happens this old buzzard's written his last play. 'Hello there, Mr. Shaw,' I said. 'Wakey wakey.'"

"Could he hear you?"

"I doubt it. And through his whiskers I could see white stuff, like brine, forming on his lips."

"How long did all this last?"

"A couple of minutes. And on top of everything else I began worrying about his heart."

"Why his heart, for God's sake?"

"He was going purple in the face. I could see his skin going purple."

"Asphyxia?"

"Something like that," Yasmin said. "Isn't this steak and kidney delicious?"

"It's very good."

"Then all of a sudden he came back to earth. He blinked his eyes, took one look at me, gave a sort of Indian whoop, leaped out of his chair, and started tearing off his clothes.

'The Irish are coming!' he yelled. 'Gird up your loins, madam! Gird up your loins and prepare for battle!' "

"Not exactly a eunuch then."

"It didn't look like it."

"How did you manage to roll the old rubbery thing on him?"

"There's only one way when they get violent," Yasmin said. "I grabbed hold of his snozzberry and hung onto it like grim death and gave it a twist or two to make him hold still."

"Ow."

"Very effective."

"I'll bet it is."

"You can lead them around anywhere you want like that."

"I'm sure."

"It's like putting a twitch on a horse."

I took a mouthful of Beaune, tasting it with care. It had been shipped by Louis Latour and it was really very fair. One was fortunate to find something like that in a country pub. "So then what?" I said.

"Chaos. Wooden floor. Horrible bruises. The lot. But I'll tell you what's interesting, Oswald. He didn't know quite what to do. I had to show him."

"So he *was* a virgin?"

"Must've been. But a damn quick learner. I've never seen such energy in a man of sixty-three."

"That's the vegetarian diet."

"It could be," Yasmin said, spearing a piece of kidney with her fork and popping it into her mouth. "But don't forget he had a brand-new engine."

"A what?"

"A new engine. Most men of that age are more or less worn out by then. Their equipment, I mean. It's done so much mileage things are beginning to rattle."

"You mean the fact that he was a virgin . . ."

"Precisely, Oswald. The engine was brand-new, completely unused. Therefore no wear and tear."

"Had to run it in a bit though, didn't he?"

"No," she said. "He just let her rip. Flat out all the time. Full throttle. And when he'd got the hang of it he shouted, '*Now* I see what Mrs. Pat Campbell was on about!'"

"I suppose in the end you had to get out the old hatpin?"

"Of course. But you know something, Oswald? With a triple dose they're so far gone they don't feel a thing. I might've been tickling his arse with a feather for all the good it did."

"How many jabs?"

"Till my arm got tired."

"So what then?"

"There are other ways," Yasmin said darkly.

"Ow again," I said. I was remembering what Yasmin had once done to A. R. Woresley in the lab to get away from him. "Did he jump?"

"About a yard straight up," she said. "And that gave me just enough time to grab the spoils and dash for the door."

"Lucky you kept your clothes on."

"I had to," she said. "Whenever we give an extra dose it's always a sprint to get away."

So that was Yasmin's story. But let me now take it up from there myself and go back to where I was sitting quietly in my motor car outside Shaw's Corner in the gathering dusk while all this was going on. Suddenly out came Yasmin at the gallop, flying down the garden path with her hair streaming out behind her, and I quickly opened the passenger door for her to jump in. But she didn't jump in. She ran to the front of the car and grabbed the starting handle. No self-starters in those days, remember. "Switch on, Oswald!" she shouted. "Switch on! He's coming after me!" I switched on the ignition. Yasmin cranked the handle. The motor started first kick. Yasmin dashed back and jumped into the seat next to me, yelling, "Go man, go! Full speed ahead!" But before I could get the gear lever properly engaged, I heard a yell from the garden and in the half-darkness I saw this tall, ghostlike, white-bearded figure charging down upon us stark naked and yelling, "Come back, you strumpet! I haven't finished with you yet!"

"Go!" Yasmin shouted. I got the car into gear and let out the clutch and off we went.

There was a street lamp outside the Shaw house, and when I glanced back I saw Mr. Shaw capering about on the sidewalk under the gaslight, white-skinned all over save for a pair of socks on his feet, bearded above and bearded below as well, with his massive pink member protruding like a sawn-off shotgun from the lower beard. It was a sight I shall not readily forget, this mighty and supercilious playwright who had always mocked the passions of the flesh, himself impaled now upon the sword of lust and screaming for Yasmin to come back. *Cantharis vesicatoria sudanii*, I reflected, could make a monkey out of the Messiah.

24

BY NOW Christmas was nearly on us and Yasmin said she wanted a holiday. I wanted to keep going. "Come on," I said, "let's do a royal tour first, kings only. We'll nobble all the nine remaining monarchs of Europe. Then we'll both take a good long rest."

Romping with the royals, as Yasmin called it, was an irresistible prospect and she agreed to delay her holiday and spend Christmas in wintry Europe. Together we worked out a sensible itinerary which would take us, in the following order, to Belgium, Italy, Serbia, Greece, Bulgaria, Rumania, Denmark, Sweden, and Norway. I checked over all nine of my carefully prepared letters from George V. A. R. Woresley refilled my travelling liquid nitrogen container and supplied me with a new stock of straws, and off we went in the trusty Citroën, heading for Dover and the cross-Channel steamer, with the royal palace in Brussels our first stop.

The effect that the King of England's letter had upon the first eight monarchs on our list was virtually identical. They jumped to it. They couldn't wait to please King George, and they couldn't wait to get a peek at his secret mistress. For them it was a fruity business. On every single occasion Yasmin was invited to the palace only a few hours after I had delivered the letter. We had success after success. Sometimes the hatpin had to be used, sometimes not. There were some funny scenes and one or two tricky moments, but Yasmin always got her man in the end. She even got seventy-six-year-old King Peter of the Serbs, Croats, and Slovenes, although he passed out at the end of it all and my girl had to revive him by throwing a chamber-pot of cold water over his face. By the time we reached Christiania (now Oslo) at the beginning of April, we had eight kings in the bag and there was only Haakon of Norway left. He was forty-eight years old.

In Christiania we booked into the Grand Hotel on Carl Johan's Gate, and from the balcony of my room I could look straight up that splendid street to the royal palace on the hill. I delivered my letter at ten o'clock on a Tuesday morning. By lunchtime Yasmin had a reply in the King's own handwriting. She was invited to present herself at the palace at two thirty that afternoon.

"This is going to be my very last king," she said. "I shall miss popping into palaces and wrestling with royals."

"What's your general opinion of them," I said, "now that it's nearly over? How do they measure up?"

"They vary," she said. "That fellow Boris of Bulgaria was terrifying the way he rolled me up in chicken wire."

"Bulgarians are not easy."

"Ferdinand of Rumania was pretty crazy, too."

"The one who had distorting mirrors all around the room?"

"That's him. Let us now see what revolting habits this Norwegian chap has got."

"I hear he's a very decent fellow."

"Nobody's decent when he's had the Beetle, Oswald."

"I'll bet he's nervous," I said.

"Why?"

"I told you why. His wife, Queen Maud, is King George the Fifth's sister. So our fake letter was supposedly written to Haakon by his brother-in-law. It's all a bit close to the bone."

"Spicy," Yasmin said. "I like it." And off she bounced to the palace with her little box of chocolates and her hatpin and other necessary items. I stayed behind and laid out my equipment in readiness for her return.

In less than one hour she was back. She came flying into my room like a hurricane.

"I blew it!" she cried. "Oh, Oswald, I did something frightful—awful—terrible! I blew the whole thing!"

"What happened?" I said, starting to quake.

"Give me a drink," she said. "Brandy."

I got her a stiff brandy. "Come on then," I said. "Let's have it. Tell me the worst."

Yasmin took a huge gulp of brandy, then she leaned back and closed her eyes and said, "Ah, that's better."

"For God's sake," I cried, "tell me what happened!"

She drank the rest of the brandy and asked for another. I gave it to her quickly.

"Lovely big room," she said. "Lovely tall king. Black moustache, courtly, kind, and handsome. Took the chocolate like a lamb and I started counting the minutes. Spoke almost perfect English. 'I am not very happy about this business, Lady Victoria,' he said, tapping King George's letter with one finger. 'This is not like my brother-in-law at all. King George is the most upright and honourable man I've ever met.'

" 'He's only human, your Majesty.'

" 'He's the perfect husband,' he said.

" 'The trouble is he's married,' I said.

" 'Of course he's married. What are you implying?'

" 'Married men make rotten husbands, your Majesty.'

" 'You're talking rubbish, madam!' he snapped."

"Why didn't you shut up right then and there, Yasmin?" I cried.

"Oh, I couldn't, Oswald. Once I get going like that I can't ever seem to stop. Do you know what I said next?"

"I can't wait," I said. I was beginning to sweat.

"I said, 'Look, your Majesty, I mean after all when a strong, good-looking fellow like George has been having rice pudding every night for years and years, it's only natural he's going to start wanting a dish of caviar.' "

"Oh, my God!"

"It was a silly thing to say, I know that."

"What did he answer?"

"He went green in the face. I thought he was going to strike me, but he just stood there spluttering and fizzing like one of those fireworks, those bangers, the ones that go on spluttering for a long time before the big explosion comes."

"And did it come?"

"Not then. He was very dignified. He said, 'I will thank you, madam, not to refer to the Queen of England as a rice pudding.'

" 'I'm sorry, your Majesty,' I said. 'I didn't mean it.' I was still standing in the middle of the room because he hadn't asked me to sit down. To hell with it, I thought, and I chose a large green sofa and draped myself along it, all ready for the Beetle to strike."

" 'I simply cannot understand George going off the rails like this,' he said.

" 'Oh, come on, your Majesty,' I said. 'He's only following in his dad's footsteps.'

" 'Pray what do you mean by that, madam?'

" 'Old Edward the Seventh,' I said. 'Dash it all, he was dipping the royal wick all over the country.'

" 'How dare you!' he cried, exploding for the first time. 'It's all lies!'

" 'What about Lillie Langtry?'

" 'King Edward was my wife's father,' he said in an icy voice. 'I will not have him insulted in my house.' "

"What in God's name, Yasmin, made you go on like that for?" I cried. "You get a really nice king for once and all you do is insult the hell out of him."

"He was a lovely man."

"Then why did you *do* it?"

"I had the devil in me, Oswald. And I was enjoying it, I suppose."

"You simply cannot *talk* like that to kings."

"Oh yes I can," Yasmin said. "I have discovered, you see, Oswald, that it doesn't really matter what you say to them in the beginning or how angry you make them, because the good old Beetle always rescues you in the end. It's always them that finish up looking silly."

"But you said you'd blown it?"

"Let me go on and you'll see what happened. The tall King kept pacing up and down the room and muttering to himself, and of course I kept watching the clock all the time. For some reason the nine minutes seemed to be going rather slowly. Then the King said, 'How could you *do* this to your own queen? How could you *lower* yourself to seducing her dear husband? Queen Mary is the purest lady in the land.'

" 'You really think so?' I said.

" 'I know it,' he said. 'She's as pure as the driven snow.'

" 'Now, just you hang on one second there, your Majesty,' I said. 'Haven't you heard all the naughty rumours?'

"When I said that, Oswald, he whipped round as though he'd been bitten by a scorpion."

"Jesus, Yasmin, you've got a bloody nerve!"

"It was fun," she said. "I only meant it as a joke."

"Some joke."

" 'Rumours!' the King shouted. 'What sort of rumours?'

" 'Very naughty rumours,' I said.

" 'How dare you!' he roared. 'How dare you come in here and talk like that about the Queen of England. You are a strumpet and a liar, madam!'

" 'I may be a strumpet,' I said, 'but I'm not a liar. There is, you see, your Majesty, a certain equerry at Buckingham Palace, a colonel in the Grenadiers, a fine good-looking fellow he is, too, with his big black bristly moustache, and every morning he meets the Queen in the gymnasium and gives her keep-fit lessons.'

" 'And why shouldn't he?' snapped the King. 'What's wrong with keep-fit exercises? I do them myself.'

"I looked at my watch. The nine minutes were just coming up. Any moment now this tall proud King would be transformed into a randy old lecher. 'Your Majesty,' I said, 'many's the time George and I have peeped through the window at the end of the gym and seen—' I stopped. I lost my voice, Oswald. I just couldn't go on."

"What happened, for God's sake?"

"I thought I was having a heart attack. I began to gasp. I couldn't breathe properly and a sort of goose-pimply feeling was spreading over my whole body. I really thought, honestly I did, I really thought I might be going to kick the bucket."

"What was it, for God's sake?"

"That's what the King asked me. He's truly a decent man,

Oswald. Half a minute before I'd been saying beastly insulting things about his in-laws in England, and all of a sudden he was deeply concerned for my welfare. 'Do you wish
me to call a doctor?' he said. I couldn't even answer him.
I just gurgled at him. Then all of a sudden this terrific
tingling sensation started in the soles of my feet and it
spread quickly all the way up my legs. I'm getting paralyzed, I thought. I can't talk. I can't move. I can hardly
think. I'm going to die any moment. Then *wham*! It hit
me!"

"What hit you?"

"*The Beetle*, of course."

"Now wait a minute . . ."

"I'd eaten the wrong goddamn chocolate, Oswald! I'd
mixed them up! I'd given him the plain one and eaten the
Beetle myself!"

"Jesus Christ, Yasmin!"

"I know. But by then I'd guessed what had happened and
my first thought was, I'd better get the hell out of the
palace before I make an even bigger ass out of myself than
I already have."

"And did you?"

"Well, that was a bit easier said than done. For the first
time in my life I was finding out what it felt like to get the
Beetle."

"Strong stuff."

"Terrifying. It freezes your mind. You can't think
straight. All you've got is this fierce throbbing sexy sensation pouring all over you. Sex is the only thing you can
think about. It was all *I* could think about anyway, and I'm
very much afraid, Oswald . . . I couldn't stop myself, you
understand—I simply couldn't stop myself . . . so I . . . well,

I leaped off the sofa and made a dive for the King's trousers. . . ."

"Oh, my God."

"There's more to come," Yasmin said, taking another gulp of brandy.

"Don't tell me. I can't bear it."

"All right, then, I won't."

"Yes," I said. "Go on."

"I was like a madwoman. I was all over him. I caught him off balance and pushed him down onto the sofa. But he's an athletic kind of bird, that old King. He was very quick. He was up in a flash. He got behind his desk. I climbed over the desk. He kept shouting, 'Stop, woman! What's the matter with you! Get away from me!' And then he really started yelling, yelling out loud I mean. 'Help!' he yelled. 'Someone get this woman out of here!' And then, my dear Oswald, the door opened and the Queen herself, little Queen Maud in all her glory, came sailing into the room holding a piece of needlework in her hand."

"Bound to happen."

"I know."

"Where were you when she came in?"

"I was leaping over his big Chippendale desk to get at him. Chairs were flying all over the place and in she came, this tiny, quite pretty woman . . ."

"What did she say?"

"She said, 'What *are* you doing, Haakon?'

" 'Get her out!' yelled the King.

" 'I want him!' I shouted. 'And I'm going to have him!'

" 'Haakon!' she said. 'Stop this at once!'

" 'It's not me, it's her!' he cried, running for his life round the room. But I had him cornered now and I was just about to fling myself at him good and proper when I was grabbed from behind by two guards. Soldiers they were. Lovely-looking Norwegian boys.

" 'Take her away,' gasped the King.

" 'Where to, sire?'

" 'Just get her out of here quick! Dump her in the street!'

"So I was frog-marched out of the palace and all I remember is I kept saying awful dirty things to the young soldiers and making all sorts of sexy suggestions and they were hooting with laughter . . ."

"So they dumped you?"

"In the street," Yasmin said. "Outside the palace gates."

"You're damned lucky it wasn't the King of Bulgaria or somewhere like that," I said. "You'd have been thrown into a dungeon."

"I know."

"So they dumped you in the street outside the palace?"

"Yes. I was dazed. I sat on a bench under some trees trying to pull myself together. I had one great advantage, you see, Oswald, over all my victims. *I knew* what was wrong with me. *I knew* it was the Beetle that was doing it to me. It must be simply awful feeling the way I felt and not knowing why. I think that would scare me to death. So I was able to fight it. I remember sitting there and saying to myself, what you need, Yasmin old girl, what you need to straighten you out is a few good digs in the backside with the hatpin. That made me giggle. And after that, but very slowly, this ghastly sexy feeling began to go away and I got a hold of myself and I stood up and walked along the street to the hotel and here I am. I'm sorry I messed it up, Oswald, I really am. It's the first time ever."

"We'd better get out of here," I said. "I don't think

these people would ever do anything nasty to us but the King is bound to start asking a few questions."

"I'm sure he is."

"I think he's going to guess my letter was a forgery," I said. "I bet anything you like he's checking it out with George the Fifth right this very minute."

"I'll bet he is, too," Yasmin said.

"Hurry up and pack then," I said. "We'll slide out of here at once and drive back across the border into Sweden. We're going to get lost."

25

WE GOT BACK HOME via Sweden and Denmark around the middle of April and we had with us the sperm of eight kings—fifty straws each from seven of them and twenty from old Peter of Serbia. It was a pity about Norway. It spoiled our record, although I didn't feel it was going to make much difference in the long run.

"Now I want my holiday," Yasmin said. "A good one. Aren't we about finished anyway?"

"America's next," I said.

"There aren't many there."

"No, but we have to get them. We'll go over in style on the *Mauretania*."

"I want a holiday first," Yasmin said. "You promised me. I'm not going anywhere until I've had a nice long rest."

"How long?"

"A month."

We had driven straight to Cambridge after disembarking from the Danish boat at Harwich, and we were having a drink in the living-room at Dunroamin. A. R. Woresley came in rubbing his hands.

"Congratulations," he said. "You've done a great job with those kings."

"Yasmin wants a month's holiday," I said. "But personally I think we ought to bash on and get America done first."

A. R. Woresley, puffing his disgusting pipe, looked at Yasmin through the smoke and said, "I agree with Cornelius. Get the job done first, take a holiday later."

"No," Yasmin said.

"Why not?" Woresley said.

"Because I don't want to, that's why."

"Well, I suppose it's up to you," Woresley said.

"You bet your life it's up to me," Yasmin said.

"Aren't you having a good time?" I said.

"The fun's wearing off," she said. "In the beginning it was a lark. Terrific joke. But now all of a sudden I seem to have had enough."

"Don't say that."

"I've said it."

"Hell."

"What both of you seem to be forgetting," she said, "is that every time we want the sperm of some bloody genius, *I'm* the one who has to go in and do the fighting. I'm the one who gets it in the neck."

"Not in the neck," I said.

"Stop trying to be funny, Oswald." She sat there looking glum. A. R. Woresley said nothing.

"If you have a month's holiday now," I said, "will you come to America with me immediately after that?"

"Yes, all right."

"You're going to enjoy Rudolph Valentino."

"I doubt it," she said. "I think my romping days are over."

"Never!" I cried. "You might as well be dead!"

"Romping isn't everything."

"Jesus, Yasmin. You're talking like Bernard Shaw!"

"Maybe I'll become a nun."

"But you will come to America first?"

"I've already told you I would," she said.

A. R. Woresley took his pipe out of his mouth and said, "We've got a remarkable collection, Cornelius, truly remarkable. When do we start selling?"

"We mustn't hurry it," I said. "My feeling is that we should not put any man's sperm up for sale until after he's dead."

"Why do you say that?"

"Great men are more interesting dead than alive. They become legends when they're dead."

"Maybe you're right," Woresley said.

"We've got plenty of ancient ones on the list," I said. Most of them aren't going to last very long. I'll bet you fifty per cent of the whole lot will be gone in five or ten years."

"Who's going to do the selling when the time comes?" Woresley asked.

"I am," I said.

"You think you can manage it?"

"Look," I said. "At the tender age of seventeen I had no trouble whatsoever in selling red pills to the French foreign minister, to a dozen ambassadors, and to just about every big shot in Paris. And just recently I have successfully sold Lady Victoria Nottingham to all the crowned heads of Europe bar one."

"I did that," Yasmin said. "Not you."

"Oh no you didn't," I said. "King George's letter did the selling and that was my idea. So you don't seriously think I'm going to have any trouble selling the seeds of genius to a bunch of rich females, do you?"

"Perhaps not," Woresley said.

"And by the way," I said, "if I'm the one who does all the selling, I think I ought to be entitled to a bigger cut of the profits."

"Hey!" Yasmin cried. "Now you just stop that, Oswald!"

"The agreement was equal shares all round," Woresley said, looking hostile.

"Calm down," I said. "I was only joking."

"I should damn well hope so," Yasmin said.

"As a matter of fact, I think Arthur should have the major share because he invented the whole process," I said.

"Well, I must say that's very generous of you, Cornelius," Woresley said, beaming.

"Forty per cent to the inventor and thirty per cent each to Yasmin and me," I said. "Would you agree to that, Yasmin?"

"I'm not sure I would," she said. "I've worked damn hard on this. I want my one-third."

What neither of them knew was that I had long since decided that I myself was the one who would take the major share in the end. Yasmin, after all, would never need very much. She liked to dress well and to eat good food, but that was about as far as it went. As for old Woresley, I doubted whether he'd know what to do with a large sum of money even if he had it. Pipe tobacco was about the only luxury he ever permitted himself. But I was different. The style of living to which I aspired made it absolutely necessary that I have a fortune at my fingertips. It was impossible for me to tolerate indifferent champagne or mild discomfort of any sort. The way I looked at it, the best— and by that I mean only the very best—was not nearly good enough for me.

I figured that if I gave them ten per cent each and took eighty for myself, then they ought to be happy. They would scream blue murder at first, but when they realized there was nothing they could do about it, they would soon settle down and be grateful for small mercies. Now there was of course only one way in which I could put myself in the position of being able to dictate terms to the other two. I must get possession of The Semen's Home and all the treasures it contained. Then I must move it to a safe and secret place where neither of them could reach it. That would not be difficult. As soon as Yasmin and I had returned from America, I would hire a removal van and drive up to Dunroamin when the place was empty and make off with the precious treasure chest.

No problem.

But a bit of a dirty trick, some of you may be thinking? A bit caddish?

Rubbish, I say. You'll never get anywhere in this world unless you grab your opportunities. Charity has never begun at home. Not in my home, anyway.

"So when will you two be going to America?" A. R. Woresley asked us.

I got out my diary. "One month from now will be Saturday, the fifteenth of May," I said. "How's that with you, Yasmin?"

"The fifteenth of May," she said, taking her own diary from her purse. "That seems all right. I'll meet you here on the fifteenth. In four weeks' time."

"And I'll book cabins on the *Mauretania* for as soon as possible after that."

"Fine," she said, writing the date in her diary.

"Then we'll collar old Henry Ford and Mr. Marconi and Rudolph Valentino and all the other Yanks."

"Don't forget Alexander Graham Bell," Woresley said.

"We'll get the lot," I said. "After a month's rest, the old girl will be roaring to go again, you see if she isn't."

"Hope so," Yasmin said. "But I do need a rest, honestly I do."

"Where will you go?"

"Up to Scotland to stay with an uncle."

"Nice uncle?"

"Very," she said. "My father's brother. He fishes for salmon."

"When are you leaving?"

"Right now," she said. "My train goes in about an hour. Will you take me to the station?"

"Of course I will," I said. "I myself am off to London."

I drove Yasmin to the station and helped her into the waiting-room with her bags. "See you in exactly a month," I said. "At Dunroamin."

"I'll be there," she said.

"Have good hols."

"Same to you, Oswald."

I kissed her farewell and drove down to London. I went straight to my house in Kensington Square. I was feeling good. The great scheme was actually coming to pass. I could see myself in about five years' time sitting with some silly rich female and her saying to me, "I rather fancy

Renoir, Mr. Cornelius. I do so adore his pictures. How much does he cost?"

"Renoir is seventy-five thousand, madam."

"And how much is a king?"

"That depends which one."

"This one here. The dark good-looking one—King Alfonso of Spain."

"King Alfonso is forty thousand dollars, madam."

"You mean he's less than Renoir?"

"Renoir was a greater man, madam. His sperm is exceedingly rare."

"What happens if it doesn't work, Mr. Cornelius? I mean if I don't become pregnant?"

"You get a free go."

"And who would actually perform the insemination?"

"A senior gynaecologist, madam. It would all be most carefully planned."

"And my husband would never find out?"

"How could he? He'd think he'd done it himself."

"I suppose he would, wouldn't he?" She giggles.

"Bound to, madam."

"It *would* be rather nice to have a child by the King of Spain, wouldn't it?"

"Have you considered Bulgaria, madam? Bulgaria is a bargain at twenty thousand."

"I don't want a Bulgar brat, Mr. Cornelius, even if he is royal."

"I quite understand, madam."

"And then of course there's Mr. Puccini. *La Bohème* is absolutely my favourite opera. How much is Mr. Puccini?"

"Giacomo Puccini is sixty-seven thousand five hundred, madam. He is strongly recommended. The child would almost certainly be a musical genius."

"I play the piano a bit myself."

"That would help the baby's chances enormously."

"I expect it would, wouldn't it?"

"Confidentially, madam, I can tell you that a certain lady in Dallas, Texas, had a Puccini boy three years ago and the child has already composed his first opera."

"You don't say."

"Thrilling, isn't it?"

I was going to have a lot of fun once the selling started. But right now I had before me one whole month in which to do nothing except enjoy myself. I decided to remain in London. I'd have a real fling. I deserved it. Throughout most of the winter I'd been chasing after kings all over Europe and the time had come for some serious wenching.

And what wenching it was. I went on a proper bender. For three weeks out of the four, I had a glorious time (see Vol. III). Then suddenly, at the beginning of the fourth and final week of my vacation, when I was really in full blood and churning the ladies of London to such purpose you could hear the bones rattling all over Mayfair, a devilish incident occurred that put an immediate stopper on all my activities. Terrible it was. Diabolical. Even to *think* about it at this distance causes me sharp physical pain. Nonetheless, I feel I ought to describe this sordid episode in the hope that it may save a few other sportsmen from a similar catastrophe.

I do not usually sit in the bathtub at the wrong end with my back to the taps. Few people do. But on this particular afternoon, the other end, the comfortable slopey end, was occupied by a saucy little imp who possessed hyperactive carnal proclivities. That's why she was there. The fact that she happened also to be an English duchess is not entirely beside the point either. Had I been a few years older, I would have known what to expect from a female of high rank, and I'd have been a good deal less careless. Most of these women have acquired their titles by ensnaring some poor benighted peer or duke, and it takes a very special kind of mendacity and guile to succeed at that game. To become a duchess you must be a prime manipulator of men. I have tangled with a fair number of them in my time and they're all alike. Marchionesses and countesses are not quite so ghoulish, but they run the duchess a close second. Dally with them by all means. It is a piquant experience. But for heaven's sake keep your wits about you while you're at it. You never know, you positively never can tell when they're going to turn and bite the hand that strokes them. Watch out, I say, for the female with a grand title.

Anyway, this duchess and I had been jouncing for an hour or so in the bathtub, and now that she had had enough she threw the soap at my face and stepped out of the water. The large slimy missile caught me on the mouth but as none of my teeth were dislodged or even loosened I ignored the incident. In point of fact, she had done it simply to quieten me down and to give her a chance to get away, which it did.

"Come back in," I said, wanting a second helping.

"I've got to go," she answered. She was keeping her distance as she dried her trim little body with one of my huge towels.

"It's only half-time," I pleaded.

"The trouble with you, Oswald, is you don't know when to stop," she said. "One day someone's going to lose patience with you."

"Frigid bitch," I said. It was a silly thing to say and quite untrue, but I said it.

She went into the next room to get dressed. I remained

sitting in the bath, silent and feeling thwarted. I didn't like it when others called the tune.

"Good-bye, darling," she said, coming back into the bathroom. She was wearing a short-sleeved silk dress, dark green.

"Go home, then," I said. "Go back to your ridiculous duke."

"Don't be so grumpy," she said. She walked over to me and bent down and began to massage my back under the water. Then her hand slid around to other areas, caressing and teasing gently. I sat still, enjoying it all and wondering whether she wasn't perhaps going to start melting all over again.

Now you won't believe this, but all the time the little vixen was pretending to play around with me, what she was actually doing was surreptitiously and with consummate stealth removing the plug from the plughole in the bottom of the bathtub. As you know, when the plug is withdrawn from a bath that is brimful of water, the suction down the plughole is immensely powerful. And when a man is sitting astride that plughole as I was at that moment, then it is inevitable that the two most tender and valuable objects in his possession are going to be sucked very suddenly into that dreadful hole. There was a dull *plop* as my scrotum took the full force of the suction and flew into the neck of the hole. I let out a scream that must have been heard clear across Kensington Square.

"Good-bye, darling," said the duchess, sweeping out of the bathroom.

In the excruciating moments that followed I learned exactly what it must feel like to fall into the hands of those Bedouin women who delight in depriving a traveller of his masculinity with blunt knives. "Help!" I screamed. "Save me!" I was impaled. I was glued to the tub. I was clutched in the claws of a mighty crab.

It seemed like hours but I don't suppose I was actually stuck in that position for more than ten or fifteen minutes. It was quite long enough though. I don't even know how I eventually managed to prize myself free all in one piece. But the damage was done. Powerful suction is a terrible thing and those two precious jewels of mine, which were normally no bigger than a couple of greengages, had suddenly assumed the size of cantaloupe melons. I think it was old Geoffrey Chaucer way back in the fourteenth century who wrote

> Ladies with titles
> Will go for your vitals

and those immortal words, believe me, are now engraved upon my heart. For three days I was on crutches and for God knows how long after that I walked about like a man who was harbouring a porcupine between his thighs.

It was in this crippled condition that I made my way up to Cambridge on May 15th to keep my appointment with Yasmin at Dunroamin. As I got out of the car and hobbled toward the front door, my marbles were still on fire and throbbing like the devil's drum. Yasmin, of course, would be wanting to know what had happened to me. So would Woresley. Should I tell them the truth? If I did, Yasmin would fall all over the room laughing, and I could already hear Woresley in his silly pompous way saying, "You are altogether too carnal, my dear Cornelius. No man can debauch himself the way you do without paying a heavy price." I didn't think I could stand that sort of thing right then, so I decided to tell them I had strained a ligament in my thigh. I had done it while helping an old lady after she had stumbled and taken a heavy fall on the pavement outside my house. I had carried her indoors and looked after her until the ambulance came, but it had all been a bit too much for me, etc., etc. That would do it.

I stood under the little porch outside the front door of Dunroamin and fished for my key. As I was doing this, I noticed there was an envelope pinned to the door. Someone had fixed it on firmly with a drawing-pin. Damn silly thing to do. I couldn't get the pin out so I ripped the envelope away. There was no name on it so I opened it. Foolish not to put a name on the envelope. Was it for me? Yes, it was.

> *Dear Oswald,*
>
> *Arthur and I got married last week. . . .*

Arthur? Who the hell was Arthur?

> *We have gone far away and I hope you won't mind too much but we've taken The Semen's Home with us, at least all of it except Proust. . . .*

Jesus Christ! Arthur must be Woresley! Arthur Woresley!

> *Yes, we have left you Proust. I never did like the little bugger anyway. All fifty of his straws are safely stored in the travelling container in the basement and the Proust letter is in the desk. We have all the other letters with us safe and sound. . . .*

I was reeling. I couldn't read on. I unlocked the door and staggered inside and found a bottle of whiskey. I sloshed some into a glass and gulped it down.

If you stop and think about it, Oswald, I'm sure you'll agree we're not really doing the dirty on you and I'll tell you why. Arthur says . . .

I didn't give a damn what Arthur said. They'd stolen the precious sperm. It was worth millions. I was willing to bet it was that little sod Woresley who'd put Yasmin up to it.

Arthur says that after all it was him who invented the process, wasn't it? And it was me who did all the hard work of collecting it. Arthur sends you his best wishes.
Toodle-oo

Yasmin Woresley

A real snorter, that. Right below the belt. It had me gasping.

I roared round the house in a wild fury. My stomach was boiling and I'm sure steam was spurting out of my nostrils. Had there been a dog in the place I'd have kicked it to death. I kicked the furniture instead. I smashed a lot of nice big things and then I set about picking up all the smaller objects, including a Baccarat paperweight and an Etruscan bowl, and flinging them through the windows, yelling bloody murder and watching the window-panes shatter.

But after an hour or so, I began to simmer down, and finally I collapsed into an armchair with a large glass of malt whiskey in my hand.

I am, as you may have gathered, a fairly resilient fellow. I explode when provoked, but I never brood about it afterwards. I scrub it out. There's always another day. What's more, nothing stimulates my mind so much as a whopping disaster. In the aftermath, in that period of deadly calm and absolute silence that follows the tempest, my brain becomes exceedingly active. As I sat drinking my whiskey during that terrible evening amidst the ruins of Dunroamin, I was already beginning to ponder and plan my future all over again.

So that's that, I told myself. I've been diddled. It's all over. Need a new start. I still have Proust and in years to come I shall do well with those fifty straws (and don't think I didn't), but that isn't going to make me a millionaire. So what next?

It was at this point that the great and wonderful answer began trickling into my head. I sat quite still, allowing the idea to take root and grow. It was inspired. It was beautiful in its simplicity. It couldn't fail. It would make me millions. Why hadn't I thought of it before?

I promised at the beginning of this diary to tell you how I became a wealthy man. I have taken a long time so far in telling you how I did not succeed. Let me therefore make up for lost time and describe to you in no more than a few paragraphs how I did in the end become a real multi-millionaire. The great idea that came to me suddenly in Dunroamin was as follows:

I would go back at once to the Sudan. I would negotiate with a corrupt government official for a lease of that precious tract of land where the hashab tree grows and the Blister Beetle flourishes. I would obtain sole rights to all beetle hunting. I would gather the native beetle hunters together and form them into an organized unit. I would pay them generously, far more than they were getting at present by flogging their Beetles in the open market. They would work exclusively for me. Poachers would be ruthlessly eliminated. I would, in fact, corner the market in Sudanese Blister Beetles. When all this was arranged and

I was assured of a large and regular supply of Beetles, I would build a little factory in Khartoum and there I would process my Beetles and manufacture in quantity Professor Yousoupoff's Famous Potency Pills. I would package the pills in the factory. I would then set up a small secret underground sales unit with offices in Paris, London, New York, Amsterdam, and other cities throughout the world. I told myself that if a callow seventeen-year-old youth had been able to earn himself a hundred thousand pounds in one year in Paris all by himself, just think what I could do now on a world-wide basis.

And that, my friends, is almost exactly what happened. I went back to the Sudan. I stayed there for a little over two years, and I don't mind telling you that although I learned a great deal about the Blister Beetle, I also learned a thing or two about the ladies who inhabit those regions. The tribes were sharply divided and they seldom mixed. But I mixed with them all right, with the Nubians, the Hassanians, the Baggaras, the Shilluks, the Shukrias, and the curiously light-colored Niam-Niams, who live west of the Blue Nile. I found the Nubians especially to my taste and I wouldn't be surprised if that was where the word *nubile* originated.

By the end of 1923, my little factory was going full blast and turning out a thousand pills a day.

By 1925, I had agents in eight cities. I had chosen them carefully. All, without exception, were retired army generals. Unemployed generals are common in every country, and these men, I discovered, were cut out for this particular type of job. They were efficient. They were unscrupulous. They were brave. They had little regard for human life. And they lacked sufficient intelligence to cheat me without being caught.

It was an immensely lucrative business. The profits were astronomical. But after a few years I grew bored with running such a big operation and I turned the whole thing over to a Greek syndicate in exchange for one half of the profits. The Greeks were happy, I was happy, and hundreds of thousands of customers have been happy ever since.

I am unashamedly proud of my contribution to the happiness of the human race. Not many men of business and certainly very few millionaires can tell themselves with a clear conscience that the accumulation of their wealth has spread such a high degree of ecstasy and joy among their clients. And it pleases me very much to have discovered that the dangers to human health of *Cantharis vesicatoria sudanii* have been grossly exaggerated. My records show that not more than four or five dozen a year at the most suffer any serious or crippling effects from the magic substance. Very few die.

Just one more thing. In 1935, some fifteen years later, I was having breakfast in my Paris house and reading the morning paper when my eye was caught and held by the following item in one of the gossip columns (translated from the French):

La Maison d'Or at Cap Ferrat, the largest and most luxurious private property on the entire Côte d'Azur, has recently changed hands. It has been bought by an English couple, Professor Arthur Woresley and his beautiful wife, Yasmin. The Woresleys have come to France from Buenos Aires where they have been living for many years, and very welcome they are. They will add great lustre to the glittering Riviera scene. As well as buying the magnificent Maison d'Or, they have just taken

delivery of a superb ocean-going yacht which is the envy
of every millionaire on the Mediterranean. It has a crew
of eighteen and cabin accommodation for ten people.
The Woresleys have named the yacht SPERM. *When I*
asked Mrs. Woresley why they had chosen that rather
curious name, she laughed and said, "Oh, I don't know.
I suppose because it's such a whale of a ship."

Quite a girl, that Yasmin. I have to admit it. Though
what she ever saw in old Woresley with his donnish airs
and his nicotine-stained moustache I cannot imagine. They
say a good man is hard to find. Maybe Woresley was one
of those. But who on earth wants a good man? Who, for
that matter, wants a good woman?

Not me.

A NOTE ON THE TYPE

This book was set on the Linotype in Janson, a recutting made direct from type cast from matrices long thought to have been made by the Dutchman Anton Janson, who was a practicing type founder in Leipzig during the years 1668–87. However, it has been conclusively demonstrated that these types are actually the work of Nicholas Kis (1650–1702), a Hungarian, who most probably learned his trade from the master Dutch type founder Dirk Voskens. The type is an excellent example of the influential and sturdy Dutch types that prevailed in England up to the time William Caslon developed his own incomparable designs from them.

Composed by Maryland Linotype Composition
Company, Inc., Baltimore, Maryland. Printed and bound
by The Haddon Craftsmen, Inc.,
Scranton, Pennsylvania
Typography and binding design by
VIRGINIA TAN